Alone With Someone

Connecting Verses for Inspiration

John E. Murray, III

Library of Congress Control Number: 2008900690

Murray, John E.

Alone With Someone: connecting verses for inspiration / John E. Murray, III.

p. cm.

ISBN-13: 978-0-9794451-1-8 (pbk.)

ISBN-10: 09794451-1-6 (pbk.)

For permission or other resources, please visit:

www.storyinstitute.com or send an email to JohnEMurrayIII@storyinstitute.com

To my wife, Teri, who enriches
my timeless tales
through every meandering path

Prelude

If perchance, you
see smiles inward,
feel warmth tingling,
or perhaps,
grow in love
while peering within,
ask yourself
how you've experienced
life differently...
because you have...
and, after hours,
maybe even days later,
ask yourself,
Why.

Chapter 1

I am so happy it is Friday. Two days of relaxing and, oh yes, grading papers. I am not quite sure why I have assignments due the day before the weekend. It gives the students a break, but takes away from that much needed down-time. I know high school students appreciate every social opportunity they get, but I can't remember the last time I enjoyed the opportunity to be social with someone other than my rampant thoughts. I'm at school all day. In the evening, I spend my time in a house that I purchased from my parents, where I usually plan and review the next major lesson for each class. The only real adult interaction I have is with other teachers. There are many female counter-parts with whom I would enjoy talking about academics, but only a couple I would even consider spending time with beyond the school day.

Lesson plans, lesson plans…the one I developed for third period sparked a lively discussion. Most of this was due to the next Shakespearean play on our list, Romeo and Juliet. The students seem to be very interested in topics from this play. I can understand why, especially at their age. Though, I do wonder whether the examples from their own lives, for which I usually ask, will really reflect the emotion Shakespeare captures so well. I even have trouble giving solid examples myself. Oh sure, I can provide insight into the themes, plots, and settings I have read in criticism and critiques. However, I do not believe that I have felt, even remotely what Romeo had felt for Juliet.

This is all rather ironic though, since I fought to make this part of the school's required reading. It took me three years to push it past a school board that doesn't know Will Shakespeare from Will Rogers. I thought that after my 30th birthday somehow, I would better be able to relate more of my experiences to this story. Numerous dates with numerous young women have really brought me no closer to personally understanding than when I was my students' age. Now that I think of it, my life seems to have the opposite theme…being alone. Eating, going to movies, and attending concerts on season tickets…alone.

Oh, yes the concert I must have missed half of it by now. What is the next piece…let's take a look here. I look at the rolled-up piece of paper that someone in a burgundy jacket handed me at the door. I smile and

1

Chapter 1

close my eyes slightly, nestling back into my seat in the hopes of enjoying this last piece. As the music begins, a calming vision appears:

The feathered ones float aimlessly by
On the soft curvaceous body of the breeze,
Gently gliding amidst the white fluffy pillows
Of the brilliant blue expanse.
Those of aqueous nature meander instinctively
Upon the smooth perpetual ripples of the waves,
Silently skimming the colorless surface
Of the mystical deep.
Wide-eyed woodland creatures roam freely
Over the peaceful verdant terrain of the forest,
Beautifully blending with the other natural residents
Of the rich earthly realm.
I can do nothing,
Except become engulfed within the placidity.

So fresh. So peaceful. So Alive!

My heavy eyelids flutter and I am thrust into yet another state of being. Fragments of thought begin to swirl around and around, searching for a sturdy place on which to rest. Words literally float by, attempting not to collide. Each concept, each idea, seems to find a suitable safe haven: "Peace"…"Insanity"…"Memory"…"Loss"…"Pure-delight"…"Sorrow."

Silence engulfs me. Before I am able to open my eyes half way, one last word comes crashing down on top of the others. It is surrounded by an intense light and a loud harmonious note: "HOPE!"

The vision fades and I am left to the silence once again.

As I drift back to a somewhat conscious state, I see the conductor's arms swing rapidly upward, then fall just as swiftly. Loud clamors of trumpets and trombones erupt with each downbeat and continue with each enthusiastic sweep of the baton. Trilling flutes and clarinets manage to squeak through every now and then with their light little doodles. The pleasant sounds of the oboe and my vision, however, are no more. I frown in somewhat of despair.

Brief flashbacks to my land of wonder occur throughout the remainder of the piece, but none as permanent or as real as before. The corners of my mouth take on a more acute angle as I say to myself, "That was the most beautiful sound I have ever..." I stop myself short considering the implications of that thought, as well as the great extent I still need to hear. It was wonderful though.

The piece comes to an end and I drift back to a more conscious state. I rise and join in the applause of my fellow audience members, showing our appreciation to the orchestra. The conductor bows a few times, turns toward the orchestra, and signals them to do the same. In unison, they rise, bow, and proceed to exit from the stage. One by one they disappear. I sit down and stare at the quickly emptying stage.

Some around me wish to leave, so I am compelled to move and impact myself into the seat until they pass. This is one of the most uncomfortable positions to be in. Yet every year, every concert, I manage to push myself back far enough into my seat so these people can get past. Many times I have asked myself, "Why don't I just leave with them?" Every concert, however, I look down the aisle and see the other unfortunate souls who remain in their seats, some of whom are much larger, so I compensate and persevere. I never like to leave until the last player is off the stage. It's like you're deserting them. They all have a right to be seen and applauded, don't they? Besides, I want at least to see the images of the people who create that wonderful music, especially the oboe player. If I wanted just to listen to the sounds, I would turn on the radio or buy a CD. The players are the ones who give the music its life. They are the ones who help create the vision.

Where is the one with the amazing sounds?

There?

No.

No.

Chapter 1

No!

The last musician vanishes behind the enormous blue curtain, and I am free to go, still no oboe player. I rise and turn toward the exit waiting for the people in my row either to do the same or sink far enough down in their seats for me to pass. The journey down the aisle is extremely slow. This is probably the only part of the performance I do not like. I simply do not have the patience to wait for each member of the audience, except the deserters of course, to decide if and when he or she may want to leave. Then, they all try to cram through the narrow doors at the end of the auditorium.

As I continue in constant hesitation, I hear a voice behind me just as I enter the main aisle, "Bill! Bill!"

I turn my head instinctively, not knowing whether or not the shouting was meant for me or someone else with the same name. I see a tall slim man with short blonde hair squeezing his way up the aisle past a number of not too enthused audience members. A voice inside my head tells me it is Frank, the band director at the high school I teach at, and I should wait to talk with him. Another voice tells me to ignore him and get out to avoid embarrassment. "It is good to see a familiar face," I think, as the redness continues to engulf my face.

Conceding to the first voice, I step aside into a row with very few people. Frank finally reaches me and says, "Hi. How come you didn't tell me you had tickets to this?"

"Umm? Uh? You didn't ask? Besides, I didn't think it was important, I guess."

"No, I guess I didn't ask. So is this your first time here? Weren't they great? Are you here with...?"

Don't get me wrong, Frank is a wonderful friend, a great teacher, and an excellent musician. He is usually quite passive, but if you catch him, or rather he catches you, after a well-performed concert, look out! He

4

becomes so full of energy, so feisty, so alive, it's hard to keep him focused. Hell, it's hard to speak.

"So are you here with anyone?" Frank pursues his last question a little further, looking around and grinning as he speaks.

"No, I..."

Frank continues to ramble on about the different musical aspects and how he only wishes the band at school could play half as well. My attention diverts back to one of his earlier questions. Who would I be here with? I haven't been out on a real date since freshman year in college, which was about eight years ago now. I've gone out a few times sure, but it was either just as friends or a business meeting (how exciting). Frank knows this, why would he be asking me if I was here with anyone?

He pauses for a moment then asks, "So would you like to go back stage with me and meet some of the players, or do you have other plans?"

"You actually know some of the players?" I ask, my eyes widening like a child who has just been given a candy bar.

"Know them? Know them?!?" Frank says. "I've either played with them or tutored them in college."

He can't be serious. He knows almost all of them? He may know the saxophone section, but the entire band?

Nah.

We begin walking toward the stage, discussing the music some more. Only a few people remain, so we don't have to push past anyone or go against the flow.

"It was very nice," I say. "I especially liked the oboe piece at the end. It was..." I hesitate somewhat not knowing exactly how to describe it.

Chapter 1

"Amazing. It was amazing. It was the most..." Again I stop myself. My eyes and thoughts betray me as they both begin to wander.

Frank stops and stares at me.

"What?" I say.

"You really liked it, didn't you?" Frank smiles. It's not one of those friendly, "how-are-you-doing" smiles either, it's more like a smirk. It's one of those expressions that says, "I know something you don't know."

"What?" I say again. "Why are you starring at me like that?"

"Like what?" Frank pauses. "Just out of curiosity, did you manage to see her when she walked off the stage?" His smile becomes wider.

"Uh, no. I missed her. It must have been when the deserters were leaving."

"The who?"

"Never mind."

Frank shakes his head and begins walking again toward the stage, "I could introduce you to her if you like."

"Who?" I ask, still trying to figure out the true meaning of his smirk.

"The oboe player," Frank replies. "That is, if it's not past your bedtime and she's still back there."

I blush again and I'm not completely sure why. "No, no, I'm fine. How do you know her anyway, the oboe player that is? Just out of curiosity, of course."

"We played in the same chamber orchestra at the university. She had just started her degree program and I was finishing mine. It wasn't an easy task to obtain a seat in that orchestra. You had to audition. Then, audition again for someone else. Finally, you played a piece with another person who was already in the orchestra or who was a graduate student."

"Impressive," I thought.

"Well, if we have time and she's still there, it would be nice, umm," again I hesitate trying to recall some of the images from the solo, "nice to meet her," I stammer out.

Finally, we reach the stairs. Frank walks up and disappears behind the blue curtain. He proceeds further ahead. I hesitate, for some reason or another, not all too sure if I want to follow.

Frank stops and shouts, "Are you coming?"

Coming? Where? Oh, yes. "Yes," I call back, "I just had to, a, tie my shoe."

"Uh huh," Frank mumbles loudly and continues walking.

"What did you say?" I ask, finally entering the backstage area.

I catch up to Frank and he is just beginning a conversation with the orchestra's director, Mr. Kay. He is about 5'9" with thinning gray hair. He isn't an extremely large nor especially intimidating man, but he has an air about him that demands respect.

Frank introduces me to him, as I extend my hand in greeting. He has a firm grip and somewhat sweaty palms. I guess it's from holding that baton so tightly. You wouldn't want to lose that little pointy thing on a quick upbeat. Heh, you might hit someone in the eye, or it may get stuck in someone's instrument. I laugh inwardly at the thought of Mr. Kay stopping the concert saying, "Excuse me while I remove my baton from this tuba here."

It's probably not as funny as it seems. Actually, it could be tragic. They may never have gotten to the oboe solo.

Chapter 1

Frank continues speaking with Mr. Kay. I nod my head and smile continuously. I'm listening to what they have to say, really. I just don't let it distract me from taking in the sights of the entire backstage, especially the most important detail, the door.

Frank finally catches on to my wandering eyes and says, "Well, we had better let you go James. I'm sure your wife and kids are expecting you."

Once again I shake Mr. Kay's hand and tell him what a pleasure it was to meet him.

Frank shakes his head and laughs as Mr. Kay turns to leave. "English teacher," Frank says.

Mr. Kay nods and smiles as if to say, "Oh, I understand."

I begin looking around again. Then, I look back at Frank, "What?" I say.

"You could have at least said 'yes' or 'no' when he asked if you were married!"

"He didn't ask me that," I hesitate, "did he?"

"Yes, he did, and you just kept nodding and smiling."

I blush an even brighter shade of red and say, "I'm sorry. My mind must still be on a, umm, the music."

"Uh huh, the music," Frank mumbles, just loud enough for me to hear, just soft enough for me to ask, "what did you say?"

Frank begins wandering around, introducing me to a few other people. No sooner does he tell me their names, however, do my eyes resume a wandering of their own. My focal point is still the door.

One by one players leave. I attempt to identify the instrument each is carrying, but there are still many people, and since I am only 5'5", I can't really see much other than faces or shoulders going out the doorway in the far left corner.

I still do not see the oboe player. Of course, I still do not know what she looks like. I only know how her fingers may have moved delicately up and down the length of her instrument, and how her smooth caress created those beautiful sounds and my vision.

"OK, that's everyone I know. Let's go," Frank says, realizing my patience is just about gone.

Without thinking, I grab his arm and say, "Everyone?" I look at my hand, somewhat surprised, and quickly release him.

He laughs, "OK, I'll see if I can find her." He looks around a couple of times. On the second sweep, he says, "I see her. Let's go."

Let's go? Go where? Oh, yeah.

My hesitation is not only pitiful but embarrassing. Frank looks at me and continues to laugh as he proceeds toward his target.

I move quickly toward him, hoping to reach him before...

I stop and say, "Umm, I guess it is getting a little late. Maybe next time."

"No, no. She's right over here." He points and moves in the same direction. "Besides, after you ignored all of my other friends, she's probably the only one who will talk to me."

I contemplate a moment about my hesitation. I guess I have my vision and my "picture" of the player, and I don't want to ruin it. Then again, does seeing any of the musicians ever destroy my enjoyment of the music? No, of course not. Sometimes, it does change it though.

Wait! I don't want to change my vision. I want to keep it the way it is. It was the...

Chapter 1

Yeah, yeah, the most beautiful sound I have, or rather might have, or rather may have ever...

Oh, never mind!

Couldn't seeing this person also enhance my vision and my enjoyment of the piece? After all, someone who plays that well, that amazingly, must be special.

I take a deep breath, tug on my sweater, and head in the direction Frank had walked a few moments ago. One last thought enters my mind before I can catch up, "Why did Frank have that darn smirk on his face?"

It was that smirk. Why did he have that...?

I reach Frank and am just about to tap him on the shoulder to ask him about it, when he says, "Your solo was played very well. In fact, a friend of mine says it was..."

"Amazing!" I say to myself.

"That's it amazing," Frank says as he turns to face me.

So much for quiet thoughts.

"I would like you to meet my friend and colleague, Bill."

She extends her hand, expecting the same from someone else.

Amazing. Simply amazing.

The visions of her solo rush into the forefront of my mind: "floating aimlessly"..."soft curvaceous body"..."smooth perpetual ripples"... "peaceful verdant terrain"..."beautifully blending."

"He teaches English at the same high school I'm at," Frank says, emphasizing the last word as he nudges me.

Alone With Someone

Oh! She's extending her hand to me, just as I did to Mr. Kay hours ago (at least that's what it seems like now).

Just as she is about to withdraw her gesture, I reach out and gently grasp her hand, turning it so her palm faces downward. In one motion, I raise her soft delicate hand and lower my spinning head, lightly touching her precious skin with my lips. I lower her hand, raise my head slightly, and admire her beauty. I stand entranced and literally engulfed by her aura, her mere essence.

Silky, long, brown hair cascades over her shoulders to about the middle of her back. Rose colored lips, slightly parted and slanting upward, form a simple, yet encouraging smile. My gaze travels slowly upward until I reach her large, innocent eyes. They are of a brilliant green almost hazel hue and glisten with a youthful exuberance and incomparable brilliance. There is something special in those eyes, something truly amazing. A twinkle, a sparkle, shining brighter and brighter as my gaze lingers, drawing me inward.

I am not entirely aware of what has or is transpiring, but I feel a sense of happiness, a sense of "HOPE." For this moment, I am happy, and that is all that seems to matter.

"And, this is the oboe player, Melody," Frank says, sounding rather distant, as he looks at both of us. Through the corner of my eye, I see his head moving back and forth, from me to her, probably waiting for one of us to speak.

I begin to shake off my daze, straighten up, and am just about to say something when a whisper escapes from Melody's lips, "Thank you."

I clear my throat, hoping I do not sound too horse, "The pleasure has been all mine."

The music. Her face. The rush of emotions. Amazing.

"Bill is a poet, who, I just found out, enjoys orchestra music very much," Frank interrupts as if he were selling some kind of product.

11

Chapter 1

I blush from Frank's comment as well as my realization that I still hold her hand in my own. I let it slowly slip away, looking once again at her angelic face, which is as red as mine must seem, if not redder.

Melody clears her throat, "That sounds wonderful."

Her voice is still rather soft, but so soothing. Little explosions erupt within me. Chills encase me.

"What kind of poetry do you write?" Melody asks.

I try to swallow and get out a reply, but before I can, Frank answers for me, "He is the last, true romantic poet."

Even I am somewhat surprised as Frank completes his sentence. I have shown him some of my poems, and believe I have used those words myself, but they still sound foreign. Most of the time when my friends say this, they are joking, but Frank sounds rather sincere here.

My eyes widen and I turn my head from Frank to Melody. "She doesn't want to hear about my boring life," I say, extending further into total consciousness.

"Your solo was truly beautiful," I say, moistening my dry lips. "And the player surely fits the piece," completing the thought in my mind and aloud.

Melody blushes again and lowers her head.

What have I done? I have embarrassed this vision of loveliness. What am I going to do? What should I say?

Frank! I turn toward Frank with one of those wide-eyed, help-me looks.

"I was telling Bill," Frank says, "how I wish our school band could play half as well."

Alone With Someone

I look at Melody. She picks up her head and seems more at ease now that the conversation has shifted. In fact, we both seem more at ease.

"I can't wait until the school's career day," Frank continues, "it will be very helpful for the band members to see 'real' musicians and get feed back other than mine."

Frank pauses for a second and looks at us. Then, that smirk graces his face again, "Did I mention that Melody has agreed to help us out on that day?"

"No, you didn't," I say, my eyebrows move upward and a smile forms on my face.

Melody smiles and says, "It should be, umm," she pauses and looks at both of us, "interesting and good for me as well. That's a week from today, correct?"

"Yep," Frank says. He looks at me and adds, "We should be finished right before our lunch break. Maybe, we all can have lunch together." Frank's eyes widen as he waits for a response.

"Sure, sure," I say. "It should be interesting."

Wait a minute. Didn't Melody just say that?

"Well, I have to get home. Cindy, is probably wondering where I am by now. It's past my 9 o'clock curfew," Frank says and nudges me.

"Oh, yes. Well, it was very nice meeting you," I say. Clearing my throat, I add, "We'll see you next Wednesday then. Take care."

"Yes, see you next Wednesday, then," Melody says as she puts on her jacket and picks up her oboe case.

"Good bye and thank you," Frank says as he tugs on my arm.

Still somewhat entranced, I shake my head and look at Frank. He has a smug little grin on his face now and mouths the words, "Let's go." His grin is different from that smirk he had before. This grin says, "Yes! I knew it." But what exactly does he know?

I move with him, stealing glances back toward Melody as she disappears through the backstage doors.

"Wednesday," I mumble, my thoughts drifting back to the visions of the night; one intangible, the other so real I was able to caress that precious hand and stare into those intensely sparkling eyes.

Chapter 2

There is a brief period of silence and then a small laughter spreads around the room. I must fight the urge to join them. After all, this is serious. This is a quiz. I settle for a very large grin and focus again on Robert.

Robert smiles, "Um, is this a trick question?"

More laughter escapes from the students.

"Just kidding," he says, "Romeo and Juliet."

Without hesitating, I shout, "Wrong!" My eyes narrow and the grin is gone.

I pause for a moment, looking at their bewildered faces.

I shuffle my papers again and smile, "No, no, you're correct." I can't keep myself from laughing now. Just the look on their faces is worth the wait.

I've done this the entire semester, and only a few seem to have caught on. I try to recall my high school days, and realize we were the same way. It must be the age. As a high school student you have responsibilities. You have to go to school; you have to go to practice; you have to work part time; you have to do your homework (sometimes). It's a difficult task to balance all that and your ever growing social life.

Social life? Oh yeah. I remember what that was.

Being a student is difficult though. At that age, your entire life revolves around the fact that you are a student. Very few adults realize the pressure and stress students undergo, even though those same people were students themselves at one time or another. As life changes so do your needs. The events which once formed your life, become meaningless, rather trivial, and someone else's problems.

I look around some more. The students are still talking and laughing. "Though Robert was correct, what did he forget?"

Chapter 2

Again, looks of bewilderment form on their faces.

I look at Robert, "Robert, what did you forget?"

He looks at me, then says, rather quietly, "I, um," he pauses, "didn't use a complete sentence."

He knows what he forgot, yet he still forgot it. Incredible. It is like putting salt on our grease-soaked fries even though we know it's bad for us.

"Right," I say. "You didn't form a complete..."

There is a knock on the door, and I stop short. In unison, the students say, "Sentence!" finishing my thought, I move toward the door, shaking my head and smiling.

Again, there is a knock. As I reach the door, I say, "Suddenly, there came a tapping, as of someone gently rapping, rapping at my chamber door." I look out the little glass window and see Frank. As I turn the knob, I face the students and ask, "Who wrote that?"

I open the door half way and smile at Frank, "Yes?"

"Do you mind if we sit in?" Frank whispers.

"Of course not." I turn toward the students and say, "Class, because of your boisterous laughter, we will have another teacher in the room to help even the odds in case of a coup."

I smile, push the door open all the way, and tell Frank, "Come in. There are a few empty seats in the back. Take your pick."

Wait a minute. Did he say "we"?

He didn't bring...?

Alone With Someone

Frank enters with a leather folder, his baton sticking out in the middle at both ends. Immediately following is...

My eyes widen as she glides into the room. Tingling sensations spread throughout my entire body. All air has escaped from within. My chest expands as I inhale deeply. As the light-headed feeling dissipates, I exhale. I lick my lips slightly and swallow a few times attempting to restore moisture to my dry, cottony mouth. My eyes remain glued to Melody, following her to the back of the room.

"Whoa! Who's the..."

"George!" I shout not letting him finish. I always seem to be disturbed when I am admiring her beauty. It appears, though, that my eyes are not the only ones captivated by this vision.

The boys mumble to each other and the girls giggle as my face turns as red as the plastic apple on my desk.

"You all know Mr. A. and the young lady with him is..."

"Not his wife!" Brian shouts.

The students laugh. I smile for a second. Then, I get that look. You know the look that says, "Enough!" My eyebrows slant downward and my lips from a straight line across my face.

I turn toward the board, grab a piece of chalk, and return to stare at the students. By the time I turn around, the students are silent. They know that if they do not quiet down they will get an extra assignment, a very long extra assignment. Most of the students have apologetic looks on their faces, but many may not necessarily know what they are apologizing for.

"As I was saying," I pause, remembering that I have not learned Melody's last name yet. How am I...?

Chapter 2

"Miss M. is helping the band out on their career day. She is a professional musician. Hopefully, she has and will continue to share her wisdom with the players."

Well, I got out of that one, I think. I look at Melody, hoping I did the right thing by calling her Miss M. Her face is redder than mine.

The students break their silence with questions for Melody:

"What do you play?"

"Where did you go to school?"

"How long have you played?"

"Are you married?"

It's the last one that really hits me. "Class!" I say, my voice slightly elevated. "I'm sure questions will be entertained after class. Right now we need to continue with Romeo and Juliet." She's not married. Is she? No, Frank would have said something.

I wait for a moment as the students grumble and take out their books. I look at Melody and mouth the words, "I'm sorry," hoping the students don't notice.

I shake my head, trying to clear it completely for this discussion. I have a job to do. The class is surely acting like high school students, I should at least compensate and act like a teacher.

I grab my book, sit on the desk, and ask, "Who would like to read?" Hands go up instantly.

"We'll start with Act I Scene V." I flip through the pages, looking for characters. "Let's see, we'll need readers for three serving men, Capulet, Capulet's cousin, Romeo, Tybalt, Juliet, Nurse, and someone to read the italicized parts."

Alone With Someone

I point at different members of the class, assigning them roles.

"OK, let's begin."

The students begin reading. I grab two books off my desk and offer them to Frank and Melody. I give Frank the page verbally; with Melody, however, I help her open the book and turn the pages. As we flip through the book, her hand brushes against mine. Chills and electricity race up my arm to my shoulders, down my torso to my legs and feet, causing my toes to curl. Then, the energy rushes directly to my head.

Somehow, I mange to point out the exact spot.

Melody smiles. "Thank you," she whispers.

I simply smile, nod my head, and walk to the front of the room.

She smiled at me.

I stop the students in spots, reminding them to check their list for Shakespearean definitions of certain words. I point out the word "portly" in line 75.

"Portly, in this case, does not mean that Capulet has put on some weight," I say as I pat my stomach and smile. "It means impressive."

"But would it mean that in your case, sir?"

The students laugh. I continue smiling and shake my head. "It's always funny when we make jokes at other people's expense," I pause, "George!"

I turn and stare at George's guilty-innocent face.

"I didn't say..."

I raise my head and widen my eyes. George does not finish his sentence.

Chapter 2

George is a good kid who receives good grades (at least in this class). He does get a little too hyper, however, and doesn't always know when to stop.

"Continue reading," I say.

I look down at my stomach. It's not that large. In fact, I'm not that much over weight. Besides, it doesn't hang way over my belt, like other members of this faculty. And? And? And, it shouldn't matter anyway.

I work out...

Sometimes.

When I can.

OK, when I feel like it, which is not very often. I've even tried to change my diet, but after a while I got tired of eating the same boring foods with almost no flavor.

I pick up my head and look around the room. The students are reading their parts, starting to add more personality and life into their characters.

When they reach a part where Romeo and Juliet are alone, Brian, who is reading Romeo's lines, stops and asks, "Can we act this out?"

"I don't think so!" Tiffany shouts. She is reading Juliet.

"Just read," I say and shake my head. I look at Frank and Melody and shrug my shoulders. I notice Frank nodding, but my gaze quickly travels to Melody who has a wide smile on her face.

She smiled at me, again.

As the students finish the scene, I take a quick look at the clock. I can hear the wheels of thought begin to turn faster and faster, though I'm not fully sure of the idea forming.

Alone With Someone

Without answering more than two questions, I push the students to proceed, assigning additional parts as we begin Act II Scene I. The scene is very short, but we do not have an especially large amount of time remaining.

"OK," I think, "this will work. Chorus, Romeo, Mercutio, Benvolio, new parts."

I keep repeating this line to myself as the students read.

Chorus, Romeo, Mercutio, Benvolio, new parts.

Benvolio's last line is read, "Go then, for 'tis in vain to seek him here that means not be found."

There is a brief pause. I can feel twenty-one pairs of eyes focusing on me. I simply sit on the edge of my desk and smile. As I fully realize the silence. I must look silly.

Brian begins to read Romeo's next line, "He jest.."

"New parts!" a loud voice echoes throughout my mind.

"Thank you Brian. That will be all," I say, my head still tilted down toward my book.

"Let's assign new parts and give someone else a chance to read." I look around the room. "We'll need a Juliet. Who would like to be Juliet?" Again I survey the room. About four girls have their hands raised.

I begin to walk up and down the aisles. "We need to pick the right young lady for this 'performance'. After all, this is the balcony scene, the most romantic scene in all literature."

I reach the third aisle and stand between Frank and Melody, facing the front of the room. "We need someone who reads well, is sophisticated, and beautiful."

"How about me?" George says in a falsetto as he stands up.

Chapter 2

The students laugh and tell him to sit down.

"I said someone sophisticated, George."

George gets the hint and sits down, pretending to cry.

"Actually, I was hoping our guest would be kind and read the part."

I look at Melody who is on my right. She looks up at me for a moment. Then, her gaze returns to the pages in her book.

"You don't have to," I say putting my hand on her shoulder. "After all, you didn't volunteer for an English class."

She looks at me again. My eyes and my mind share the same thought, "Please?"

Melody clears her throat and says, "Well, um, OK. I'll be Juliet." Her voice is just as sweet sounding and quiet as I remember from her concert.

I take a deep breath and escort Melody to the front of the room, motioning for her to sit on my desk. She does so without hesitating or complaining. She just looks at me and smiles. Her eyes say, "I trust you."

I smile at her and turn toward the class, "OK, who would like to be Romeo?"

Almost every male hand in the room goes up.

"Maybe this wasn't such a good idea," I think.

"Well, Romeo must also be someone who reads well and is sophisticated," I say, glancing around the room.

"That rules George out again," a voice shouts.

Alone With Someone

"This person should also know the part rather well, and since most of you probably didn't read your assignment for today, I would be willing to bet you haven't even looked at this scene."

Many hands go down as I scan the room again.

"Well, I can't decide," I say. Many of the boys begin to grumble.

"I guess I'll have to be Romeo then." I pause for a second and look at Melody, "That is unless you object?"

She blushes and shakes her head, "no."

"Mr. A., could you read any italicized parts and keep an eye on the time please?"

Frank smiles and says, "Sure."

"Let's begin," I say as I walk to the back of the room.

Frank reads the stage direction, "Romeo comes forward."

With my back still facing the front of the room, I say, "He jests at scars that never felt a wound."

I slowly spin around to gaze at Melody.

"But soft, what light through yonder window breaks? It is the East, and Juliet is the sun."

I continue with the speech, barely looking at the page, trying to capture the moment as well as Melody's innocence and comforting warmth.

With each word, each metaphor, Romeo uses to depict the fair Juliet, the vision in my mind and the vision in front of me blend more and more.

"Two of the fairest stars in all the heaven...dost entreat her eyes...Oh, that I were a glove upon that hand...Bright angel...winged messenger of heaven."

Chapter 2

Then she speaks, softly at first, "O Romeo, Romeo..."

As she continues, I hear and feel her hesitation lessening. Her voice becomes more audible and her words become more clear.

With each line, I seem to move closer. My movements are short and almost unnoticeable. It is as if I am being drawn to my magnetic source, physically and mentally.

As I reach the front of the room, I sit on the edge of a student's desk, staring directly at those dark sparkling mirrors.

Melody recites her next line, "Thou knowest the mask of night is on my face, else would a maiden blush bepaint my cheek."

And blush she does.

Melody breaks with my gaze and tries to find Juliet's next few words. She continues, her eyes escaping from the page only briefly this time.

I hear only parts of her speech as I ponder her actions as well as my own.

"In truth, fair Montague, I am too fond...But trust me, gentleman, I'll prove more true."

"O blessed, blessed night!" I hear myself saying as I look up toward the ceiling. "I am afeard, being in night all this is but a dream, too flattering sweet to be substantial."

This all seems so pleasant, almost dream-like. What exactly is happening? This all feels so pleasing, so comfortable, so amazing.

"Three words, dear Romeo, and good night indeed," Melody says, her eyes still rising only slightly above her book.

"So thrive my soul," I say enthusiastically, lifting my arms upward.

Alone With Someone

"A thousand times good night."

"A thousand times worse to want thy light. Love goes toward love as school boys from their books, but love from love toward school with heavy looks."

"Romeo," Melody says.

"My dear," I reply.

"What o'clock tomorrow shall I send to thee?"

With that, I glance at the ever ticking time piece on the wall.

"Not much time," I think.

I move even closer towards Melody. As she finishes her line, I place my hand under her chin and lift her head.

"Let me stand here till thou remember it."

"I shall forget, to have thee still stand here," she says, hesitating only for a moment.

Her eyes maintain their contact with mine, even as she steals quick glances at the book.

We continue our gaze, my hand still on her chin, though no longer supporting its weight.

"I would I were thy bird," I say as I begin to withdraw my hand and take a small step backward.

"Sweet, so would I," Melody says taking my hand in hers.

My thumb delicately caresses her fingers and the top of her hand.

Chapter 2

"Parting is such sweet sorrow," Melody's eyes continue to shine, still focusing on mine as she completes her thought, "that I shall say 'Good night' till it be morrow."

Without breaking the bond between our hands or eyes, I speak my final words, "Sleep dwell upon thine eyes, peace in thy breast. Would I were sleep and peace sweet to rest. Hence will I to my ghostly friar's close cell, his help to crave, and my dear hap to tell."

I blink, and my closed book falls from my hand onto the floor. The bell rings in the halls, sounding very distant, almost worlds away. Then, it stops.

Voices from the hall manage to leak into the silent room.

As my mind returns to full consciousness, I hear clapping behind me. It starts with just one pair of hands, then two, then three, then...

I shake my head and look at Melody. Her face is just as red as before.

My eyes move from her face down her entire body. Amazing.

Once again I stop and stare at our clasped hands.

It is real. It isn't a dream.

I hold out my other hand toward Melody, offering to help her off the desk.

She moves her head from side to side, her silky hair rippling from the motion. She looks at my hands, then at my face. She accepts my gesture, sliding down with grace and ease.

After a few seconds of stillness, I let her hands slip out of mine and turn to face my class. No one has left. Everyone is standing and clapping.

"Thank you," I say, my face returning to its most recent natural red color. "We'll see you tomorrow."

The students pick up their books and head out the door.

I overhear some students talking as they leave:

"Wow!"

"Intense."

"I actually understand now."

Again, it's the last comment that gets me. "Brian," I call, motioning him toward me, "I was just wondering, what do you understand now that you didn't the last few days?"

He looks me straight in the eye and says, "The love. I understand the love Romeo had for Juliet. You guys were great."

I want to ask him more questions, like "why?" or "how?", but I only manage to say, "Thanks. See you tomorrow."

Brian turns to exit.

I walk toward Melody, who grasps the desk behind her as she leans against it; her head faces the ceiling.

"Oh yeah, you were great too, um, Miss M.," Brian says.

I spin around to see him wink and walk out the door. "Brian!" I shout, maintaining about a medium volume.

From the corner of my eye, I see Frank making his way up the aisle towards us.

"So how about some lunch?" he says as his hands clap together.

Chapter 2

That clap seems to snap Melody out of her daze. She stands up straight and levels her head. Being so close, I notice that she is a couple of inches taller than I am.

"Lunch?" Melody says then looks at Frank and me. We both smile.

"What?" she says.

"Are you OK?" Frank asks.

"Yeah, um, yes," Melody whispers. "Just hungry I guess."

Frank swings his arms toward the door a couple of times saying, "OK, let's go."

"Ladies first," I say looking at Melody.

She moves towards the door. I follow with Frank close behind.

As we near the doorway, I feel a hand on my shoulder. Frank begins to pass on my left saying, "Nice, very nice, and smooth."

There's that grin again, that 'yes-I-knew-it' grin.

Maybe, he does know something.

Chapter 3

We turn left out of my classroom. Frank and Melody are rather quiet. Then again, so am I.

I look at the carpet and my slowly moving feet.

Wow! What am I doing?

I have never acted like that.

What was I thinking?

I'm not too sure, but it was exciting and...

And, not over yet.

I pick up my head and notice we are now at the corner of the hall. I take a quick look around in order to get my bearings; to the right are the doors to the outside and the cold; to the left is another hall that leads to the gym, cafeteria, more classrooms, and the teacher's lounge.

"So, what's for lunch?" Frank says.

What?

Lunch?

I just performed the balcony scene of Romeo and Juliet, with someone I met only once before, and he wants to know "what's for lunch!"

We begin walking again, heading left, down the other hallway. I am next to Melody and Frank is immediately behind us now.

"I don't know," I say. "What would our guest like?" I turn toward Melody and smile.

"I'm sorry?" she says. "Did you say something?"

29

Chapter 3

"Lunch? What would you like?" Frank says, putting a hand on each of our shoulders. "We could either sample the fine cuisine of the cafe or go down the street to Kirk's."

We stop. Frank and I stare at Melody.

What is she thinking?

What thoughts are racing around her intriguing mind?

Is she upset about the scene?

Did I embarrass her?

"How's the cafe food?" Melody finally says, biting her lower lip.

"Well...?" Frank says.

"They have good soup," I stammer out, figuring I had better say something positive.

"That's about it," Frank says sarcastically.

Another negative, not good.

"They have, um, a," I pause, hoping to come up with something. "They have cold soda."

I smile and wait.

Melody smiles and says, "Well, what's Kirk's?"

"It's a nice little place just west of here," Frank says. "Bill went to high school with the owner. We usually go there to relax and unwind after school."

"Don't you have classes after this period?" Melody asks. "Do we have enough time to get there before you have to be back?"

"Actually," Frank says, "Bill has next period off and since I have not been given a sub assignment yet, so do I."

"Well, how's the food there?" Melody asks, looking at both of us. "Do they have more than 'good soup'?" She smiles.

I turn red as I try to come up with a reason not to go. That's right, not to go. It's a great place, but I don't think I want to take someone I just met to a place that has developed into a tradition, a home away from home, a place where the food, beverage, and music are very good (well, pretty good at least). I'm not too sure if I want to bring a beautiful, innocent, young lady like Melody to a place where... well, where, my closest friends are.

"Um, I have papers to grade," I hear myself saying. "I was hoping to get some finished next period. Besides, I don't think Kirk is there today."

"Sure he is," Frank says now on the opposite side of Melody. She turns her head toward him. "Besides, you..."

I shake my head and mouth the word "no" at Frank.

Frank stops speaking, his eyes widen, and he shrugs his shoulders as he stares directly at me.

Melody turns and looks at me as well.

"What?" she says. "What's going on?"

"Nothing. Nothing," I say, my hands moving slightly and my eyes widening as I attempt to look innocent.

"Uh huh, um," Melody says and looks around briefly.

Great, she knows I'm lying.

"Um, I'm going to use the ladies room. Wherever you two decide to go is OK, I'm not really that hungry." Her voice becomes slightly softer.

Chapter 3

Melody walks to the restroom, which is just a few feet from where Frank and I are now standing...alone.

She pushes open the door and turns to look at us.

I smile at her as she enters.

The door closes and my smile turns into an angry frown as I face Frank.

"What?" he says shrugging his shoulders and giggling.

I continue to stare, not saying a word. It is like I'm either trying to send him a message telepathically or sear a hole through his head with infrared vision.

"I just asked where you wanted to go for lunch. Is that a sin?" He continues smiling.

I shake my head as I look downward and close my eyes briefly.

"If you don't want to go to Kirk's, just say so," Frank adds.

I pick up my head and speak to him, never really making eye contact, "Yeah right, I'm going to say, 'I think we should eat in the cafe today in order to save time' and she's going to say, 'OK, do they have good salads' or something, 'I feel like a nice salad today.' Then I say, 'no they don't, but Kirk's does.'"

Frank shakes his head and laughs. "Why don't you just say you don't feel like going to Kirk's? I'm sure she'll understand."

"Sure, sure, I just tell her, 'sorry Melody you get stuck with our misidentified cafe food because I don't feel comfortable bringing such a beautiful young lady, whose last name I don't even know, to a place where my closest friends meet, talk, and will undoubtedly ridicule me with comments days from now as I think about your large illuminating eyes.'"

Alone With Someone

"OK, OK, we could just call the deli down the street. I think they deliver," Frank says, hitting me on the side of the shoulder.

"Uh huh," I mumble, my thoughts becoming lighter as I recall Melody's eyes. They are beautiful. So big, so intense, so alive. I saw so much energy, so much hope in those eyes.

My frown turns into a smile and my head moves from side to side in small motions. Kirk's wouldn't be that bad after all. I could deal with the comments, if there are any. All I have to do is remember those amazing...

Melody exits the restroom and my head snaps quickly toward her.

"We figured we would just call the deli down the street," Frank says. "That way we don't lose any time and still get decent food."

Though I face Melody, I can't seem to pick up my head very high. It's like my own embarrassment and the wonderment of her have become a weight, which is forcing my entire body to decrease in stature.

I manage to lift my head enough to see her right foot gently brushing the carpet. My gaze somehow wonders upward. She raises her bowed head slightly as she seems to sense my stare.

"Um, actually, I'm not hungry," Melody says, her head maintaining that downward angle and her eyes becoming larger. "I forgot to feed my cat anyway. I should be going home."

Wait a minute! She's going to leave. No, I can't let this happen. Just a few more min...hours. Think! Think!

"You have a cat? What's her name?" I say, hoping to stall until something better comes to me.

"Midnight," Melody replies softly.

"That's a good..."

Chapter 3

"Well, I guess it's not yellow then," Frank interrupts.

With that comment, the weight around my neck breaks off and I look at Frank whose large smile diminishes. He mouths the word 'what?' I just shake my head.

"It's been interesting," Melody says.

My head turns quickly toward her.

She looks at Frank, "Thank you for inviting me."

"You're welcome," Frank says, "but you helped me out. I should be the one thanking you."

"I enjoyed it. You have some good players."

She's leaving and I can do nothing except stand here.

Melody turns to me, picks up her head and says, "Thank you." She pauses. "Your class was..." again she stops, bites her lower lip, and completes her thought, "very nice. I haven't read Romeo and Juliet since high school. Thank you."

She extends her hand. I do the same. Our contact is brief. We both seem to slide our hands back almost immediately upon touching.

"You're welcome," I say still a bit perplexed.

We begin walking again, though I am not too sure of the destination.

"Let's get your coat and instruments out of the band room," Frank says. "You can go out down there."

We walk past the trophy case and the glass doors of the gym, both to our right. We proceed to a bi-level staircase, almost parallel to the doors and just a few feet away.

Alone With Someone

We reach the twelfth stair, I count them now to maintain a small amount of control, and enter onto the gym floor through a set of double doors.

Directly on the other side of where we are is the band room, Melody's belongings, and my solitude.

We seem to have reached the doors in no time at all. I still have not come up with any ideas that will keep Melody here even just a little longer.

Frank unlocks the doors and pushes them open allowing Melody and myself to enter before him.

Melody virtually glides to the chair where her coat is draped over its back and two instrument cases lie, one on the floor, the other on the seat of the chair.

So smooth.

"She's leaving!" a loud voice echoes throughout my head.

Frank has passed me and is unlocking the doors to the outside when I shout, "Wait!" There is a slight sense of urgency in my voice.

Frank turns and stares.

Melody stops and almost drops one of her instruments.

There is silence.

After a few seconds, Frank and Melody still have not moved. They are probably waiting for me to say something. What can I say? Think!

"Um, I forgot to thank you properly for helping me out in class. Your performance was extraordinary." I step toward Melody, hoping to continue with this line of thought.

Melody has not moved and as far as I can tell neither has Frank.

Chapter 3

"In fact," I continue, "if Brian learned something after only one reading, you must have seemed just as amazing to them as you did to... Frank was she not amazing?" I spin on my heals to face Frank who is on a small set of stairs still staring at me, or at least in my direction.

"Um, yeah, Melody was very good. You both were..."

"See," I say not letting Frank finish. "Thank you again. I'm sorry that I put you on the spot. I shouldn't have done that. Thank you. I really appreciate it."

Great! I'm babbling. I can't believe it, I'm babbling. I don't babble unless, unless, I'm nervous and I don't have anything to be nervous about. Do I? What am I doing? What is she thinking? What...?

"You're welcome," Melody says, her voice at a very low level, almost the exact level it was at a week ago when we first met.

"I did enjoy it," she says clearing her throat. "It was unexpected but..."

Wonderful! There's a 'but.' There's always a 'but!'

"But I felt...I, a, thought it was sp...um, it was nice," she says blushing.

Huh? I missed something, right.

I must be spacing out again. I missed half of what she said.

Melody picks up the two cases and heads toward the door.

I look at Frank. He just shrugs his shoulders.

As Melody nears him, Frank holds the door open for her and says, "Good bye and thanks again. We'll see you at the next concert. Cindy will be at that one."

Melody smiles, nods her head, and takes one step outside.

Alone With Someone

"Take care. Be careful!" I shout.

Melody stops and turns around. She smiles at me and says, "You too. Thanks again."

Then she disappears through the doorway.

A smile graces my face and even though part of me is confused, I feel mostly content.

Frank taps me on the shoulder and says, "OK, Romeo let's get lunch."

"Huh?" I mumble. "Sorry, what did you say?"

"Lunch. Did you forget about lunch?" Frank says as he takes a bite out of the imaginary sandwich he has created with his hands.

"Sorry," I say, "I'm not really focused today."

"You could say that again," Frank mumbles.

"Huh?"

"Point!" Frank exclaims.

"I'm not especially hungry any more," I say, my head tilted downward.

"You're not what?" Frank says. "After all that, you're not hungry?!?"

All what? After all of what?

"No," I tell him. "Actually, I'm kind of tired."

Tired? Where did I get that from?

"Tired?" Frank replies. "Guess it's all that exercise you've been getting." He pats my stomach.

Chapter 3

"Hey! I get plenty of exercise." I look at him. He has that 'yeah-right' look on his face.

"Well, enough," I say trying to diverge from the topic.

Frank mumbles something and heads toward his office which is behind the large glass windows to my left.

"What did you say?" I ask following him.

"Nothing," he replies, "nothing."

"Did Melody have two cases with her?" I ask somewhat unsure even though I distinctly remember seeing two cases.

"What?" Frank asks as he sits down behind his desk.

"Two instruments. Melody had two instrument cases with her, yes?"

"Oh, yeah," Frank responds rummaging around the insides of his desk.

"Yeah what?" I ask.

"What exactly are you talking about?" He asks, still going through papers inside the wooden piece of furniture. He has a perplexed, looking-for-something expression.

"What instruments did she have?" I ask, not seeing a reason for him not to understand what I was trying to get at.

"Huh? Oh, she had an oboe and..." Frank pauses as he opens another draw.

"I know she plays the oboe. What other instrument does she play?"

"Actually, it is instruments," Frank says. "She plays alto and bari sax and the clarinet."

"Incredible," I mumble under my breath. "I didn't know she was that talented."

Frank picks up his head and looks at me. I blush, though I am not too sure why.

"Well, I mean I didn't know she could um..." I stop and try to come up with a convincing excuse for my prying.

"She did go to the same university I went to, and she is in the orchestra. Many performers..." Frank pauses and pulls a piece of paper out of the bottom drawer. "Here it is. Anyway, many of the performers play more than one instrument."

Frank scribbles something on the bottom of the paper he just pulled out. He looks at me, waiting.

"Oh, really?" I say, trying to get a look at what he wrote. "I didn't..."

"Anything else you wish to know about her?" Frank asks smiling. "She's single, lives alone in an apartment, plays four instruments, and..."

Frank stops for a moment and looks directly at me.

"I, um, was just wondering about the cases," I say stumbling over my words and thoughts.

She's not married.

"Oh, yeah, and she has a cat named, um?" Frank pauses.

"Midnight," I mumble.

"What?" Frank asks, his smile widening.

"I said, I know that."

Whew, got out of that one.

Chapter 3

I think.

"Uh huh. Excuse me a minute. I need to use the washroom," Frank says, moving from his desk toward the office door.

"Sure," I say. "I'll be here."

Frank shakes his head and laughs lightly.

I hear the bathroom door close and begin to pace the room.

What's going on?

I feel excited, enthused, yet somewhat exhausted.

It must be that sugar and caffeine from early this morning really kicking in.

Why did Frank tell me that Melody was single?

Why would he think I would want to know that?

He knows I haven't...

Were my actions earlier that evident, that reflective?

So many thoughts. So many questions. So few...

Wait a minute. What did he write on that paper?

I move toward the desk, my head shifting from the door to the paper lying on top of the pile.

Just a few inches away now. I look directly at the place Frank had written, or at least where I think he had written. The words "You're welcome" are scrawled with his initials underneath.

"You're welcome?" I say.

For what?

My gaze travels upward to more writing on the top half.

It's a name, address, and telephone number.

It's Melody's.

I think.

"So that's her last name," I say softly, as if I knew it all along.

But what would Frank...?

Nah!

Have I been that interested?

What am I going to do with it anyway?

"Write it down," a little voice inside me says.

I fumble through my pant's pocket for my pen.

I don't have paper! I'm a writer without paper!

I look at Frank's desk for a small scrap, one he will not miss.

Attendance slips!

Yes! I could use one of the attendance slips. He won't miss any. He has about twenty-five in this stack alone.

I quickly tear off a sheet of the three by five paper and look at the door.

Good, he's not coming.

I write down the information quickly.

Chapter 3

Melody...Apt 3c...Phone #

OK Done.

"So, are you hungry yet?" I hear Frank say.

I flinch upward and turn to see him entering the room, rubbing his hands together.

"Did I scare you?" he asks.

"No, I, um," I say, still hoping he didn't see me writing.

"What do you have there?" Frank says smiling.

Attendance slip!

"Oh, this? It's just the attendance slip I forgot to turn in last period."

The bell rings and I flinch again.

"I'll bring it up for you," Frank says.

"No, no," I say. "I'll do it. I'm headed that way anyway. Besides, you said you were, um, hungry."

Does he buy it?

Will he let me go now?

"You're right," he says. "I could use some food to go with my lunch." He pats his stomach and smiles.

"Well, I had better get going to um," I pause thinking of where it is I have to go, "in order to get this upstairs before they wonder whether the students were missing or just me. I mean, well you know what I mean."

I fold the paper and put it in my pocket along with my pen.

Alone With Someone

Frank laughs and nods his head.

I move toward the door. "See you later," I say. "Thanks."

I take one step out of the office when, "Oh, Bill."

"Yes," I say abruptly not turning around. I simply freeze and lift my head toward the ceiling.

"What..." Frank says pausing briefly.

Great, he saw me writing down Melody's information. I know he did. He's going to say something.

"What kind of soup do you think they'll have in the cafe today?" he asks.

What?

"Chicken with rice," I say. "Today's Wednesday, they have chicken with rice today."
Why do I know this?

"Thanks. Maybe I'll get some," Frank says.

"You're welcome. See you later."

Even though I can't see him as I exit through the band room doors to the gym, I know he's smiling. He's leaning back in his chair, hands folded across his stomach, and he's smiling.

I can feel little beads of perspiration on my forehead as I make the journey back to my classroom. The second bell has rung and the halls are clear.

So what if he saw me? I didn't do anything wr...

Still in a daze, I reach my classroom, open the door, and enter. I close the door and remember the words at the bottom of the paper Melody's address was on, 'You're welcome.'

I smile, shake my head, and begin to laugh. I am not too sure what I'm going to do with the information now, but I can think of nothing better to do except smile and say, "Thank you."

Chapter 4

"Let's see which key is it?" I fumble with the long mental string in my hand. You would think I would have a separate keychain for the house and garage keys, one for the car keys, and one for miscellaneous keys, like this one. I grab a short circular object with very few grooves on it. What is this for anyway?

It seems that I have decided to save full key chains and have somehow managed to link each set in no apparent order. The only keys not on this strand are those for the school.

"Ah, here it is," I say inserting the key into the lock and turning it to the left. Then, I twist the knob and attempt to push open the door with my shoulder.

Thud!

Oh yeah, left locks it. I look around hoping no one is watching.

This is silly. I can't even open a door. Worse yet, I can't open a door that I've opened hundreds of times before.

I turn the key to the right, push the door open, and enter the house, shaking my head and smiling. I slide my briefcase along the floor toward the kitchen cabinets directly across from the door. I place my backpack on the L-shaped counter to my right and begin to close the wooden barrier which most recently denied me entrance into my own home.

"Wait! The keys are still in the lock," a small voice in my head shouts.

Again, I shake my head as I remove the long chain and toss it on the counter alongside my backpack. I push the door shut and take off my coat, hanging it on the hooks between the counter and door.

I spin around and head toward the darker front room area. I glance at the dining room table on my right, pausing for a moment to look at the scattered pieces of paper with notes and lesson ideas and/or objectives on them. There are literature and psychology books as well, placed haphazardly among and intertwined with the papers, creating a rather discouraging scene.

Unable to bear the sight any longer, I close my eyes briefly and move forward slowly.

I reach the front room in a few steps and look around at the darkness. The thick drapes are closed and the timer for the lights has not kicked in yet. To my right is the cabinet where the TV, VCR, and stereo system are kept. The thought of opening the cabinet's wooden doors and turning on the television crosses my mind. Taking only a second of thought, I let the idea pass and continue to gaze into the ever darkening room.

Surrounding the TV cabinet are shelves with statues and little figurines. There are some clowns, some cartoon characters, and many dogs. I started collecting them when I was in eighth grade. That was some time ago now.

Wow. How many years ago was that? Let's see, I'm...

Ah, forget it. It was a while ago.

My eyes shift to the brown recliner on my left. Thoughts of sitting down in the relaxing chair quickly pass as my eyes wonder first to the lamp resting on a dark brown end table, then to the couch next to it.

That couch looks so comfortable.

I take a couple of steps forward. I could just lay right there and not move for days. OK hours. Half an hour. Fifteen minutes?
OK, a few seconds. I get antsy and need to move at least some part of my body.

Just as the previous two ideas passed, so does the thought of collapsing on the couch.

Alone With Someone

I shake my head and smile as I look at the large mirror above the furniture. I stare at my image. My eyes widen as I turn from side to side, inspecting my all too familiar frame. I pat my stomach and let out a short laugh. I move toward the chair again, still watching my reflection.

"Who would be interested in someone looking like this?"

Like what?

I'm not too sure.

I chuckle briefly and sigh. She was beautiful though, wasn't she? I close my eyes, envisioning her again: long silky hair, soft delicate hands, luscious lips, and...and those eyes, so intense, so peaceful.

My eyelids open slowly and I quietly whisper her name, "Melody."

I hear a click and the entire room lights up. I look at myself in the mirror and drop to the floor, grabbing an arm of the chair. I push my back up against the chair's front and look around, expecting to see someone laughing at me.

I try to hold back the laughter, but it is no use. In fact, I can't help but laugh.

HAHAHAHAHA...HehHehHeh...HAHAHA!

My laughter becomes somewhat lighter as I reach behind me and grab a rectangular, plastic object from the end table. I feel the buttons on its surface. Without looking, I depress the big orange button in the center. I hear a low click as my stereo comes alive. I then begin feeling the remote for other buttons. Again, without thinking or looking, I turn on the CD-player and start the first disc in its six CD-changer. I return the remote and listen.

My laughter has ceased, but I continue to smile. The music plays and I listen.

Chapter 4

"Better get to work," I tell myself. After all, I did miss lunch in order to grade papers I still haven't even looked at.

I push myself up from the floor and head toward the kitchen where my backpack still rests. As I pass the dining room table, I stop and stare again at the, the, um, research material scattered about it. "Well, I guess I'll have to straighten this up somewhat."

I move toward the table and stop. "Nah, I'll just use the kitchen table."

I take one more look at the scattered papers and shrug my shoulders as I head toward the kitchen, still listening to the smooth classical sounds emanating from the front room.

I grab my backpack off the counter, sling it around my shoulder, and make my way to the square wooden table just on the other side of the barrier. This table seems slightly better, though it still has some scattered pieces of paper and a metal framed container with more paper inside it. You know, if I would fully trust my computer, I would save so many trees.

I toss my backpack on a chair and begin to gather a few of the papers left on the edges, placing them into the metal thing. Before I actually set them down, I take quick looks at what I had written. There are many individual thoughts on one paper in particular. I stop and read some of them:

"It is not
External beauty
Which is the soul means
Of inspiration";
"Identity is truly not known,
Nor is the falsehood accepted";
"It is within
And I am without".

"What is?" I ask myself.

Alone With Someone

I take out my pen and scribble "Expand" on the top of the paper. I finger through those sheets which were already in the container. Most of which are half or full page poems written about three months ago; some are ideas that need more elaborating. I look again at the first paper of thoughts and notice the dates are recent, in fact, within the last couple of days.

"I'll have to work on these later," I say, moving the metal container to a distant section of the table, though still within reach of the chair I will be sitting in.

I unzip my backpack, take out the papers I need to grade, and drop them onto the table.

Whomp!

I stare somewhat amazed at the stack. This is only one assignment for two classes. Most students wrote more than I thought they would. Or at least it appears that way. Sometimes, they like to play with the margins or character sizes. This makes the paper appear longer, but the expression of ideas always seem to be lessened. I admit, I did it when I was in school. Though I only did it after I had stuffed many ideas into the paper as well as much support for each one and somehow still came up short on the page requirements. At least that's what I always told myself.

I look around for my briefcase, spotting it just where I slid it, against the cabinets just where I slid it earlier. I move toward it, pick it up, and lay it on the counter. Without even bothering to check the combination, I flip the little latches upward and open the case. I look inside it briefly, then grab a blue folder and a red one.

I always like to check the assignment as I grade papers in order to make sure I am grading the students on what was actually assigned, not what I would like to see. It would be like a supervisor evaluating an employee on how quickly he/she drinks a soda. It isn't part of that person's job, but the supervisor thinks that if one drinks quickly, the person is sloppy and neglective in his/her work and they should not deserve a raise or in this case an "A."

Chapter 4

I like having the assignment paper in front of me, so I can comment directly on areas the students may have missed or just areas that need more clarifying. I tend to use words and phrases directly from the assignment so the students can't say, "You never said we had to do that." Of course, there is always that one who tests the boundaries of creativity and fulfilling the writing requirements.

I do, however, always include my immediate reactions in the margins as well as more lengthy explanations and examples at the end of the paper in the hopes of showing the students how to improve or rather how to drink their soda more slowly, savoring every slurp.

I am rather thirsty now.

I smile and shake my head as I move toward the refrigerator, hoping to quench my self-induced thirst. I open the frig and look at the top shelf where the 2-liter soda bottles usually rest.

I select a bottle that is half full and close the door. Then I reach into the sink, adjacent to the frig, and grab my "cup" which is resting upside-down. Inching the lever on the faucet upward with a free finger, I rinse out my "cup." I then turn off the water and begin to fill the glass with the dark bubbling liquid.

I wash this "cup" before I leave for school every morning, and everyday, it seems, I rinse it out before I use it again. I use the same "cup" for everything. It's not as if I do not have other cups. In fact, the two cabinets to the right of the sink are full of them. I am content, however, to use one "cup" each time I have something to drink. Except for hot tea of course. That goes in my "mug."

The papers.

I should at least start them I guess.

On my way back to the table, I flick on the light switch, realizing that this room is becoming just as dark as the front room was when I came in. There are no timers in here. Thank goodness.

Alone With Someone

I sit down in the chair I had pulled out earlier. I place my drink to the upper left, the folders to the upper right, and let the papers rest directly in the middle. I slide the chair forward slightly as I open the first folder and begin reading the assignment:

Since you have already written papers on where and what your home is, who your family is, and who you believe yourself to be, I want you to draw from those ideas and tell me about a dream or rather an aspiration you have now. Tell me also (yes, also) about how you intend to make that dream a part of your reality.

Remember from your previous papers how your concept of the world can be different from any and everyone else's, but (yes, there's a 'but') you must explain your actions and/or thoughts in order for them to seem realistic to your reader(s).

Therefore, do not write, "Well, I just snap my fingers and I have a million dollars."

This will one, not happen because none of you are politicians, yet, and two, you will not fulfill the page requirements.

One last point, do NOT tell me about a dream you may have had a few nights ago and then attempt to analyze it. Tell me about your hopes. Tell me about your dreams.

I guess I was trying to be specific on this one. Yet, I tried to leave it open so the students had enough room in order to incorporate their individual styles and personalities, because those are the aspects which make any writing interesting.

Before moving on to the first paper, I glance at the assignment once more. I remember explaining to the students that Joseph Conrad once wrote, "We live as we dream, alone." I remember telling the students that although I respect Mr. Conrad very much, I must disagree with his statement. Human beings need other human beings in order to survive, they are gregarious by nature; it is just a part of being human. Therefore, if we share our dreams and attempt to make them real, real for us at least,

51

we may in turn solidify the dreams of others. The roles may alternate in the future, supporting the idea that we can't do it by ourselves.

If we keep our dreams to ourselves, how will we truly know if they have been fulfilled, or at least satisfied? Putting it simply, we need to dream and be dreamed about. This is the nature of our beast.

I also remember that it took me almost an entire class period to give the assignment and explain this concept. I elaborated and gave examples from the students' lives as well as my own. The time was well spent and worth it when just about every student had a look of understanding. They smiled, saying silently, "Oh, now I get it."

This is why I became a teacher, for that look. I actually would have settled for just a few faces like that, but when you get almost the entire class, it just sends shivers up and down your spine.

I gave them the opportunity to write in the ten minutes that remained in class. Everyone wrote something. Some jotted down ideas, others wrote phrases or sentences, and there were even a few who wrote a paragraph or two.

I shake my head, dispelling my remembrance daze, and stare at the first paper. I nonchalantly read the first two lines. The words seem garbled as my gaze travels back to the assignment, "Tell me about your hopes. Tell me about your dreams."

My eyes again shift quickly and rest upon the metal basket I had moved earlier.

My dreams.

I look back to the assignment, then to the students' papers. I move the pile to the right and grab the basket.

My dreams?

Alone With Someone

I take out the first paper, the one on which I had written "Expand." I glance at the page and close my eyes. My ears pick up some of the soft sounds emanating from the CD-player, which is probably on the second or third disc by now. My mind and thoughts drift back to the concert and the soothing sounds of the oboe as well as the beauty and purity of the player; "float"…"meander"…"roam"…"engulfed," hair, lips, eyes...eyes.

My dreams.

A group of words at the top of the page catch my eye again:

"It is not
External beauty
Which is the soul means
Of inspiration."

"How true," I say softly. "I have seen and have spoken with many attractive women What makes her different though? What makes Melody so special?"

I should attempt to reason this out before I get further into it. I have written many poems which were inspired by women with a pleasing outward beauty, but the inspiration seemed to fade when I came to know more about the person inside. They turned out to be self-indulged, lethargic, or just plain boring.

What makes Melody diff...special?

Well, I've only met with her twice now and it seems that everything new I learn about her sounds interesting and positive. She plays four instruments and performs in an orchestra. She probably needs to practice quite a bit, so that shows she's not lethargic.

"Uh huh. What else?" I hear a tiny voice in my head ask.

Well, she didn't tell me most of what I know about her, Frank did. In fact, she is rather quiet. I guess I can say she's not self-indulged or arrogant then. The only thing she really told me was that she hadn't read

Chapter 4

Romeo and Juliet since high school and, um, and...Oh yeah, she has a cat named Midnight.

"Wait a minute, you hate cats." The voice returns.

I don't really hate them, I, um, just, a....

Haven't been around many that's all.

"You dislike cats!" This time the voice is more forceful and insisting.

I pause for a moment, trying to think of a way to, to...

Hold on. I'm being inspired by the person, not the animal which the person possesses. The cat has nothing to do with the inspiration.

"Yet," the voice says. And, if it had a face, I'm sure it would be grinning.

Anyway, am I going to be hurt again if I try to make this a continuous inspiration? With most of the others, I knew the sensation was only going to last for a brief period of time. So, I jotted down my thoughts and expanded on them. There have been only two times in which I wanted to sustain the inspiration while maintaining contact with its source. Both times I felt when it was going to end even before I was told, "You're a nice guy, but..."

"But" what?

I got over them, fairly quickly actually, and still consider them friends, well, acquaintances more than true-everyday friends. We talk only every once in a great while. I think they believe it is much easier on me for some reason or another.

What is?

I admit, unlike the majority of writers today, I need an outside inspiration in order to write and write well. Most of my close friends know this and kid me about it, calling me the last true romantic poet, just as Frank did when he introduced me to Melody.

The Romantic poets drew from others as well as nature to compose their emotional, thought-provoking creations. As far as I'm concerned though, I can not even compare to the likes of Keats, Shelley, or Wordsworth, but my friends enjoying stretching my literary explanations and comparisons.

Will I lose this inspiration the same emotional way I lost the others? I have learned to control my emotions and do not want to test that control.

I pause.

At least not yet.

It should not matter how it will be lost, it's an inspiration. I need to draw from it as much as I can. I'll just have to deal with the ending when or if it happens to come.

I hear a ring. It echoes at somewhat of a distance as I continue to contemplate my recent thoughts.

I guess it shouldn't matter who or what the inspiration is, especially since I have not written anything of value in about four months.

The ringing sounds again, this time somewhat louder and closer.

"The phone," a voice says, "answer it."

I have an answering machine. I might as well use it for something. I don't usually receive calls during the day because anyone who usually phones me, knows I'm at school.

"But it's late," the voice says. "Pick up the phone."

Chapter 4

The device sounds a third time and I realize that if I don't pick it up before the next ring, the machine will take the call. The machine is rather impersonal and I really hate to be that rude, especially if it's a friend.

I jump from my seat and move swiftly toward the phone on the wall directly opposite the windows and where I was sitting. The silence between the rings is just long enough to get there before the fourth sound is made and the machine picks up.

"Hey Bill, how's it going?" the voice on the other end says.

My head is not fully clear from my earlier thoughts, but I recognize the voice to be Steve's, a good friend from high school and a fellow writer.

"Fine. How ya doin'?" I know my voice sounds somewhat wavy and unsure because my thoughts continue to shift.

"How are classes going? Did you hang any students today?"

"Um, a, no, not today," I comment not really paying attention to what either of us has to say. My mind is cloudy and my concentration level is at a minimum.

"What are you doing next Wednesday?" Steve asks.

"I, um, a," I pause, trying to comprehend the question and attempting to come up with an answer.

"Teaching," I manage to blurt out.

"Yeah, yeah, yeah. At night?" Steve says.

"Um," I think for a second longer. "Steve, you know I rarely plan a day, let alone a week ahead."

"Oh yeah, you're too busy doing lessons, grading papers, exercising, dancing..."

Alone With Someone

"Funny," I say softly.

"Never mind," Steve says laughing slightly. "There's this poetry reading I've been invited to, and I thought you might want to come." He pauses. "If your not too busy of course."

"Ah, yeah, sure," I say. "When and where?"

Steve rambles on about the exact location and time as well as how a girl he just met got him involved.

It always seems to be like this, Steve finds a girl, he shows her his poetry, she finds him sensitive, and I get roped into doing something "different" with them.

I'm not too sure how they find him "sensitive." Understanding maybe, but sensitive? He's a six foot one inch blond with hair down past his shoulders who writes about the most depressing times of life. It's the way he writes about them that makes him so effective. He seems to choose just the right words, just the right story line, and just the right genre. He sticks to science fiction for the most part, because he is able to twist and turn the psyche of his characters while rationalizing and justifying it using his own sense of reality. He is able to create his own little world in the stories as he draws from the ever-changing present for examples.

It was only after many years, many diverted conversations, and even a few threats by me to actually kill him and published his works posthumously, that he began "sharing" them with a large number of people and having them put in print by someone other than himself. Now, he seems to be branching out, developing more, and refining his style even more. He makes fairly decent money writing short stories, poetry, and editorials for a few magazines.

"So?" I hear a voice say.

"Oh sorry," I mumble, "I was just..."

Chapter 4

Steve speaks again, "Are you writing? You're working on something right now, aren't you? Bring it with next Wednesday. I doubt these people have ever heard anything by a..."

"Steve!" I say before he can finish. I can almost feel his grin as I finish my thought, "I'm not writing anything." I reach across the table and grab the piece of paper I had become involved with before he called, turning it over.

"OK, what's her name?"

"What?"

"Her name?" Steve says enunciating each word. "Or do you not know it this time either?"

"There's no one," I say, hoping that I sound somewhat assuring. "And what do you mean, 'this time either'?"

"Well, there was the time at the dance club, the time at the New Year's Eve party, and the time at Kirk's after which one of us, not me, wrote a poem entitled 'Your Name' in which the writer sought only to find out the girl's name. Should I go on?"

"Hey, they were inspirations. I couldn't just let them pass, could I?" I pause hoping for some kind of understanding. "You at least should understand inspiration."

"Yeah, yeah," he says and pauses. "So who is she?"

I say nothing. I look at the paper I grabbed moments earlier and flip it over, so that I can see the words. Once again, I scan the phrases. Once again, the visions of Melody and the pleasant sounds of the oboe return to the forefront of my mind.

I want to tell Steve that I am going to write about a beautifully simplistic, intoxicating women who...who...

58

Alone With Someone

Instead I say, "No really, there is no one."

My thoughts betray me and begin to drift even more. They wonder back to the question I had asked myself earlier, "What makes Melody so special?"

Steve says a few things, but I do not comprehend him as I look at the paper yet again.

Why?

Why?

Why?!?

"Bill!" Steve bellows.

"What?" I shout back, somewhat upset that my thoughts are being disturbed. After all, I am...oh yeah, on the phone.

"All right, just tell me this," Steve says sounding moderately perturbed and concerned, "are you working on or thinking of working on something right now?"

"Um," I say, still not wanting to admit to anything, even to myself. Why? I don't know exactly. Maybe it's because I can't really justify the intensity of the inspiration yet.

"Come on! I've known you since high school, I can tell when you're writing something."

So what if I admit that I'm working on something. I'm an English teacher, I should be writing.

"Yes, I am, but it's not even passed the first thoughts yet, so that's all I'm going to say."

Chapter 4

It was as if I was hiding something. I don't have anything to hide. I'm just not sure yet, that's all.

"Fine," Steve says. "I'll let you go then. You gonna be at Kirk's on Friday?"

"Um, yeah," I say, shaking my head, hoping to lose more than my apparent dazed state. "I'm always there. Where else would I be?"

Yeah, that'll teach him. Where else would I be?

"Just checking. See you Friday then. Later," Steve says sounding somewhat disappointed.

"Bye," I mumble.

I hear a click, and still continue to hold the plastic receiver against my ear.

I manage to hang up the phone and return to my seat, still grasping the paper with the ideas on it.

How would he know if I'm writing something? What would he know about my inspirations?

"Hello! He's a writer, remember?" The little voice inside speaks again.

I smile inwardly at my different levels of consciousness, lowering my head to stare at the paper again.

I attempt to relax and look at the first idea. I grasp the paper with both hands now. Slowly, I pick up my head and freeze as my body tenses up. I do not move or rather can not move. The thoughts have stopped. I stare straight ahead, feeling only the flutter of my eyelids as they descend and rise quickly.

Silence...
I sense the stillness.

Alone With Someone

Solitude...
I feel the cold.
Nothingness.
Then...
Wonder...
My eyes widen.
Understanding...
My body relaxes.
Appreciation...
My mind erupts.

An intense light hits my thoughts and I hear a loud harmonious note as the word "HOPE" floats in front of me.

With a flash, the word disappears.

As I readjust my inner sight, I see the word has been replaced by a vision.

It is Melody. Or, rather Melody's face.

The sight remains for only a few seconds, just enough though to make my heart pound quicker. It moves closer and closer toward me.

Finally, the vision stops, and I can see nothing more than her large illuminating eyes.

Astonishing. Simply astonishing.

Another flash and my vision completely fades. My eyes blink twice. I look around quickly.

Nothing.

Her eyes. It's her eyes that send the sparks swirling within me. It's her eyes that make her special. I have never seen such innocence, such purity, such hope in anyone else's eyes before. Never.

Chapter 4

For a brief moment, I feel and know that this inspiration will last. Last, for as long as the intensity remains.

I am the one who must maintain that intensity.

"Write!" I hear the little voice say.

Without questioning or commenting, I grab a loose piece of paper from the basket, take out my pen, and write.

> *If I were granted*
> *A place to gaze*
> *For an eternity,*
> *It would be*
> *In those large*
> *Luminous mirrors*
> *That link*
> *Your world*
> *With mine.*
> *Reflecting,*
> *Glistening,*
> *Radiating,*
> *The simplicities*
> *Of life,*
> *The intricacies*
> *Of living,*
> *Into my*
> *Never ending dream.*

I know that I pause between lines, but other than that, the words seem to flow readily from my mind, to my hand and pen, and onto the paper.

I look over the words a couple of times, take a deep breath, and let out a sigh of satisfaction.

I need a title still. I look through the piece again. The words "luminous mirrors" seem to stand out slightly more than the rest. I stare at those two words.

"Mirrors." Yes. "Mirrors" for what?

I sit in silence, constantly staring at the recently written work.

It's not "mirrors for" it should be "mirrors of...of..."

"Life?"

No.

"Of...?"

Something inside oneself. Something deep.

"Heart?"

No.

I pause and then scribble some words at the top of the piece: "Mirrors of the Soul."

I look at the words I have just written and then scan the other lines hoping to feel that sensation, the sensation that both blend together.

"Yes," I finally whisper.

I lift my head and scan the room. It is slightly darker than when I entered. The only illumination emanates from the neon lights above the stove and table.

I turn my body around in order to take a look at the clock on the microwave, 12:00.

No, that can't be correct.

I look at my watch. Same time.

What seemed like seconds, maybe minutes at most, appears to be hours.

Chapter 4

I rise taking my new creation with me and move toward the small square room adjacent to the kitchen and across from the table, where my computer lies dormant and awaits my touch. I open the accordion-like door and proceed to turn on the components of the machine, awaiting it to come alive.

I maneuver to my word processor and select "New". I begin typing my work, slowly at first, picking up speed with each letter and word. I still have not sat down.

I finish quickly and look at the piece on the screen. It seems a slight more lifeless there. I look back at the hand-written paper and smile. With a few key strokes I place my letterhead at the top, save it, and print it.

I have yet another copy within seconds. I inspect this one too.

"Send it," the little voice says, returning.

What?

"Send it to her."

What? I...I...can't.

"Send it."

I contemplate the thought and look around the room, almost expecting to see Frank standing at the door smiling.

I do have her address now. Besides, I don't actually have to make verbal contact with her again. My guess is that she'll be hidden in the crowd again at the concert.

Without thinking any further, I grab an envelope off the shelf next to the computer, fold the newly printed piece and place it in the envelope. I take out the attendance slip I had written her address on and begin copying it onto the envelope. I put a stamp on it, leave the small room, and head toward the door.

Alone With Someone

I grab my coat and open the door. No problem this time. I shut the door, but do not lock it as I leave the house. Then, I walk down the steps through the open gate (whoops, must have forgotten to close that when I came home), and head toward the mailbox.

I expect to feel happy, sad, indecisive, but I feel nothing.

I reach the mailbox at the end of the block, about fifty yards from my house which stands in the middle of the block.

Slowly, I open the lid and place the envelope inside. One hand on the envelope, one hand on the lid, I close it more slowly than I had opened it. At the last possible second, I pull the envelope out and shake my head, keeping the lid open slightly.

"What am I doing?" I whisper. One can not have a continuous inspiration if an initial attempt at maintaining it is not made. If she accepts it, there should be many more opportunities to compose. If she puts it aside, it was only one piece and I can at least feel content that I didn't waste the inspiration.

"Send it," the voice says.

I pull the lid open a slight bit more and put the envelope back inside. Once again I do not let the paper object slide down into the blue metal container.

I can't. Not now at least.

I turn and head back toward my humble abode.

"If not now, when?"

I ignore the voice and continue home.

Chapter 5

"It's been a week; OK a little over a week; nine days to be exact, but who's exact these days, certainly not me."

So it's been over a week.

"Nine days."

Nine days, since I wrote that first poem and decided not to send it.

"Wouldn't send it."

Couldn't send it. It just wasn't time yet.

I have composed a few other pieces since then and have been rather happy. However, I know I must seem somewhat distant to my friends.

"It's kind of chilly today, maybe we should have driven," a voice says, and I know it is no longer my own.

I turn my head to the right and say, "It's not that bad."

"Distant?" my inner voice says sarcastically.

I am with Frank walking the all too familiar path from the school to Kirk's. He is carrying nothing, while I have my black backpack thrown around my right shoulder. We have said very little so far.

Actually, I think Frank has been talking, I've just been nodding my head and walking, responding every once in a great while, when I am able to pull myself away from my almost constant justification process.

It seems that I am only able to break the chain when I am teaching. I seem capable of rambling on and covering questions about grammar, vocabulary, and even Romeo and Juliet without any apparent problem. At least, I think I can.

Chapter 5

When the bell rings, however, my thoughts are my own once more. I sit at my desk until that next bell sounds and up I go again. It's like a boxing match where neither fighter shows signs of considerable fatigue, and the referee will not stop the fight, due to the lack of any punishing blows.

We are about a football field's length away from Kirk's. I pause my thought process and look at it's outside. It's about the size of a one story house, though wider. Its dark brick surface contrasts the white concrete of the mini-mall directly behind it. Its pitched roof adds to the feeling of "home."

About four years ago, before they started building the stores, Kirk bought the tavern and half of what is now the mall parking lot. The group that put the shops in, ended up paying almost as much for the parking lot as Kirk did for the entire area.

Kirk never really thought that his place would be that busy or that it would require that much parking space, but the guy who sold it to him was leaving the state and wanted to get rid of it. It all sounded rather fishy, literally. The guy was moving to Alaska. He made Kirk an offer, and Kirk took it.

I remember all of us joking with Kirk saying, "Hey, we have a place to play football now"; and "Yeah, this would be a great place for a truck stop, if we were even close to the expressway"; and "Hoping to pay off that lone a little quicker, huh?"

Man, were we wrong. Kirk used the money from the parking lot sale to expand on the older style tavern. He modernized almost everything inside and added a small stage and even smaller dance area. Of course, we were all there helping move stuff in and out, shaking our heads in disbelief and satisfaction that one of us was that much closer to his dream.

Frank and I reach the doors, I shake my head, smiling.

"What?" Frank inquires.

Alone With Someone

"Nothing," I say, still smiling. "Just thinking."

Frank opens one of the doors, smiles, gestures me in, and says "Isn't that dangerous?"

"Funny," I think.

The moment I step in the doorway, I can almost reach out and touch the aura. I feel rather comfortable and at ease. My constant thought process recedes more than if I was teaching.

The room is dimly lit by fluorescent lights, hanging high above the simple wooden tables which are covered with checkered cloths; a slight aroma of liquor seems to have settled in to remind the occupants of where they are; the soft sweet sounds of a saxophone and the light brushes of a cymbal are heard to remind us why we are here.

A combination of sounds stir up the many memories we have shared and the emotions which went along with them. The deep vibrations of the bass bring about thoughts of difficulties and sadness, while the high pitched squeals of a sax, which are the trademark of the player, cause the times of joy and excitement to make their way to the forefront of my mind. No song is without those uplifting shrills. It is those, mostly brief, interludes which manage to hold the entire piece and us together.

The mesmerizing music comes to an end. I smile and nod approvingly. Raising my hands toward the musicians, I clap lightly, the fingers of my right hand gently striking the palm of my left.

Almost instinctively, Frank and I move toward and reach a table directly in front of the simple stage and dance floor which is in the middle of the room. The musicians move toward us smiling, Joe with his wooden sticks in hand, and Jerry with his classic Marc VI saxophone. Joe is about 5'11" with dark curly hair, veins protrude slightly from his arms, outlining his muscle tone, and a pair of thin dark-rimmed glasses, which are removed when he plays an intense piece, rest upon his nose. Jerry is 6'3" with broad shoulders, dark thinning hair, tan skin, and a "trust-me" smile.

Chapter 5

We have been together since high school. There have been many moments of joy and sorrow, some of which struck at and shook the very foundation of our friendship. Those moments, however, are an important reason why we are here today and every other day for that matter. This is our place of respite. Here, we are able to get away, escape if you will, from the monotony of our everyday lives; Jerry from small gigs and the police station, where he has followed in his father's footsteps; Joe from his morning radio show on the local WOMP; and Frank and I from the halls which continue to bring us together. Frank is rather new to our group, but just as it was at our high school lunch table, he is a much welcomed addition.

We shake hands, pull out our chairs, and sit down, all without saying a word. I slide my backpack under the chair, positioning it between my feet. Before we can motion for our usual round of drinks, Kirk is placing them down in front of us. He is of medium height, about an inch shorter than Joe, somewhat heavy set, and a true embodiment of his Scottish heritage. He must have jumped off the stage after that last number because our drinks are here much quicker than usual. He has taken much criticism from us, but has proven that luck is much more than a four letter word.

Kirk grabs a chair and sits down. We all look at each other, raise our glasses, and say, "Salute."

Jerry sips from his glass of Chablis. Joe and Kirk take gulps of their beers. Frank tastes his lemon-lime concoction (only he and Kirk know exactly what is in there). And, I drink from my mug of root beer. I gave up drinking right before I started teaching, only touching the stuff on very special occasions. Alcohol just doesn't satisfy my caffeine driven taste buds.

"So, are we fully awake today?" Joe asks, quickly looking at each member of the group, resting lastly and longest on me.

Within a few moments it seems, everyone's eyes are on me.

Alone With Someone

"What?" I say smiling and almost bursting out with laughter, though I'm not particularly sure why. "I wasn't that bad last week."

I look around the table. Everyone has that look on their faces. You know, the look that says, "Oh, yes you were. How could you even ask?"

"No, no, you weren't that bad," Joe says, as a fake smile forms on his face and he begins to nod his head.

"No, I think it was more like this," Jerry says, almost mimicking Joe, except he lifts his head up toward the ceiling more and bobs his head slightly less.

Kirk joins in saying, "You both have it wr..."

"OK, OK, I get it. I was just tired I guess," I say cutting Kirk off.

"Tired? Tired? He's been doing that for a few..." Frank says, his voice diminishing as he attempts to finish his thought.

My eyebrows are raised and my left hand is rubbing my chin slowly. My heart pumps faster and my face reddens. I do not want Frank to say anything or give his reason for my recent actions. It is bad enough I have to put up with his looks and smiles. I don't especially need the comments of the others as well.

Please don't say anything, Frank.

My eyes widen and I stare directly at him, my heart still pounding and my hands resting on the table.

"It must be all that exercising," Frank finally says as he turns his head away from me.

Please don't...Hey, he didn't say anything. Thank goodness.

Whoa, wait a minute. What was there to say? What was he going to tell them that would have been so bad?

Chapter 5

The little voice returns saying, "Well, there's M..."

"We've all had those days," Joe says, thankfully disrupting the comments within.

"Especially Bill," Jerry adds.

"Maybe, you should try what Frank's drinking. That should wake you up," Kirk says, nodding at Frank's glass.

"Wake him up? Hell, it'll wake him up and give him the exercise he keeps saying he gets. What's in that thing anyway?" Jerry says sarcastically.

I frown. My eyes widen and slant downward.

"He's got that look again, guys," Kirk points out.

"What look?" I inquire, maintaining my expression.

"You know, that innocent-child look," Jerry says.

"The look that some women give you when they want something or did something they think you will not like. You know, puppy-dog eyes," Joe says, not feeling the need to justify the point any further.

"So, you're saying I'm a puppy-dog?" I say with a straight face.

"No, no, just that..." Joe adds, stopping short of completion.

"So, you're saying that I'm a female then," I say still maintaining no distinguishable expression.

"No, no, I, um, mean..." Joe stumbles with his words briefly.

A small smile forms on my face and I look directly at Joe.

"Why you!" Joe exclaims.

Alone With Someone

We all laugh.

We always seem to laugh.

"Ah, don't," Joe says, putting emphasis on the second word.

"What?" I say smiling and shrugging my shoulders slightly.

"I guess he's awake today," Kirk says.

"You should have walked here with him," Frank says, starting to nod and smile.

I flash a quick blank stare at him and he stops.

"OK, OK," Jerry says, "I think we've picked on Bill enough today."

"Bill's not fun to pick on anyway," Joe says. "He always makes you feel guilty, and he doesn't even have to say anything." Joe laughs a little.

"Yeah, I know what you mean," Frank chimes in.

"We could pick on Kirk," Jerry says. "It's always easy to make fun of Kirk or something he did. And, he takes it so well." A malicious grin forms on Jerry's face as he turns toward Kirk.

"Now class, we shouldn't pick on anyone," I say. "How would you like it if..." I smile and begin to laugh.

"If what?" Joe asks in a loud whining voice. "If someone was to pick on me? Huh? Huh? Well, go ahead. I can take it." He folds his arms and looks at all of us.

No one moves or says anything. After what seems like about five minutes, we all burst out laughing. We each look around at the other tables.

Chapter 5

Still chuckling somewhat, Kirk says, "Can we keep it down just a bit? You'll chase away my paying customers."

"I think I pay enough by drinking this thing," Frank says lifting up his glass and swishing around its contents.

"Frank's OK," Kirk says, "but the rest of you free-loaders..."

"Free-loaders?" Joe shouts.

"Free-loaders?" Jerry reiterates. "Who provides quality entertainment...free?"

"I'm not sure, it's either the cook or that clock over there," Kirk shoots back still laughing a little. "No, no just kidding. Actually, I'll be sorry when you get a regular gig. I haven't been able to get any good musicians in here...cheap."

"Well, Frank plays about fifty different instruments," I say, my laughter ceasing. "How about Frank sitting in sometime?"

Though the thought has crossed my mind before, I don't believe I've ever verbalized it. Frank is an excellent music teacher and a very good saxophonist, but I have never pictured him on stage with Joe and Jerry, playing jazz or rock.

It might be because most of the pieces I've heard him play have been either technical or classical. Even now, I find it difficult to see him performing without any music in front of him and very little if any practice with the other members of his group.

"Hey, why not?" Joe says. "Why haven't you sat in with us before?"

"No, no, I couldn't," Frank comments. "Besides, you never asked before."

"How about next week?" Jerry asks.

"No, you guys sound great," Frank responds. "I wouldn't want to ruin it."

"We've had a few other people sit in," Joe says looking at me, smiling. "Some of them didn't quite click the first time."

I just shake my head and look at Frank. "What do you have to lose. Besides, it will be an experience."

"Yeah, an experience I won't live down for a while. I don't know what you guys play anyway," Frank says shifting his gaze between Joe, Jerry, and myself.

"Come on," Joe says. "We play the basic sets every time, then we just jam." He raps his sticks on the table and looks at Kirk, "Sorry."

Kirk smiles and says, "It's OK, just don't leave any more dents."

"So, you'll sit in next week," Jerry says. "No more arguments."

"Not next week," Frank says abruptly. "How about in two weeks? It'll give me more time to um, a..."

"To what? Practice?" Joe says laughing. "Bill says you're very good. Right, Bill?"

"Um, yeah," I say surprised to be in on the conversation again. "He's great." I smile at Joe. As I turn toward Frank, my lips form a grin, a grin much like Frank had after Melody visited my class.

"You got him," my little voice says.

"All right, two weeks," Jerry says, "but then you'll play even if your students have to drag you here bound and gagged. I'm sure they'll like that."

"Fine, fine, two weeks," Frank says downing his drink. He stands and brushes off his pants.

"Where are you going?" Joe asks. "You said two weeks, not two seconds."

"Um, I forgot," Frank stammers out, "I promised Cindy we would um, go to the movies tonight."

He is met with a chorus of "Yeah, right," from all of us.

Who does he think he's kidding? He's going home to practice. Practice what, I'm not too sure. He can hum or whistle almost their entire set.

I watch Frank make his way to the door we had most recently entered. Just as he pushes the right door open, Steve enters from the left. He is about 5'11", has long blond locks and a very white complexion. He is carrying a leather folder with him.

"Where are you going?" Steve asks rather loudly. "It's still early."

Frank mumbles something, then leaves. The door swings slightly back as a small vacuum effect occurs finally sealing the entrance once again.

Steve crosses the room to our table and sits downs at the same chair Frank just vacated.

"So, what's up with him?" Steve says, motioning for his drink.

"Oh, nothing," Joe says and starts to laugh.

Seemingly holding back laughter of his own, Jerry adds, "We invited him to play with us in two weeks."

"Invited?" Kirk says. "You insisted!" He too chuckles.

Kirk's bartender sets down two shots in front of Steve and heads back toward the bar.

Steve picks up one of his shot glasses and holds it up in the air. We all pick up our drinks and do the same.

"Salute," Steve says and proceeds to down the first shot. We all take sips from our drinks, though somewhat smaller than that first one.

"So, you guys going to do a classical piece or what?" Steve asks.

"We may have to," Jerry says. "I don't know if Frank knows anything else. After all, he's been teaching for a few years now and he has a masters in classical music."

Classical? The sweet sounds of the oboe; "soft curvaceous body"; "placidity"; Melody; deep intoxicating, "large luminous mirrors."

"Isn't that right Bill?"

"What? Huh?"

"I said, isn't that right?" Jerry enunciates each part of his question this time.

"Is he still at it?" Steve says sarcastically.

"He wasn't a few minutes ago," Joe says, waving a hand in front of my face.

"Maybe, he's been possessed or something," Kirk adds.

"I'm fine," I say, hoping to stop this avenue of conversation. "Besides, who or what would want to possess this body?" I pat my stomach and lean back in my chair.

"Is he still doing the head bobbing thing?" Steve asks as he mimics the actions the others performed earlier.

"I said, I am fine!" I say, this time widening my eyes and looking at each one of them.

"OK, OK," Joe says laughing a little. "We believe you."

Chapter 5

"I think I know why he spaces out," Steve says as a devilish grin forms on his face. "Last week, I called him and he was like this on the phone. I didn't think anything of it until he acted the same way last Friday here, and again when he came to a poetry reading with a friend and me."

Steve continues to explain how a few people tried to ask me what I thought of a particular poet, but I said very little, nodded my head, and seemed to be taking notes.

They weren't notes at all. They were lines from poems I had started earlier.

I remember everything that happened that day, but I reacted to very little if anything. I wanted so much to capture the picture I had in my head before it disappeared. Once it's gone, it's gone. I guess, I get somewhat selfish when I'm inspired.

Steve has finished his story and I have done nothing to stop him.

"The only time he gets like this is when he's insp..."

"Steve!" I shout, pleading to him with my eyes.

"What?" Joe interrupts. "When does he get like this?"

"Yeah, it's happened before, but not for this long," Jerry adds.

I feel like an outsider, even though I am the main topic.

"He's inspired," Steve says shrugging his shoulders at me.

"So?" Kirk says, "What's that got to do with him..." He stops, smiles, and nods his head. The others laugh briefly and softly.

"Do you remember the other times he was like this?" Steve asks.

"Yeah," Joe says, "that time we went to the bar, and..."

Alone With Someone

"Say something!" the little voice echoes throughout my head.

What? What can I say?

"How about the time after the jazz concert," Kirk adds.

"Which one?" Jerry asks. "We've been to so many."

"You know," Joe says, "that concert you almost got up on stage to show the guy how to really play a saxophone."

"There were so many," Jerry says again, laughing. "No, no, I remember now."

"Are you just going to sit here?" the little voice says sarcastically.

What am I going to do, leave like Frank? That would be ridiculous.

"So, you're just going to sit here?" the voice asks.

"And, what was at each one of those places?" Steve asks, evidently trying to draw a conclusion for everyone to see.

"Music," Jerry says.

Yes.

"Yes, but what else," Steve adds, looking at each one of them, avoiding me.

There is a moment of silence and again, though I am sitting right next to them, I feel half way across the room.

Joe looks at me, smiles, and says, "Women!"

"Ding, ding, ding," Steve sounds. "We have a winner."

Wait a minute, that's my line.

Chapter 5

They all look at me as if waiting for a response.

After a few moments of silence, I say, "What?"

"So, who is she?" Joe asks leaning toward the center of the table.

"Yeah, who is she?" Jerry echoes.

"He wouldn't tell me last week either," Steve says.

"You mean you knew about this last week and didn't say anything?" Joe asks.

"Hey, I thought it was just one of those temporary things again," Steve says. "All I got out of him last week was that he was writing something."

"OK, where is it?" Joe pushes.

"Who? What?" I say innocently, my mind spinning somewhat.

"Ah, come on!" Joe says. "You've always let us see your stuff."

There is another moment of silence. At least, it feels only like a moment.

Ah, what the hell, I'll tell them.

"They'll laugh," says the little voice.

They're my friends. We've known each other for how long. They will not laugh...at me in particular at least.

"It's your call," the voice says fading to the back of my mind.

"Do you have a copy of what you wrote?" Jerry asks.

I shake my head quickly, attempting to clear my thoughts. "I, um..."

"Of coarse he does," Steve says. "He's a teacher and a writer. I carry only my current pieces with me," he says patting the dark brown, leather folder to the right of him on the table. "But, Bill here, carries everything he has ever written."

The others chuckle at Steve's comments, but I just sit back in my now rather uncomfortable, hard wooden chair.

"That's not true," I say. "I only carry some of it, the good stuff, or the pieces I may need to add to."

"Has anyone ever seen him come here without his backpack?" Steve asks, pointing at my black bag on the floor.

I forgot it was there. I'm glad I didn't get up and leave. I probably would have forgotten it...OK, maybe not.

"So, pull it out Billie," Joe says, motioning me to do so.

"Yeah, let's hear it," Jerry adds.

"I um," I say trying to think of something. "It's not really finished yet." I manage to blurt out, my face turning bright red.

"Ah, come on. We've heard your stuff before," Joe persuades, reiterating one of his earlier comments.

Yes, they have heard many of my other writings. In fact, they've heard or read just about everything I've written since high school. I've used them as my test audience. Even though they're my friends, they are honest about my writings. I think.

This one's different though. This one's...she's... she's sp...

I shake my head again and reach for my bag, placing it on my lap. Instinctively, I unzip it and pull out a green folder. I take out one piece of paper from the front of the thick stack.

Chapter 5

"Wow, you do have everything in there," Kirk says smiling.

I am just about to put the paper back when Joe says, "Kirk was just kidding. Go ahead, read it."

"It's not really finished," I say swallowing hard.

"Neither is our music most of the time," Jerry says reassuringly, "but we still play it in front of strangers. We just want you to read it to us."

"All right," I say, swallowing again.

I proceed to read from the poem exactly as I wrote it nine days ago. My head remains angled downward and my eyes are glued to each word.

I finish and pause briefly. I raise my head and look at my friends. They're not laughing. Then again, they're not saying anything either.

"Anyone want another round?" Kirk says as he gets up and moves toward the bar.

Was it that bad?

"So, who is she?" Steve asks staring blankly at me as if he was still trying to comprehend parts of the piece.

"Yeah, who is she? Or, are we going to have to figure that one out too?" Joe asks smiling.

"No one," I say. "It's just someone I met at a concert."

"Here we go again. What concert?" Jerry says. "And, how come we weren't invited?"

"Come on, you know that I go every year to..."

"Yeah, yeah, that's right," Joe says. "He has season tickets or something. It's like once a month from January to June."

"Oh yeah," Jerry says somewhat enlightened.

"Isn't that the symphony?" Steve asks.

"Yes, it is," I say. "So?"

Kirk returns with the drinks, passes them out, and sits down again. "So what did I miss?"

"Bill's inspired by some chick he met at a symphony or something," Steve says.

"She's not a 'chick'!" I say defensively, my heart pounding.

"Oooh, I think we've hit a nerve," Joe retorts.

"She's just not a 'chick', OK?" I say looking around the table, my heart rate still elevated.

"So, do you know her name this time?" Steve asks.

"Yes," I say quietly.

"Yes? And, what is it?" Jerry asks, sipping from his second glass.

"You've done it now," the little voice says returning.

"Melody," I say. "Her name is Melody and..."

"And, what?" Joe says. "What's up Bill?"

"And she plays the oboe in the orchestra," I somehow ramble out.

"Have you even talked to her?" Jerry asks.

"Um, yes," I say.

"Yes?" Joe adds.

Chapter 5

"Man, this is like getting a "A" from Mr. Z," Kirk says taking a gulp of his beer.

"Frank, um, Frank introduced us," I say feeling a slight more at ease.

"So that's why you were giving him those looks," Jerry says.

I nod my head.

"Why didn't you just tell us?" Joe asks. "Hell, you haven't gone out on too many dates lately."

"Don't remind me," I say smiling somewhat.

See, they didn't laugh. They seem concerned and I finally get to talk about the situation with someone other than myself.

"So?!?" my little voice says sarcastically and then fades.

"So, have you gone out with her yet?"

"What's she look like?"

"Is she hot?"

"Kirk!" Joe shouts.

"What?" Kirk responds. "I was just asking.

"I haven't actually been out with her yet, but we performed Romeo and Juliet in my classroom," I say smiling.

There is another brief silence. Then, everyone laughs including me, though I'm not too sure why.

"I bet you did," Kirk says.

We all stop laughing and stare at Kirk.

Alone With Someone

"So let me get this straight," Jerry says, "you've played Romeo and Juliet, but you haven't gone out on a date yet? Am I missing something here?"

"Ah, yeah," I say, my smile and eyes widening.

They laugh again. I just continue to smile and sit back in my chair, patiently waiting the next question.

"So have you given her the poem yet?" Steve asks.

"Um, no," I say becoming somewhat intrepid again.

Joe, Jerry, and Kirk stop chuckling and stare at me.

In unison, Joe and Jerry say, "What are you waiting for?"

"Um, I..." I say trying to think of the reason I gave myself nine days ago.

"Don't you always give your poems to the inspiration if you know where they live and if you write more than one piece?" Steve asks smiling or rather grinning.

I swallow, my mouth is rather dry now, so I take a drink of my rootbeer.

There, that gave me another moment.

"Do you know where she lives?" Joe asks.

"Yes, yes, I do," I say with conviction. "In fact, I have the envelope all addressed and ready to be mailed."

"So?" Joe says.

"So what?" I say, taking another sip of my beverage, hoping for a boost of caffeine or something.

"So when are you going to give it to her?" Joe says, this time a little more adamantly.

Chapter 5

"Well, I was going to um, wait..." I say.

"Wait?" Jerry says. "Wait? You find a girl, you write a poem about her, you're spaced out for over two weeks, and you haven't even asked her out?"

"Um, yeah."

"So, it was easy to do the Romeo and Juliet thing, but you can't send a simple poem?" Steve adds sounding somewhat upset. "What happened to the last 'true' romantic?"

"Don't start," I say. "Besides, it doesn't quite work that way any more."

"Start what?" Steve responds, shrugging his shoulders. "What doesn't work what way?"

"You know and stop with the last 'true' romantic thing."

"He's just trying to help," Joe says. "Listen, if you can't send it, give it to me, I'll do it."

"No, no, I'll do it," I say as if it were some sort of burden.

"When?"

"Later."

"Come on," Jerry says. "When's the next concert?"

"Next week, Wednesday," I respond.

"So you have to send it now," Joe says.

"Just send it," Kirk says.

"Look at it this way," Steve says, "some guys pick up girls in bars with one-liners, you, you on the other hand, write poems about them. And, speaking as a fellow writer, girls seem to really enjoy it when you write something 'deep' about them."

"Yeah, look at the other girls you wrote poems about. They appreciated them, didn't they?" Jerry says winking.

"Yeah, but where are they now?" I ask. "Sure it was nice to have someone around for a short time, but Melody is different. She's... she's...I don't know." I shake my head and look around the table for a response.

"Just send it and worry about what will happen later," Steve says. "Enjoy the moment now."

"Yeah, what have you got to lose?" Jerry adds.

"Well, let's see, you have Nicole, Kirk has Crystol, Steve has his harem, and Joe can go out with just about anyone. What do I have right now? A good education and quite a few 'friends.' That's what I got." My tone is very sarcastic and I can feel it.

"Yeah, but what have you got to lose?" Jerry says again, enunciating the last word.

There is silence.

I look at each one's face, hoping to find another reason not to send the piece. I pause at each person, looking directly into each one's eyes, hoping.

"OK, I'll send it," I say finally. "And, what do I do if..."

"If what?" Steve asks. "If she says it was a lovely poem, but she's not interested? Or better yet, she falls for it? You've still lost nothing!"

"But I would have lost the inspiration and..." I say, not able to put my finger on what else.

87

Chapter 5

"Think of how more intense it could be if you two hit it off," Joe says smiling.

"Yeah," Jerry says. "You might even be able to finish that book you started in high school."

Jerry laughs, then Joe, then Kirk and Steve, finally I join in.

"You're right," I say still giggling.

I pull out the sealed envelope from my bag, zip the sack back up, and rise from my chair.

"I'll go with you," Joe says and stands.

"Me too," Jerry chimes in and rises from his seat as well.

"Might as well," Steve says, pushing himself upwards.

"Well, someone's got to stay and watch the bar," Kirk adds.

"Thanks guys, but I think I need to do this by myself."

"I think we should go with you, just to make sure," Jerry says.

"I'm not in high school any more," I say. "Besides, I'm much too old to have an entourage with me as I mail a letter."

"But you do teach high school. Some of it may rub off," Steve says sarcastically.

"Funny," I say. "No, I'll do it. I promise."

There are times when being with your friends makes you feel so young. I've taught hundreds of students these past few years, and I still act much like a teenager when it comes to these situations.

I say good-bye and head toward the door.

Alone With Someone

I reach the door and stop. I turn around and face the table, and smile. They are all sitting again watching me leave. "Just kidding," I say, turning back toward the door and exiting.

I walk to the big blue box about fifty yards or so from the front door of Kirk's. "How convenient," I think.

For some reason, I feel like eyes are staring at me from a distance, but I don't turn around.

I pull open the hatch, place the envelope inside and pause.

Hum, I wonder if this could be considered de ja vu? Different mailbox, same scenario.

I laugh inwardly.

There's something missing, however. I can't quite remember though.

I let go of the envelope and watch it slide down into lifeless container.

I close the door and open it again.

Gone.

"Now what?" my little voice says.

"We wait," I say, recalling what was different.

Chapter 6

I don't want to be here.

Why am I here?

Did she receive the poem yet? I hope not.

I shouldn't be here.

"I told you to wait," says my little voice.

Wait? Wait, for what? Besides, the guys said I should have sent it.

"The guys?"

Yes.

"Point!"

Funny.

"Did you hear that flute solo?"

Huh?

"What?" I say out loud and look around. I am at the concert hall, walking toward the stage with Frank and his wife, Cindy.

"I said, did you hear that flute solo?" Frank reiterates.

"Um, yeah," I stammer out. "It was nice."

"Nice? Nice?" Frank questions sarcastically. "Last month, the oboe solo was incredible, this time the flute is 'nice'?"

"Yeah. I should really be going home," I say quickly.

91

Chapter 6

"Why?" Frank asks. "You don't have any papers to grade. I talked with some of your students and they said you've returned everything they've written, including the five paragraph essays they turned in two days ago." Frank laughs and shakes his head.

"I like to return their papers as soon as possible," I say hesitating in my steps. "I'm actually kind of tired. I should just go home."

"Scaredy cat," Frank mumbles, slurring the words.

"What?" I say.

"Nothing," Frank replies as Cindy hits his arm.

"Ow! What was that for?" Frank asks smiling and holding back his laughter.

"That's enough," Cindy says shaking her head.

I look at her and smile. Cindy is about an inch shorter than Frank, has short blonde hair, and wears a medium-width, brown-rimmed pair of glasses. She too teaches music but at a private high school for girls where they have an excellent woodwind ensemble.

As we reach the stage and are just about to disappear behind the giant blue curtain, I notice them whispering back and forth.

Frank smiles and says, "So, do you think you could be a little more social this time?"

"Frank!" Cindy exclaims.

"Sorry," Frank says laughing and taking the first steps backstage. "Would you like to meet more of the players?"

"Um, sure," I say, hesitating even more as I follow them further backstage.

Alone With Someone

We take a few steps and I notice Mr. Kay about ten feet in front of us. Though my thoughts are still somewhat clouded with concern, I manage to wave to him and smile.

He sees me and waves back. We move closer and I see him look at Frank, bring his hands together, palm against palm, and move them apart a few times, keeping his pinkies together.

What does that mean?

I look at Frank and remember, "English teacher."

Frank laughs a little and Cindy taps his arm again.

We meander through the crowd in some direction, though I'm not too sure what...it...is.

Oh, no, he's bringing me right to her again.

"Run!" my little voice shouts.

I let the thought pass and before the idea is able to complete another cycle...

"Hi, Melody," I hear Frank say. "You remember Cindy, don't you?"

"Oh, hi. Um, yes. How are you?" Melody reaches out and shakes Cindy's hand in one downward motion.

That voice, so sweet, so soft, so...

"And you remember Bill, of course," Frank says motioning toward me and moving Cindy to the side.

I put my head down, then pick it up quickly, gazing at Melody's innocent face.

She turns a bright shade of red the moment my eyes meet hers.

"Placidity."

How true!

I smile at her and bow, not wishing to risk physical contact, yet.

She smiles and does somewhat the same.

"She received the envelope," my voice whispers.

How can you tell?

"Look at her. She probably has it with her now."

"Cindy and I were wondering," Frank says, "if you two would like to join us for some dessert?"

I want to reply, but I can't seem to open my mouth or break my gaze.

"Um, I, um," Melody says, turning away and taking a deep breath.

With the trance broken, I am able to respond. I turn my head toward Frank and say, "Really, I should be getting home, but..."

"Yeah, I should be getting home as well..." Melody says quickly, her words trailing off toward the end as if she has something to add.

"Don't be party poopers," Frank says. "We'll just go to the restaurant down the street, have a sundae or something, chat, and head home."

"Well, I don't..." I pause, looking at Melody and waiting for some form of response.

"Um, well, I guess," Melody says softly. "But, I can't stay too long. We have an entirely new set to go over tomorrow."

"She said she's going?" my little voice remarks.

Alone With Someone

Did she say she's going?

"Good," Cindy says. "Frank and I like to treat ourselves every once in a while. It reminds us of when we were dating." Cindy turns her head and smiles at me.

What does that mean? She's been taking lessons from Frank.

"So, Bill," Frank jumps in, "you are going as well, right?"

"Yes. I mean, I guess so," I say trying to control any enthusiasm I might have.

"Good," Frank says and walks toward the backstage door.

I don't move. I watch Frank and Cindy take a few steps and...

Wait a minute. Frank and Cindy?

Where's...

I turn to my right and see that Melody is standing still as well. At the same moment that I notice her, she seems to spot me and hurriedly grabs her oboe case, almost dropping it to the floor.

I react and help her catch the case before it hits anything else except her knees. With my hands on the top and bottom and hers on both sides, we bring the case up to about chest level.

Our heads must rise simultaneously, because when I look at her she is staring at me.

We are just standing still staring.

I'm not sure what she's looking at or what thoughts are racing around her beautiful head, but then again, I'm not too sure why I can't move. I seem fixated by her eyes, though there are moments when I seem to be staring right through her.

Chapter 6

"Are you two coming or not?" a voice asks.

What? Where?

I turn my head to the left, breaking my gaze, and notice Frank and Cindy are standing a few feet away from the stage door, waving.

I turn back toward Melody again and notice that our hands still rest upon the case.

"We had better get going," I say not moving much.

"Um, yeah. We should," she says.

"I could, um, carry your case, if you like," I say looking at the middle-size, hard, black case.

"Um, it's OK, I'll be fine," Melody says as she begins to put her coat on. She fumbles through her pockets a few times, frowns, and says, "Darn, I left my gloves in the car."

I quickly take off my fur-lined, leather gloves and offer them to her. "Here, use mine. I have warm pockets."

Actually, the gloves aren't 'fur-lined'. It's just fake fur, but they feel very soft and warm.

I move my gloves toward Melody again.

"I'll be all right," she says biting her lower lip.

"Please take them," I reiterate. "I'm fine. Really."

Fine? Fine? I think I could be in the middle of an ice age right now and still feel nice and toasty.

I pick my head up and look Melody straight in the eyes, my arm is still extended.

Alone With Someone

She smiles.

Melody slowly takes the gloves and says, "Thank you." Her head slants downward as I see her blush again.

Has it gotten hot in here or is it...

"Were you two going to order out?" Frank says tapping me on the shoulder.

"Um, yeah. I mean no," I say shaking my head, finally turning to look at him. "I was just helping Melody with her coat."

"Whatever. Let's go," Frank says and turns back toward the door.

This time we follow. I know Melody is right next to me, though I don't turn my head. My peripheral vision and the continuous emanation of warmth from that direction, enable me to sense she is there.

We reach Cindy, who is by one of the doors. She just smiles and shakes her head.

"What? Why did she do that?" the little voice questions.

We walk through the doors and into the back parking lot area.

So, this is where all the performers park. I scan the lot. There are still quite a few cars here. I wonder if any of them saw us standing there. I wonder if any of them saw us leave, together. I wonder...which car is hers.

"What?" my little voice echoes through my mind.

They say you can tell much about a person by what type of car he or she drives.

Chapter 6

"Who's they?" the voice asks. "Are these the same people that say, 'It's raining, you might get wet'? If it's raining and you're outside, of course you're going to get wet."

I giggle and it appears to be out loud, because Frank, Cindy, and Melody all turn their heads and look at me.

"What's so funny?" Frank asks.

"Nothing. Nothing," I say beginning to laugh a little louder and longer, though I don't know why. It wasn't that funny.

Frank shakes his head and laughs a little as well.

Cindy starts to giggle and says, "Whatever it was, it sure is funny."

I turn my head to the right and see Melody giggling as well, moving her head up and down as if agreeing with Cindy's statement.

Laughter can be so contagious. It's kind of like yawning, except more so.

I stop laughing and take a look around. We have made it to the front of the building and are heading toward a restaurant. I think.

We all become quiet and only the sounds of the buses, cars, and their brakes squealing can be heard around us.

My eyes wonder to Frank and Cindy who are still in front of me. They are holding hands. I smile as if content. Then, Frank turns his head and whispers something to Cindy. She smiles. My gaze travels back to their clasped hands. They seem a little tighter than before.

That's nice.

I turn my head to the right, toward Melody. She too is looking at Frank and Cindy. She is smiling.

My smile widens.

Melody's head turns toward me and she seems to know she is being watched as well. Her eyes widen and her smile diminishes, briefly, then returns larger than before.

"Say something!" my inner voice exclaims.

"Um, are you sure you don't want me to carry your eystrument, um instrument?" I say hoping she didn't notice my unintentional Freudian slip.

Now is definitely one of those times when you would like to find the nearest brick wall and beat your head against it. Look there's one. And another. And another.

"I hear that it burns about 150 calories every 15 minutes," my inner voice jokes.
Melody smiles and says, "No thank you. It's really not hat heavy. Would you like your gloves back? It's really not that chilly tonight."

"I know what you mean," I say.

"What?" she asks quietly.

"Um, I mean, I agree that's it's not that chilly. It seems rather warm," I says adjusting my jacket.

Gee, that wall right there will do nicely.

"Well, if you think this is warm," Frank says turning his head slightly backwards, "then you're going to be roasting tomorrow when it's supposed to be five degrees warmer." Frank smiles.

Thanks for the weather report, Frank.

I look at Melody and shrug my shoulders. She is still smiling.

We reach the front of a restaurant, though I'm not too sure it's 'the' restaurant, because Frank and Cindy slow down only slightly.

Chapter 6

Without warning they turn left into a set of doors, pushing them open quickly. Melody and I almost run into each other as we attempt to compensate for our forward progression and sudden change in our intended direction.

Yeah, that sounds good, 'progression' and 'direction.'

"I'm sorry," I say grabbing Melody by the shoulders in an attempt not to run her over.

"It's OK, " she says shaking her head and beginning to laugh.

"I guess you two were awake after all," Frank says also laughing.

Cindy joins in the amusement which has become Melody and me.

How can they be laughing? I almost ran Melody over! And, they're laughing!

I look at all of them. A smile forms on my face and I too start chuckling.

"What's wrong with you?" my little voice asks.

I'm not too sure. It must be the yawn effect again. I continue to laugh.

"Can I help you?" an unfamiliar voice asks.

I look ahead and see a middle-aged woman in a black frilly skirt and a white shirt.

"Yes, a table for four, please," Frank says still chuckling a bit.

"Right this way," the woman says as she leads us to our table.

The restaurant is rather small, but very clean and well kept. It's not as modern as some of the other restaurants around here, but it's peaceful and pleasant. The counters are completely white and so are the booths and chairs. The floor, ceiling, and tables, on the other hand, are black. They even have the old silver fountain handles behind the counter.

This place looks too nice. Can I afford a sundae here, let alone an entire meal?

"Well, first of all, you're only getting dessert," my little voice says. "Secondly, you haven't spent any money this week except for gas and milk. So, you should have plenty."

Maybe, I should check.

"You'll look silly," the voice says.

Right. I'll excuse myself as soon as we sit down and check in the restroom.

"Oh brother!"

We reach our destination. It's a booth. Frank lets Cindy slide in then follows. I bow slightly and motion for Melody to go in first.

She looks at me briefly and smiles. She slides in putting her instrument on the seat by the wall. I sit down. Menus have already been placed in front of each of us.

Almost simultaneously, it seems, we all begin to remove our coats. Frank and Cindy seem to slip out of their garments quickly. As I pull an arm out of my sleeve, I brush up against Melody. Realizing my error, I put my arm back in my coat and say, "I'm sorry, let me help you with your coat."

I hold one sleeve as she pulls her arm out. I then reach around and hold up her other sleeve as she slides out her other arm.

"Great! You've made her feel helpless," my inner voice says.

I was just helping. I think.

Chapter 6

"You just helped yourself finish before you even got started."

I pick up my menu and look at the desserts on the back.

"So, do you know what you are going to have?" Frank's voice breaks my thought barrier.

I look at him and shrug my shudders.

"I'm going to have a hot fudge sundae," Cindy says, "with lots of whipped cream."

"I thought you were on a diet," Frank says, a smile forming on his face.

"I am," Cindy responds. "This will be my breakfast, lunch, and dinner for the next week."

"You don't need to diet," I say. "If anyone needs a health program, it's Frank. He's got to eat more or something."

"Well, if some people wouldn't keep me from my lunch," Frank says as his glare passes from Melody to me and back again.

I look at Melody, smile, and shrug my shoulders.

Melody smiles and shrugs her shoulders as well.

"Uh huh, whatever," Frank says grinning. "I'll probably have a banana split. If that's OK with everyone."

Frank looks around the table smiling. We all seem to be smiling and nodding as his gaze reaches us.

"So, have you decided yet?" Frank asks looking directly at Melody.

"Um, I was thinking about some jello," Melody says softly.

Alone With Someone

"Jello?!?" Frank exclaims. "What's so exciting about jello? It's not fattening and half of the times it tastes like gelled plastic." Frank turns his head toward Cindy on this last statement. She looks at him somewhat offended and hits him on the shoulder.

"You deserved that one," I say laughing, figuring the reference was to the way Cindy has made jello at home.

Our waitress, the same woman who lead us to the table, is at our table now staring at us. The name on her badge reads, 'Theresa.' "Hi, have you decided yet? Or do you need a few more minutes?"

Our eyes seem to diverge from the menus to Theresa and the words she just spoke.

"I'll have a banana split," Frank says.

"I'll take a hot fudge sundae," Cindy follows.

Theresa moves her eyes to Melody and me. She seems to have a questioning look.

"Hello! Tell her what you want!" my inner voice exclaims.

"I'll have some jello," Melody says and turns her head toward Frank, staring at him with widened eyes.

I laugh slightly and say, "I guess I'll have some rice pudding."

Theresa says, "Thank you. I'll be right back with your order." She collects the menus, turns, and heads toward the counter.

"Rice pudding?" Frank questions. "That's even more blah than jello!"

"Not with the right amount of cinnamon and whipped cream," I smile and say correcting Frank.

Each of us seems to chose this moment to observe some sort of silence.

Chapter 6

I look around the restaurant taking in the same sites as when we entered. I'm not too sure what Cindy or Melody are doing, but I know Frank has picked up his silverware and has started tapping out a tune on his small empty bread plate and full water glass.

"Will you stop that?" Cindy says grabbing Frank's hands, causing him to stop tapping and begin conducting.

I look at Melody, shrug my shoulders, and say, "Band directors."

She laughs and shakes her head.

"Hey, wait a minute," Cindy says laughing a little. "Don't include me in that category. We're not all like him."

Again, there is a moment of silence as my eyes wonder once more.

A few seconds pass and we are disturbed again by more tapping, this time with one utensil. I look at Frank. He is drinking his water. My eyes travel to Cindy who is bouncing her spoon off the top of an empty coffee cup.

I turn my head quickly toward Melody. As a smile forms on my face, a duplicate is found on hers. A few brief seconds seem to pass and we begin to laugh.

By now, Frank has realized that our recent outburst was not meant for him. He too laughs.

We stop and look at Cindy.

"What?" she says still tapping.

My gaze travels down to her echoing spoon and I'm almost positive Frank's and Melody's eyes have joined mine.

Cindy stops and says, "Alright, maybe it does happen to all of us. Or maybe, just those who are around Frank everyday."

Alone With Someone

All of us laugh.

"Hey, don't blame me for your compulsive behaviors," Frank says chuckling.

"Compulsive? Compulsive?" Cindy says. "What about your little conducting routine you do with your spoon in the morning before you eat your cereal?" Cindy mimics the act with a phony grin on her face.

"Now children," I say, shaking a finger at Frank and Cindy. "Remember, what is done at home, stays at home."

Again, we laugh. Man, is this stuff contagious or what.

I conduct with my spoon, look at Melody, who picks up her spoon and does the same. I look over at Frank and Cindy. Their looks go from straight faces, holding in laughter, to wide-full-faced smiles. They then begin to tap out a little tune on their water glasses again.

"OK, who had the banana split?" a cheery voice asks.

I stop swinging my arms and look to my right. Theresa is standing there with two sundaes and appears to be waiting for something.

"Right here. I did," Frank says.

I blush. Why? I do not know. Frank opened his mouth first. Didn't he?

"And, the hot fudge sundae?"

"That's me," Cindy says still giggling.

"I'll be right back with the jello and rice pudding," Theresa says as she turns around and heads toward the counter area.

I look at Frank and Cindy as they 'eye' their large icy creations. My eyes widen as well. I turn to Melody, smile, and whisper the word 'pigs.' She shakes her head and laughs.

Chapter 6

She is so beautiful when she laughs.

"You're just saying that," my inner voice says. "Will you cut that out."

No really, the way her smile stretches her entire face and how her big, beautiful, intoxicating eyes glisten...

"Let's see, you had the jello, and you had the rice pudding."

I turn my head and see Theresa placing a bowl of rice pudding in front of me. It's a little bigger than I expected, though still much smaller than Frank's or Cindy's sundaes. Usually, you get a small sundae type container and there is a sprinkle of cinnamon and some whipped cream on top.

Hey, wait! There's no whipped cream.

"Is there anything else I can get you?" Theresa asks.

"Ask for some whipped cream!" my little voice shouts.

"Um, would it be possible to get a little more whipped cream for my sundae?"

Huh? I didn't say anything. Besides, I don't have a sundae.

"What?" Cindy says looking at Frank.

"Nothing," Frank replies. "I didn't say anything. Did I?"

"It's that look," Cindy says.

"I know what you mean," I say rather quietly.

"What?" Cindy says looking at me this time.

"Um, nothing," I say. "I was just agreeing with you about his looks."

106

Alone With Someone

"Alright, who would like some more whipped cream?" Theresa asks shaking the red and white container she has returned with.

"Since I asked, I'll take some first," Cindy says raising her spoon.

Theresa sprays the foamy substance all over Cindy's sundae. Back and forth she moves the container. Back and forth. Until the entire bowl is almost completely covered.

"Anyone else?"

"I guess I'll have a little more," Frank says smiling as he looks at Cindy then at her bowl.

Theresa repeats the same process with Frank's split then turns toward Melody and me, "How about you two?"

What? What about us two?

"I'll have just a little," Melody says.

Theresa reaches over me and squirts a small mound of whipped cream directly in the center of Melody's bright red jello.

"And you?"

"Huh? Oh, yeah, sure. I'll have a little too, I guess. I don't want to be left out," I say knowing how silly I must sound.

Theresa begins to put the same white mound on my rice pudding as she had with Melody's jello, when she lurches forward, covering my entire dish as well as the short distance to Melody's bowl.

"Oh, I'm very sorry," a voice says. "I didn't see you."

I turn my head and see another waitress standing behind Theresa with a full tray. She leaves and proceeds to another table.

Chapter 6

I look back at the path of whipped cream and begin to laugh. "Whipped cream for everyone," I say.

"I'm very sorry," Theresa says. "Let me get a towel." She walks away shaking her head.

"Well, I sure hope you're hungry," I say turning my head toward Melody.

Melody looks at me wide-eyed and still somewhat astonished. Then she looks back down at the whipped cream and begins to laugh with me. "All we need now are some cherries," she says pointing to the path with her spoon.

I hear Frank and Cindy laughing. I pick up my head to look at them.

How contagious is laughter? Ah, never mind.

"Only you, Bill," Frank says. "Only you."

"Here, let me get that," Theresa says as she puts a damp towel on the table and begins to wipe off the whipped cream.

"Actually, we were wondering if you could just bring us a couple of bananas and a bottle of those little red cherries. We'll be happy to take care of the entire thing," I say scooping some whipped cream with my fork off the table and into an empty coffee cup.

Theresa smiles and shakes her head. "I'd have to charge you for four extra sundaes with this mess," she says laughing a little.

As I scoop another fork full into the cup, my hand hits something soft and some of the whipped cream flies from the fork.

I turn my head and see Melody's hand by the cup. It appears that she too was cleaning up. "I'm sorry," she says as she points her utensil across the table and begins laughing.

Alone With Someone

I turn my head quickly and see Frank staring at me, melting whipped cream dripping down his nose.

"You can give the cherries to him," I say pointing at Frank and laughing somewhat sarcastically.

"Funny. Funny," Frank says grabbing his napkin.

"Here, let me get that," Cindy says wiping Frank's nose with her own napkin. "If you wanted more, I could have given you some of mine, Frank. After all, I am on a diet." She begins to laugh a little louder than before.

Frank's look of shock at being bombarded with whipped cream turns into a smile and he too laughs.

"Again, I'm very sorry about the mess," Theresa says finishing her cleaning and still giggling at Frank. "Is there anything else I can get you now?"

"Maybe a bib," Cindy says.

"Or a shield," Frank jumps in, pretending to duck an imaginary flying object.

Theresa turns around and heads toward the counter again, still laughing.

See, it's very contagious.

I look at Melody. She continues to smile. How small, yet sultry. How simple, yet comforting.

She reaches for her spoon and attempts to lift out some jello from her bowl. "I know there was jello in here earlier," she says discarding some more whipped cream into the ever filling coffee cup.

Chapter 6

"Hey, if we just had some coffee, we could make espresso or cappuccino," I say spooning some whipped cream from my rice pudding into the same cup.

"You two be careful over there," Frank says. "We have enough problems with food fights in the cafe."

"Huh?" I say still observing Melody, but looking around enough to keep her from suspecting I'm watching her.

I think.

"You know, the cafe," Frank says. "The place with the 'good soup'."

Melody lets out a short, but loud, burst of laughter.

We all join in somewhat, but I don't think any of us know exactly why.

"You know," Melody says, "for the past couple of weeks, every time I've gone to a restaurant and the waiter tells me what kind of soup they have, I need to hold my breath so I don't burst out laughing. In fact, I was in the grocery store the other day, passed by the shelves of soup, stopped, looked right at them for a few seconds, and started laughing uncontrollably. I thought they were going to throw me out of the place."

Great, she thought it was funny. I try to come up with excuses to eat the questionably edible cafe food and she thinks...

"That means she thought about you," my inner voice says. "And, when she received the poem..."

I blush and look at Melody. She's blushing too. Why?

"Maybe because no one else is really laughing," my little voice buts in.

I attempt to fake a laugh in order to make her feel better. Frank does the same. At least it sounds fake for him.

"What's all this about soup?" Cindy asks innocently, eating another spoonful of hot fudge.

"You'd better ask Bill," Frank says smiling taking a chunk of banana from his elongated dish.

"So?" Cindy inquirers.

"Um, it's nothing," I say. "For some reason, I mentioned that the cafe had good soup."

"From what Frank has said, that's about all they have that's good," Cindy says smiling.

Great! We should have just went to Kirk's.

I think Cindy realizes that I am somewhat uncomfortable with the topic because she turns her head toward Melody, who has become rather quiet since her little out burst. "So," Cindy says, "Frank tells me you'll be tutoring some of the students on a weekly basis."

No, not me. I tutor the students on a daily, no hourly basis.

"Um, uh huh," Melody says trying to swallow the jello she has just placed in her mouth. "I thought it would be interesting and a way to help improve striving musicians."

'Striving'? Did she say 'striving'? Some of those students are there because they have some talent and think the class will be an easy 'A.' Boy, are they usually wrong. Frank grades on level of performance as well as skill.

They are kind of like some of the students in my creative writing class. They come in thinking, 'this will be a breeze.' By the second day of class they've changed their mind. I grade them on the work they actually do, not the work that they're thinking of doing or have already done. I keep telling them, 'this is 'creative' writing, not 'potential' writing.'

Chapter 6

"I was going to volunteer my time," Melody says, "but Frank said since I have a degree and performance experience, I should charge something." She half smiles, half grimaces.

"Yeah, Frank said you weren't going to require the usual lesson fee and he talked you out of it," Cindy says glaring at Frank who is smiling innocently.

"I would just feel better if I didn't, though. It's so...so...committal," Melody says now frowning somewhat and biting her lower lip.

"What do you mean," Cindy says taking another spoonful of ice cream.

"Well, what if they don't get better?" Melody asks. "I would feel so bad, like I was cheating them."

"Believe me," Frank says licking his spoon, "some of those kids couldn't get anything but better. Besides, most of them haven't had a private tutor in a few years. Any help you can give them would be an improvement. You saw how well they listened when you were there for career day. Sure they have some talent, but it's difficult to show them how to use it when there's just one person and such a large group."

"Yeah, but..."

"Are you going to say anything?" my inner voice asks. "Or are you going to sit here feeding your face?"

I look down at my bowl of...of almost nothing and then quickly switch my gaze to Melody. "I'm sure that if you just show up, you'll do them more good then they could hope for." I smile and blush.

"Now would be a good time to hold her hand," my inner voice says.

I resist.

Melody's face is red and her hand rests on the top of the table just inches from my own.

"Thank you," she says, "but I hope I can show them why I enjoy music so much. I mean it's so exciting, so inviting, so comforting." Her eyes glisten brighter and brighter with each example.

I want to reach out, hold her hand, and say, 'Yes, I understand.' Instead, I sit, stare, and nod my head as if following some business plan being presented.

"I would like to give them something to remember," Melody says. "Kind of what you did." She turns toward me, blushes even more, then lowers her head.

We all pause and wait for her next words.

"When we observed your class, the students seemed to have a respect for you and you for them. The minute we walked in, I felt comfortable and saw young minds working."

My entire body feels warm and I can't really explain why right now.

"Actually, they were just being nice because we had visitors," I say. "It's like when you were younger and your parents had company coming over. You were always on your best behavior when the company was there. You may have even helped with the dishes. When they left, however, you took out your toys and left little remnants all over, showing your parents whose house it really was. Or rather, whose house you thought it was."

"Oh, come on," Frank says. "Those kids do respect you and so do the other teachers. Some of us get frustrated with the students that give up or just fail to try. But you, you get even. You try for them. There are some that just can't be reached, but you try anyway."

"I'm, a , just doing my job," I say rather sheepishly.

"No, I mean it," Frank says. "I keep thinking how easy I have it. Most of the kids that are in the band have some talent, they just need the direction. I remember when I was in high school, I hated Chemistry and

113

had to be tutored. I worked my butt off to earn my grade. It's got to be the same for some of these kids in English, especially if it's not their native language. I've seen you handle the material and present it in a way that everyone understands something."

Great! He's made me a miracle worker!

"Um, I'm still just doing my job," I say my hands moving slightly. "Besides, who turned a band program around so far, that it's actually competing again in marching band competitions rather than just wondering aimlessly along the streets?"

I pause for a moment and look at Frank and Cindy. Then, I turn to Melody and add, "I enjoy seeing that light click on inside the students. When they seem to understand some part of my incessant rambling, they are happy and they learn."

"Exactly," Melody whispers and leans in toward me on the table.

I blush and stare...and stare...at the wall behind Melody.

"What are you doing?" my inner voice shouts. "Look at her!"

"Here's your check," a voice says. "Is there anything else I can get you? Some coffee? Tea? More whipped cream?"

I turn my head from Melody and see Theresa standing by the table smiling.

"No, thanks," Frank says. "I think we're just about finished."

I look at Frank and stare at him perplexed. He has that grin on his face again. This time it reiterates his verbal statement, 'yep, we're done all right.'

Without thinking or hesitating, I grab the check off the corner of the table and say, "I'll get this one."

"Oh, no you don't," Frank says. "We invited you." He tries to grab the piece of paper from my hand, but I pull it back and stand up.

Frank stands as well and proceeds to follow me to the register.

"Come on, Bill. Let me pay. You can get it next time."

I stop at the register and stare at him as we wait for someone to take our money. I pull out my wallet from my back right pocket, extracting one bill.

"See, you had more than enough," my little voice says.

Funny. And, what did he mean by next time?

"You leave the tip," I say to Frank as I smile at the host who has just stepped behind the register.

"Why don't you leave the tip? You were the one who got all that extra whipped cream," Frank says smiling.

"I hope everything was OK," says the medium height, tanned man behind the register as I give him the check and my money.

"Very good, thank you," I say nodding my head and smiling again.

He takes the check and money, counts back my change, and says, "Thank you. Have a nice night."

Frank and I walk back to the table. Cindy and Melody have already put on their coats and are waiting for us to return.

"So, did you get it?" Cindy asks Frank.

"No, old money bags here said we should get the tip."

"Well, that's OK. We'll just get it next time," Cindy responds.

Chapter 6

I look at Cindy bewildered. Then, as I grab my coat and begin to put it on, I look at Melody. She has almost the same look as I do. We seem to look at Cindy and Frank at the same moment. I can see Melody's head turn and lift up from the corner of my eye. Frank and Cindy have their coats on and are smiling.

"Sure," I say putting my right arm into the sleeve and shrugging my shoulders.

Frank puts some money on the table. I'm guessing that's the tip. That should be enough.

"Have a good night," Theresa says as she passes by with a tray of desserts for another table.

"You too," we all seem to say simultaneously.

I move away from the table and offer my hand to Melody as she rises from the table.

She smiles and accepts my gesture. Her glove covered hand touches my bare skin. She stands a little more, and exits the booth, grabbing her instrument with her free hand. We all walk toward the doors.

Hey, she didn't say anything about the poem all this time. We got out of that one. And, I was worried that...

"Maybe she didn't get it yet," my inner voice says.

Yeah, maybe it got lost in the mail or something.

We reach the doors, exit, and walk a few steps in the direction we came in, when Frank says, "Do you mind walking Melody to her car? We're parked on the other side." Frank points in the opposite direction we must head in.

"Um, no," I say. "I mean, no, I don't mind. I guess."

Alone With Someone

What am I saying?

"Well, I'll see you tomorrow then," Frank says shaking my hand.

"It's been nice seeing you again, Melody," Cindy says giving Melody a hug. "Oh, and you too Bill."

I extend my hand. Cindy does the same. Instead of shaking, however, I grasp her fingers. She bends her wrist slightly. I bow and she curtsies. It's the kind of action one may do in a ballet or when dancing a minuet.

A what?

"Cute," Frank says. "Can we go now?"

"I'm sorry," Cindy responds, straightening up and running her fingers through Frank's hair, messing it up slightly.

"I'm sorry, I forgot it was past your bed time," Cindy says in a pouty voice.

Frank and Cindy turn and walk away, waving one last time as they turn the corner. Melody and I still have not moved nor looked at each other.

"Hello! I think we should be moving here!" my inner voice shouts.

"So, which way to your car?" I ask turning toward her.

Her eyebrows are angled upward and her eyes are glassed over as if she is thinking about something else. But what?

"Um, this way," Melody says extending her hand in the original direction and proceeding to move that way. She still does not seem very focused.

What is she thinking?

"Maybe she did get the poem," my voice says.

117

Chapter 6

Nah, she would have mentioned something earlier.

"Would she?" my inner self questions.

Chapter 7

What thoughts...What ideas...What visions are forming...shaping... solidifying?

What am I thinking? She's probably just tired. Yeah, that's it, tired.

"Look at her again," my inner voice says. "Does she really look tired?"

Well, she could be. A concert takes so much out of me, and I'm just a member of the audience. And, Frank...

"What about Frank?"

He's always sweating after conducting and seems at least somewhat exasperated.

"Well, here it is," a soft soothing voice says.

"Huh? What?" I say aloud.

"Here's my car," Melody says rather quietly.

"Great! You've walked the entire distance back and still have not said a word!" my inner voice shouts.

"Sorry," I say looking beyond her into the darkness. Slowly, I turn my head toward her. She is holding the car door handle with her left hand and her oboe case with her right. She still has not opened the door. She is biting her lower lip and staring...staring right past me.

"What?" Melody asks, continuing her blank stare.

What does that look mean? What is she staring at? Is there something back there?

"Sorry, I wasn't very talkative," I say moving around a little, my head turning left, right, and left again. "I guess I'm just tired."

"Um, yeah, me too," Melody responds. She shakes her head a little and lifts up the handle on her door. "I guess I'm very tired. I should be going...home," she adds hesitating on her last words. She opens the door partially and places her case on the back seat, closing the door just enough so the light goes off.

"She's leaving," my inner voice says. "Again!"

"Yeah," I say aloud, trying to shake off my own cloudy thoughts. "It's rather late, and I have some writing to do yet." Melody seems to pick up her head. She stares at me somewhat inquisitively as I finish my sentence.

"I'll see you later," I say. "Maybe we all could have lunch one of the days you tutor."

"Good one," my little voice says.

Melody smiles and begins to laugh slightly. "Would we have some of the 'soup' I've heard so much about?"

"Only if you're not lucky," I say joining Melody in her laughter.

"Beautiful," I whisper as my laughter dissipates and I continue to gaze at Melody.

"What?" Melody asks becoming somewhat quieter and blushing slightly.

"Um, nothing," I say, not realizing I was that loud.

I'm just going to say 'good-night', turn around, and leave.

"What are you going to write?" Melody asks shyly.

"What?" I respond.

"You said that you have some writing to do," Melody says swallowing hard. "What are you going to write about?" Her eyes widen as I gaze directly into them.

"Um," I say shaking my head, "I usually try to write about the music. There are so many images and visions. I try to get some of them down before they fade or blend."

"Oh?" Melody says sounding somewhat inquisitive, yet searching for what to say next.

"But, tonight," I say attempting to find the right words myself. "Tonight, most of them have disappeared or changed. It's the time lapse. It's too long." I smile as if amused by this little explanation.

"Changed?" Melody says. "How have they changed?"

"OK," my inner voice says, "how are we going to get out of this one?"

"Well," I say attempting to moisten the inside of my very dry mouth, "you don't 'hear' a piece the same way when you first play it at practice as you do when you perform it for an audience, do you?"

Melody shakes her head, smiles, and says, "No," seemingly waiting for more.

"It's like that," I continue. "In the beginning, your view of the music is basic, simple, pure. You try to look for the right way to perform it, so you experiment slightly each time you practice." I look at Melody with the hope that she is understanding this analogy, even though I'm not completely sure about its validity.

"Yes," she says nodding her head and smiling, still seeming to expect more.

"It's also like that when I write," I say moving my hands up and down and side to side as I continue to gaze at her. "When I hear 'good' music, I try to write down the images almost immediately in the hopes of

121

capturing some of the music's purity. It's always those first, simple images that help bring life to my poems."

"But, how would the images change?" Melody asks.

"Well, just as you expand on your musical interpretation and play it differently, sometimes only slightly differently from when you first played it, the ideas I get from the music have a chance to blend with the other images in my head..." I stop and rap my head with my knuckles as if knocking on a door.

Melody smiles. "Isn't that good?" she asks giggling. "Don't you get longer pieces of writing that way?"

"Well, yes and no," I say trying to come up with some further explanation. "The simplicity of the original thoughts is usually lost within the expanded ideas. Then, the images which should give the piece its life, fade into what confounds so much of modern literature, its supposed 'deeper meaning.'"

"What do you mean 'supposed'?" Melody asks biting her lower lip.

"Let's see," I say still searching for a phrase. "Oh, yes. Freud once said, 'sometimes a cigar is just a cigar.' Sometimes, when a poet writes about a tree, he is just writing about a tree, not about the plight of humanity, nor the stages of life, but a tree. It's when people start 'thinking' about a poem before 'reading' it, or even 'listening' to a piece of music before 'hearing' it, do they miss its initial beauty, its purity."

"So, you don't usually include a deeper meaning in your writing?" Melody asks seeming somewhat confused and concerned.

But, why? Why does she seem confused? Why is she asking about my writing? Why am I rambling on as if teaching a class?

"Actually," I say blushing, "I usually have a deeper meaning. However, when I write down the initial phrases or the first few lines, sometimes even an entire rough draft, I'm not thinking about what certain words

122

could mean. Only after I revise, and revise, and revise, does the full piece come together. Most of the time...well, usually... OK, sometimes."

I look at Melody, shake my head, and shrug my shoulders. "To tell you the truth," I say, "I just hope that something hits me in the head and says, 'this is the deeper meaning.' Then, I will not have to revise the piece. " I laugh a little and look at Melody.

She smiles and nods her head. Her body shakes briefly as if chilled.

"I'm sorry," I say. "I've babbled on about my personal views on writing and let you stand out here freezing."

"I'm fine," Melody says smiling. "So, have you written anything recently?" She adds quickly still smiling.

OK, do I play along? Do I lie and say, 'no, nothing especially good'?

My inner voice says, "You should probably..."

"I wrote on some students' papers the other day, does that count?" I say sheepishly shrugging my shoulders.

"You know what I mean," Melody says, this time blushing as her eyes widen and a look of concern wonders over her beautiful face. It's a look that says, 'I might be wrong. I'll go a little further then drop it.'

"Tell her something. Make something up," my little voice instructs me.

"Um," I say blushing and hesitating for what seems at least an hour. "Why do you ask?" My eyes widen and a half smile, half frown forms on my face.

"What are you doing?" my inner voice shouts. "Say, 'no,' 'good-bye,' then leave!"

"I was, um, just wondering," Melody says. "Um, actually..." She stops and puts her right hand in her pocket, moving it around as if searching for something.

A cold breeze blows through the parking lot, and I shiver even though my face is burning with concern. I swallow, hoping that my mouth will moisten, will loosen up, will move. There are many different levels of thought, concern, words, to be communicated, but I am not able to verbalize anything.

I'm acting childish. I should say something, before...before...

"Well, I received something in the mail the other day," Melody says as she manages to pull out a folded piece of white paper from her pocket. She pauses and stares at me.

As she unfolds the paper, I say, "And...?"

"And, I was wondering if you really sent it," Melody says finishing a thought rather that answering the intended question.

I shake my head quickly and say, "No, no...I mean, yes. What I'm trying to say is..." I take a deep breath and hope to start my speech over.

I smile and continue, "What I'm trying to say, if my mouth and brain can work together for a few seconds here, is, um, I..." I pause again. Then add, "May I see it?"

Sheepishly, Melody hands me the paper. I look it over and smile. The rush, the sensation, the inspiration, comes back to me as I close my eyes for just a few seconds. I pick up my head, opening my eyes wide as I hand the piece back to her.

Still smiling, I take another deep breath and look at her. She is waiting for some sort of response.

"I wrote that," I say. "But, I was hoping you wouldn't get it so soon."

Alone With Someone

Melody has a look of puzzlement on her face, but says nothing.

"It was just something I wrote...about..." I pause, still debating whether to tell her the entire truth, yet. "I wrote it after your first concert."

Well, that's half right.

"Oh?" Melody says looking confused.

"And, after you visited my class," I say, my smile becoming even wider than before. I feel myself moving closer to her.

"Oh?" Melody reiterates, this time looking more tentative.

"Just as the music inspires me to write, I attempt to capture the essence from other things as well."

"Like?" Melody says as if understanding more than I have actually said.

"Well," I say, hesitating again, hoping to choose the right words. "Well, I use objects and...and people. If someone inspires me, in one way or another, I try to give them a copy of the piece or pieces."

Melody's smile becomes larger as she seems to be waiting for more.

"Anywho, I used you and your solo as an inspiration. That poem is a result of the inspiration." I swallow hard and continue hesitating though somewhat less than before. "When I heard your solo that night, then finally got to meet you, my mind raced and expanded. It was amazing!" I smile, look at Melody, and laugh a little.

"It wasn't until you 'played' Juliet, did I finally let the images take form. I wrote down ideas and images between the two times, but when you...when I...when we..."

"Yes?" Melody asks innocently blinking her eyes as her gaze widens.

Chapter 7

I look at her, smile, then frown. "I'm sorry...I..." I pause and just stare, unable to come up with words that will escape from my mouth.

"I'm flattered," Melody says. "But..."

Great! There's a 'but.' I knew it. She's seeing someone. Or, she's not interested in someone like me; someone short; someone lacking in one-liners; someone lacking in needed spoken words.

Melody's eyes have become larger, rounder, and have compacted a few times during my self dismissal. She says, "But, why me?"

"I know, I'm sorry to...have..." I pause and shake my head quickly. "Why you? Why you?" I pause and stare at Melody. She nods her head innocently.

Do I tell her that I asked myself the very same question? Do I tell her anything? Do I tell her the guys coaxed me into sending it? What do I say?

"You know, if you would have listened," my little voice says sarcastically.

Then what? I would still be wondering and hitting myself over the head and a few other spots for missing this emotionally draining, thought provoking, intoxicatingly inspirational, experience.

"I still don't understand," Melody says softly as she leans against her car.

"I'm sorry," I say waiting for the words. "Um, well, I'll be honest with you. I thought about why I was being inspired by you. For the first time ever, I questioned an inspiration. And, I'm not too sure why."

I look at Melody hoping for some form of nonverbal response. The only thing I can sense is her attentiveness to what I am saying.

I continue, "I have had very little outward sensation lately, and for a poet, or rather a verser, who draws from others in order to compose, this is not positive. So, the recent surge was welcomed, immensely. I wrote down ideas, knowing I would get back to them later. It was only after that day in my class, did I reason out what makes you diff..." I stop short and look at Melody. I smile and look into her eyes.

"...what makes you special. Each time I see your large, beautiful eyes reflecting, glistening, radiating, I feel that great sensation of inspiration. It's incredible!"

Did I just say that, aloud?

My heart pumps faster. My face becomes redder (if that's possible). My mind wonders as I search for an appropriate analogy.

"It's like...it's like..."

Though I am excited, elated, and want to tell her the inspiration is like being stalled on a train track with a train coming, and you are able to start the car and jolt forward just as the locomotive zooms past, horns blaring. Or it's like having a baby smile at you even though you haven't done anything. And, it could even be like feeling the eyes of a thousands, no millions, of people staring at you as you sing or even play the Star-Spangled Banner at the Olympics.

Instead, I just grin and think a while longer.

"When the inspiration is strong and positive, it's kind of like what we were discussing in the restaurant."

Melody has an intrigued but uncomprehending look on her face.

Without waiting for an actual response, I continue my analogy, "When a student realizes what you have been trying to get across to him for an entire class period, a light clicks on and his eyes light up. Your job then seems that much easier, that much better, that much more worth it."

I smile and hope Melody has understood somehow, even through my verbal ramblings.

Chapter 7

Melody stares at me with a smile on her face. Then she says, "I think I understand what an inspiration might feel like for you, but why me? I'm not..." She pauses.

I beg her with my eyes and thoughts, not to finish her thought.

"I just...well, I'm...me," Melody says noticeably and understandably searching for words. "I mean, I'm just not sure. No one has ever written a poem for me, let alone about me." She bites her lower lip and looks at me as if waiting for a response of some sort.

"Don't ever underestimate the beauty others might see in you," I say as I blush and a half smile forms on my face. I move closer to her and the urge to hold her hand crosses my mind just as it did in the restaurant.

I let the urge pass somehow and proceed to speak again. "I think the poem tries to say so much of what I find beau...inspiring about you. Besides, I owed you something for playing such a beautiful solo. Poetry is one of the ways I can compensate for that." I'm not too sure of my movement, but I feel even closer to Melody than before.

"I enjoyed the poem very much. Thank you," Melody says averting her gaze downward. "In fact, I had thought that Frank was playing a joke on me or something. You know how Frank is. So, I tried to find the poem in some books I have at home, as well as others in the library. I even looked on the Internet. No one had seen it before." She picks up her head slightly and stares at me.

So many words and lines run through my mind: 'Well, they've never seen someone so beautiful'; 'They had its source right in front of them'; 'others have seen the idea before, just not in those words, not in that particular way, not with your visage.'

The only response I manage to verbalize, however, is, "If Frank was playing a trick, you could have just opened an English text book and it would have been the first poem in there." I laugh outwardly slightly, but inside, inside, I'm throwing myself against a wall.

"Yeah, I guess you're right," Melody says smiling and giggling softly.

We grow silent. The air around us seems to be extremely light, and the darkness seems to be diminishing greatly.

I begin to look around, though I do not seem to be focusing on any object or area.

"So?" Melody says thankfully breaking the silence.

My head snaps back toward her and my eyebrows move up rapidly as if saying, "Yes."

"Ask her out!" my little voice shouts.

I become slightly perturbed at the disturbance from within.

"You said you wrote other things as well," Melody says, seemingly continuing where she started from. Her tongue quickly runs over her red lips, and she brushes back her silky hair with a slow, somewhat instinctive movement of her hand. "Have you written any other poems? Or was it just that one?"

Have I written anything else? Have I written anything else? Of course I have.

"Tell her no. Save them for latter," my inner voice suggests.

"Um, actually," I say reverting to my verbal hesitation instead of babbling. "Actually, I have written a few other pieces, but..."

I pause and look at her again. She is beautiful. She is...

"She's waiting for an answer!" my little voice shouts, not seeming so tiny any more.

"But they don't really capture exactly what I'm fee...thinking," I say hoping to avoid any further embarrassment. "The first one doesn't really capture everything about you, just one point. The other poems I've worked on try to do the same thing. They seem to have blended more, however."

Yeah, they try, but nothing could...

"Do you remember any? Or do you have any with you?" Melody inquires rather innocently.

Do I have any? Do I remember any?

"Not really," I hear myself saying as I attempt to moisten my lips, hoping not to sound too dry and pitiful.

Melody's eyes are angled downward again and a look of disappointment forms on her face.

"I think I remember most of the one I had written immediately after I sent you this poem," I say pointing to the paper she is still clutching in her delicate hand.

"If I remember correctly, I tried to tie into the music more for a slightly better flow." I hold up my thumb and forefinger, slightly parting them directly in front of my squinting eyes as if trying to see what is in between.

Melody picks up her head and brushes back her hair again as a smile replaces the disappointment. "If you don't mind, I'd love to hear it."

"As I looked for this one," Melody says moving the paper upward, "I read quite a few others and found them more enjoyable now than I did in high school and college. I realized, especially through your piece, that poems can say so much."

"And, there are as many meanings as there are readers," I say staring directly into Melody's eyes, searching for some courage in order to go through with this.

Alone With Someone

"Um, I don't know if I can remember the entire thing," I say, finally breaking my gaze with a slight, but quick twist of my head.

"That's OK," Melody says rather energetically. "Whatever you can remember, I'm sure will be very good."

"Well," I say moving the corners of my mouth from side to side. "Try not to judge it too harshly. It's not really finished yet."

"I'm sure it'll be fine," Melody says as a look of reassurance covers her face.

"I'm sure you'll make a fool of yourself," my inner voice interrupts.

I frown briefly. Then, to spite myself, I say, "OK, but give me a few seconds to recall it."

I take a quick, yet deep look at Melody, turn my head, close my eyes, and attempt to 'see' what I wrote only a few days ago.

I open my eyes, but do not look at her. I say, "The title, I believe is 'Sweet Sounds.'"

I mouth the first few words a couple of times and blink. I pause, squint, and wait a few more seconds. I can actually see the piece as I wrote it. I begin to speak. I hope this is what I wrote, but right now, I'm not too sure because I am still trying to clearly focus on the piece and its layout.

Chapter 7

Shivers,
Chills,
Sensations,
Ravage my inner being
With each
Semblance of sound
From your
Soft luscious lips.
Beats begin;
Melodies meld;
Symphonies surge;
Devouring my very soul
With each
Intoxicating note
Of your
Soft harmonious voice.

I stand motionless and blink a few times. Slowly, the picture of the piece fades. I smile, somewhat satiated.

"So?" I say turning my head toward Melody again.

Her eyes are closed, but they seem to open very quickly as the sound of my voice finally reaches her. She looks so peaceful, so content. I can do nothing except stare.

Melody blushes and shuffles her feet as she realizes I am looking at her. Simultaneously, it seems, we both turn our heads away and clear our throats.

"Could you possibly write that one down for me?" Melody asks softly.

"Sure," I say still fighting the dryness that has settled in my mouth. I am reassured of my sanity, however, as I did not repeat her question this time.

"I was wondering," I say not hesitating one bit and not waiting for my mood to change. "I was wondering, if I were to ask you out for dinner or something, what would you say?" I turn my head to face Melody. My heart is racing. My entire body is burning up.

"When?" She asks before my eyes actually reach hers.

No 'yes,' no 'no,' just 'when'?

"How about Friday? Saturday? Sunday?" My voice trails off with each day.

"Oh, I have practice those nights," Melody says still smiling, yet seeming somewhat disappointed.

"Well, how about next Friday then?" I ask and without waiting for a response, revert to babbling again. "We could go to Kirk's. We roped Frank into playing with Jerry, Joe, and Kirk for the first time. They play jazz and rock, while Frank, well Frank plays how Frank plays. It should be interesting."

"Let me see," Melody says elevating her head slightly and staring upward. She lowers her head after a few seconds and says, "That should be OK. What time?"

"We usually get there around four or five, but we're going to make Frank sweat until about six or so."

"That's right down the street from the school, right?"

"Yes. It's actually just east of there, by that new mini mall."

"Would it be OK if I meet you there?" Melody asks biting her lip seemingly trying to make this work.

"That would be wonderful," I say still not too sure of what is going on or what I am feeling.

Chapter 7

"I'll introduce you to the guys. Most of us have been friends since high school. In fact, the same high school Frank and I teach at. Joe plays the drums, Jerry plays the..." I stop and look at Melody.

"I'm sorry," I say. "I was babbling again. You'll meet them next Friday."

"That's OK," Melody says smiling. "I do that myself sometimes."

She babbles? I surely haven't noticed. Then again, I haven't noticed much lately.

I smile and say, "Very well, next Friday it is."

"Next Friday," Melody reiterates almost inaudibly.

We just stand there. I begin looking around hoping for something to break the silence.

I look down and happen to notice the time on my watch. My head does a double take as I bring up my watch closer to my eyes. The big hand and the little hand are very close together at the top of the time piece.

"I'm sorry," I say switching my gaze from my watch to Melody and back again. "I didn't know it was so late."

Melody looks at her own watch and appears to be somewhat surprised herself.

"I had better get going," Melody says softly as she pulls open the car door slightly. "We have a new set tomorrow."

"I know," I mumble, smiling a bit wider.

"What?" Melody says opening the door about three-fourths of the way and moves around it to get in.

Still in somewhat of a daze, I move toward her until we are centimeters apart.

Alone With Someone

"Thank you very much," I say taking her hand in mine. "I had a wonderful night, especially the last couple of hours."

"So did I," Melody says as her eyes appear to become extremely shinny appearing glassed over.

Holding and now caressing her hand with my thumb, I close my eyes, lean toward her slowly, and attempt to touch her soft cheek with my lips.

I open my eyes slightly when I feel that I am close to my desired destination. I notice and feel Melody's full red lips touch my own. Electricity runs throughout my entire body; a flame ignites within; a soothing cool engulfs me. I close my eyes briefly and enjoy the sensation. My lips know what to do almost instinctively as our embrace continues.

I open my eyes and see that Melody has closed hers. Her eyelids flutter and slowly open. Our intimate gazes meet and the passage of reality ceases.

I slowly begin to realize what I had just done. My eyes widen and my lips contract and stopping their movement. Melody seems to do the same. I move my head back, as does Melody, and we stand here. We both sigh heavily.

My head is light and floats on each new wave of emotion. My mind is empty and void of words and little voices.

"I'll see you next Friday then," I say, my words sounding blocks away and echoing through my less vacant mind as I help Melody into her car, still holding her hand.

"Yes, see you then," Melody says almost inaudibly accepting my gestures as she situates herself in the driver's seat.

Slowly, I let her hand slip from mine. Melody looks at it briefly, smiles, then places it on the wheel as I slowly close the door.

Chapter 7

The metal barrier clicks shut, her engine starts, and she turns to face me. Through the clear, yet somewhat frosty glass, I can see her still smiling face and sparkling eyes. The corners of her mouth somehow manage to extend outward slightly more than usual as she waves to me.

I step back from the car and watch as she disappears across the parking lot and onto the street.

"Did she let it warm up? It might stall and she might..." the little voice returns.

I shake my head and laugh softly at my unwarranted contemplation. Then again, if it's as hot as it feels, I guess a few seconds is long enough. Though time has really not been that much of a measurable quantity for me lately.

I do not move as I reflect on what just happened. I close my eyes slightly and try to visualize her eyes, her hair, her lips...ah her lips, and her hands.

My eyes pop open at the last thought, her hands, and I look down at my own. My smile seems to extend from its already full form as I see her hand sliding from mine, onto her steering wheel...still wearing my gloves.

I shrug my shoulders and put my hands in my pockets, more for comfort than heat. I stroll to my car, thinking not behind, nor ahead, rather on the present, which seems very warm and soothing.

Chapter 8

How beautiful...

How soft...How smooth...

How...

"Hey, thanks for taking some of the heat off."

"What?" I say aloud turning my head to face Frank.

"Are you going to tell them before she gets here?" Frank asks. "Or, are you just going to introduce her afterwards?"

"It's no big deal," I say, hoping he believes it more than I do. "Besides, Cindy's here," I continue, turning my head and smiling at Cindy who is sitting at our table.

"Well, let's see...Cindy's here," Frank says imitating my expression and smiling in Cindy's direction. "And the guys don't say anything about her..."

"Yeah," I say swallowing hard.

"Yeah, and she's my wife!" Frank stresses the last word.

I blush as I realize my false comparison.

"What I meant was that, um, both of you know her. It shouldn't be that big of a deal."

"So, what are you going to do, ignore her and let Cindy sit with and talk to her?"

"Well..." I say, not really considering the idea, just trying to stay away from any real answer, an answer I do not have right now.

Chapter 8

"Bill, don't do this to yourself," Frank says shaking his head.

"What? Do what?" I say beginning to look around.

"Bill! Are you listening? Melody's a very nice young lady and a friend. Besides, I've seen the way you two look at each other." Frank pauses.

I look at him again and say, "What do you mean by that?"

"Come on. I'm not one of your students. I can see that sparkle you write about."

"What sparkle? I say swallowing hard again, trying to defer his analogy.

"Whatever," Frank says apparently trying to move on. "Just act as if this wasn't a place filled with your closest friends, where one of them is going to make a complete fool of himself...even more than usual."

A smirk forms on my face and my recent concerns subside somewhat as I remember exactly why we are all here, besides the fact that it is Friday.

Frank and I move away from the stage and toward the table, which is slightly larger than usual and surrounded by more chairs. We have pushed together two of the center tables anticipating a few more members of our group for this performance. Cindy and Steve are already sitting down and talking as we approach.

"So, are you ready to make some great squealing noises?" Steve asks Frank as we reach the table.

"Funny," Frank says half smiling, half frowning.

"You'll do fine, honey," Cindy says taking Frank's hand and rubbing it between both of hers.

"At least someone came to support me," Frank says bending down and kissing Cindy.

Alone With Someone

My thoughts wonder back to Melody's lips and our embrace. I sigh softly and smile.

"But why?" my inner voice inquires.

Why what?

"Why did she kiss you?"

I am somewhat confused and slightly concerned. I really haven't thought about that. I do not know why.

"Hey guys," a familiar voice says as a hand hits my shoulder. "What's going on? How come the table is so big? Are we having a party or something?"

I turn and see Jeff standing to my right. He is about 6'3" tall, rather thin, and has short brown hair. He removes his hand from my shoulder and begins to take off his black leather gloves and leather bomber jacket, which has a flying tiger on the back. Jeff is a pilot and an assistant golf coach at our school.

"Actually, Frankie here is going to play with Joe, Jerr, and Kirk," Steve says smiling, and almost bursting with laughter.

Jeff's eyes widen as he looks at Frank, then Steve, and finally at the stage. He points from the stage, to Frank, and back again.

"You're kidding, right," Jeff says chuckling slightly.

"No, he's not!" Frank says rather forcefully. "What's so funny? I am a music director. Or, have you been away so long, you've forgotten?"

"I'm sorry," Jeff manages to blurt out between fits of laughter. "I just...well, you...you're Frank! How long did they give you to practice?"

Chapter 8

Jeff shakes his head and sits down next to Steve. He holds up two fingers toward the Kirk, who is standing on the other side of the room. Kirk seems to see this gesture and goes behind the bar.

"Hey, you're rather quiet today," Jeff says looking at me.

I know, I'm just standing here smiling.

"Are you still there? Hello," Jeff says, this time waving his hand in front of my face.

I blush and say, "I'm fine..."

"He's been like that for a few weeks now," Kirk says as he puts down drinks for Steve and Cindy, then hands Jeff his red-colored drink in a medium size glass.

Number two? Red? Mai Tai.

"He met this g..." Kirk says and stops.

"What's her name?" Jeff inquires quickly.

"Um, well," I say still focusing on his earlier question as well as mine.

"I believe it was Melody or something," Steve says. "We did get to hear a poem he wrote for her."

"It's Melody," I correct quickly, making sure they don't get it wrong.

"What's she look like? What's she do?" Jeff spouts outs questions rapidly.

I ignore most of his inquiries. Jeff's a great friend who is always there for you, but at times, he asks too many questions or pushes when I do not want to be pushed. Though more often than not, it is his prodding that makes me act.

Alone With Someone

Speaking of actions, why did she kiss me?

"Does it matter?" my inner voice asks sarcastically.

Yes, it does. Was she kissing me or was she kissing someone she thought I was?

"What?!?" The voice shouts.

No, really. If she was kissing me then I only need to worry about why.

"Yeah, and..."

If she was kissing someone she thought I was, or rather am, who is this person? Am I really him? Can I be him? And, why would she kiss him instead of me?

"This is crazy," a voice says.

"Exactly!" I say, pointing my hand, palm up, in the direction of the voice...at Jeff.

I blush as I realize that my thoughts were wondering again. I've been so together since that night. Why am I losing it now?

"She's coming," my inner voice whispers.

I turn toward the doors and feel everyone's eyes follow mine.

A door opens and in enters...

In enters a man. He is about my height with dark, thinning hair, and wearing a pair of thick, dark-rimmed glasses. He smiles in our direction and makes his way toward us with short quick steps.

"Hey Mark. How's it going?" Jeff asks rather loudly as Mark finally reaches the table.

Chapter 8

I shake my head, trying to overcome my uncertainty and surprise. I actually thought it would be her.

"So, did they tell you about Frank's little performance here? Or did they forget to call you too?" Jeff turns in my direction on the last few words of his question.

"Well..." Mark starts.

"I'm sorry," I say. "I've just been a little busy. You're both here anyway, so it works."

How could I forget to call Mark? He's actually the only one who would come for the show and not to ridicule Frank, besides Cindy of coarse.

"It's OK," Mark says taking off his jacket. "Joe called me. He said you've been spacing out more than usual and...."

"And, I would forget to call," I say quickly, completing a thought Mark probably didn't have. My eyes widen and I look at Mark to make sure he's not going to say more or change the subject.

"So, are you going to try something daring tonight, doc?" Kirk asks Mark. "Or, are we just going to have water as usual?"

"I'll just have water," Mark says. "And, how about some potato skins?"

We all look at Mark briefly. Then, burst out laughing.

Mark's not that heavy. He's thinner than I am, though I'm not really that large. Recently, however, he's been concerned about his weight. He says those gowns at the hospital are very revealing. Ever since his internship, he's been worried about his appearance one way or another. He's an excellent doctor, though he prefers the research aspects of his current position, and he's a very trusting and responsible friend. He was the only one in high school whom I didn't mind losing to for any academic or humanitarian competition. He graduated valedictorian of his undergraduate college and in the top ten percent of his medical school.

Alone With Someone

He is incredible at retaining knowledge, which he then applies to life and the many things he somehow finds time to do.

"Coming right up. Someone will bring it out once we start playing," Kirk says shaking his head, still laughing.

Mark puts his coat on the chair to the left of Cindy and sits down.

"I was running some tests before I left and didn't have enough time to eat. After all, I didn't want to be late," Mark says looking up at Frank who has his sax draped around his neck and is still holding one of Cindy's hands.

From the stage in front of us, come the reverberating sounds of a bass drum, two quick thumps, a pause, then two more thumps.

"Well," Frank says looking at all of us, "I had better get up there. They want to warm up before...before..."

"Before, you get too warm," Jeff says, taking a drink of his Mai Tai.

Frank lets go of Cindy's hand and moves slowly toward the stage.

"Are you going to stand for the entire thing?" Steve asks. "I don't think the people behind us are going to like that."

I move to a seat across the table from Cindy, close to Jeff, and facing the door. I can't help but take in the entire room as I move. There seems to be a few more people than usual. The couple behind us don't look harmful, slightly older than the usual crowd, but not harmful.

Just as I sit down, Kirk hops on stage. A high pitched note echoes around our confinement. It is followed by a soft harmonious note. At this moment, for one reason or another, I feel sorry for Frank. I hope tonight does go well.

Chapter 8

Two more notes wonder from the stage, this time blending. I turn my head toward Cindy and give her a thumbs up sign as if to say, "It'll be OK."

I pick up my head slightly and see...and see... my own harmonious note. My eyes widen and my hands become limp.

Cindy seems to notice my actions and turns around. She motions to Melody, who seems to be looking for a familiar face.

Melody smiles and moves toward us.

Part of me thought she wouldn't show up. Part of me hoped she wouldn't show up. The majority of my instincts tell me to jump up and lead her to the table, but I am interrupted by another voice.

"We'd like to thank you for coming tonight," Jerry says. "It looks a little more crowded than usual, which means it is a very good day to introduce a fellow musician and a friend, Frank."

Frank steps forward and takes a small bow. Kirk snaps a couple of strings on his bass and Joe clashed his cymbal.

We all stand and applaud. Melody reaches the table and claps with us. Cindy motions for her to sit down next to me.

"Wake up!" my little voice shouts.

I shake my head and stare at Melody.

"Her coat!" the voice echoes.

"I'm sorry," I say helping her take off her coat.

Melody smiles as I place her garment on the back of a chair. In the same motion, I manage to pull out the chair for her and motion for her to sit. She does so, turns toward Cindy, smiles, then faces the stage.

Alone With Someone

Everyone else seems to have sat down as well. Somehow, I join them and position myself so that I can see the entire stage as well as Melody. It's not that difficult considering I am at the end of the table and she is at the side still close, very close.

"Beautiful," I whisper.

Melody turns her head toward me and smiles again.

"So, if the people down in front are done playing musical chairs," Jerry says grinning, "we'll begin. Feel free to eat, dance, submit requests, anything. Just don't get too rowdy."

Joe pounds on the drums a few times and Jerry adds, "Especially if you've paid your bill already."

Joe adds a cymbal crash as Jerry's attempt at a joke is met with groans from those of us watching...

Watching much more than...

"Their best friends on stage!" my inner voice shouts.

I can feel my face turn red. I look around the table quickly to see if anyone else has noticed the recent increase in temperature.

I turn and look at Steve and Jeff. They are staring blankly at the stage and smiling. They continue their stare as they simultaneously take a sip from their glasses.

Joe clicks his sticks together and takes off with a rock beat. As I look back at the stage, I see Jerry smiling and wetting the reed on his sax. Kirk slides his fingers lightly along his metal strings. Frank shakes his head. They usually start out with a slower song, which is probably what Frank was expecting and hoping for.

"Let the games begin," Steve says softly and chuckles.

Chapter 8

I take a deep breath and frown.

Steve taps on the table as Jerry begins to spout out a series of upbeat notes, some that were written for the piece and others that seem to fit in just as well, if not better.

Melody turns around and looks at Steve. He smiles, she blushes, and looks quickly to me.

I want so much to reach out and caress her hand, to hold her. Instead, I let the initial sounds of Frank's alto sax pull the thoughts right out of my mind. I just smile, reach out my hand, and...and tap on the table.

"You could listen to the music and not worry about what she's doing," my inner voice suggests.

Sure, and I could just stop breathing!

Melody has turned her head in order to watch the stage. Frank, who after trying to catch up with the other guys has not only fit in but made them adjust somewhat to his interpretation.

The first tune comes to an end. We all clap. It's one of those moments when you expect the lights to get brighter, but this isn't a movie. Or is it?

I look around expecting to see cameras or a director yelling, "cut."

Instead, I see Steve and Jeff whispering. They stop and take another drink as my gaze hits them. They seem to stare blankly again at the stage as another song begins, it's a slower one this time. What are they doing?

Cindy is still in her chair, a smile graces her face. Mark has his arms crossed and his eyes seem to scan the stage over and over.

Funny, it may have even gotten darker in here. The people beyond our little group seem to be less in focus.

"Maybe, it's because you don't have on your glasses," my little voice says sarcastically.

I smile and shake my head. My focus returns to the stage. Joe lightly brushes his cymbals. Jerry's eyes are closed as the notes flow from his tenor sax. Kirk bobs and sways as the deep sounds escape from his bass. Frank's eyes are half open, half closed, and a few beads of sweat roll down each side of his forehead.

Right in front of me, closer than those on stage is...is a figment of my imagination. She has to be an illusion, only my imagination could create such a vision. Only my mind might see the way her eyes sparkle and shine with...with this limited lighting.

What am I doing?

"So, why did she kiss you?" my inner voice asks.

I close my eyes and listen. The music courses through me. The notes cease to be high or low. They maintain a simple melodic tone as my thoughts drift back to that night. Her eyes glistening in the moonlight.

"How bright was the moon?" my inner voice asks. "Was there a moon at all?"

What?

My eyes open briefly and close again, catching a small glimpse of reality, a miniature, framed picture of my vision. The music overpowers me again.

I'm leaning inward absorbing the scent of her perfume, the warmth emanating from her entire being, the aura...

"What did her perfume smell like?" the voice interrupts.

I don't even bother opening my eyes as I try to ignore my more annoying self. The song changes, quickening in pace.

Chapter 8

I am so close, so near to this "figment," this creation of my imagination. I can feel her soft skin, her silky hair, her full red lips...

"But, why did she kiss you?"

I shake my head and open my eyes half way.

Why?

"That's my question," the voice says.

No, no, why am I doing this? It shouldn't matter.

"But, it does."

No, it doesn't.

"Does it?" I whisper.

"Does it what?" a voice sounding like Jeff's asks.

My eyes open completely and my head turns to the left, toward Jeff.

The music has stopped and I am staring at Jeff and Steve. They are both clapping. I join in, hoping to avoid answering the questions again.

I turn my head again, this time toward the stage. Frank, Joe, Kirk, and Jerry are walking toward us, each with at least part of his instrument.

Great. I wasn't really listening again. The first thing they're going to ask is...

"So, what did you think?" Frank says reiterating my thoughts.

"Are you sure this isn't a movie?" my little voice asks.

"You might consider using a mike after the break. We couldn't hear you," Steve says leaning backward in his chair.

"You did very well," Cindy says taking Frank's hand.

Frank bends down and kisses her. "Thank you. At least someone was paying attention."

Out of the corner of my eye, I can see Melody smiling. I turn my head to look at her, just as she does the same. Her smile broadens.

"So, Bill what did you think? You're the critic, and you did rope me into this," Frank says.

I hear his voice, but do not look directly at him.

"Um, it was very good," I say.

I pause then shake my head, breaking my gaze with Melody.

I turn my head toward Frank and say, "I mean you did better than I thought you would. You have proven your greatness." I bow slightly even though I am sitting. I move my open hand in small circles in front of my face a few times.

"Thank you, sir. I am not worthy of your praise," Frank says clicking his heals together and returning my bow.

"You can say that again," Jeff mumbles.

By now, Joe and Jerry have sat down, Joe to my left and Jerry between Mark and Melody.

Melody! I almost forgot to...

"And, who is this lovely young lady?" Jerry asks looking at Melody.

"We were wondering the same thing," Jeff says inquisitively.

Melody's face turns red as she realizes the conversation has shifted to her.

Chapter 8

"Um," I say hesitating in more than my words.

"This is..." Cindy says, pausing herself for some reason.

"She is an even better musician that Frank is," I blurt out.

Did I just say that aloud? I think I did.

"You must be Melody then," Joe says.

Where did he get that from?

Melody moves her head up and down but doesn't say anything.

There is a silence at the table and I can feel everyone's eyes shift from Melody then to me.

"Hey, how many sets we doing tonight?" Kirk asks as he sets down drinks for Joe, Frank, and Jerry. He turns to Melody and asks, "And, what would you like young lady?"

We are all quiet again.

"Kirk," Jerry says wetting his lips as he sips his drink, "this is Melody." He winks and motions with his head toward her.

"Melody?" Kirk says stumbling over his words. "Oh, yeah. Nice of you to, um, stop by. Would you care for anything?"

Melody shakes her head and moves her lips, but nothing comes out.

"Don't worry, it's...what did you call it Bill?" Joe asks tapping me a few times on the arm.

"A chimney," I say softly.

"That's right, a chimney," Joe reiterates.

Alone With Someone

Melody's face changes again. This time it asks, "What is a chimney?"

"A chimney is..." Joe pauses, taps on the table with his sticks, and looks around.

"On the house," everyone except for Melody and myself says.

I shake my head and wonder why we still use that joke.

"Actually..." Kirk begins to say.

"Actually, Kirk makes us do dishes," Jeff says looking at Kirk and frowning.

"Dishes? Dishes?" Steve questions. "Who gets to do dishes? I get stuck with the trash."

"If the shoe fits," Jerry says pointing to Joe for a cymbal crash.

"Ha, ha," Steve says sarcastically.

"The only one who doesn't have any chores is Mark here," Joe says pointing a stick in Mark's direction.

Melody and I move around slightly to look at Mark. I am trying to see his reaction. Melody is probably trying to see who they are talking about. She still has not said anything aloud.

"That's because he only gets water," Steve says reaching across the table and with his forefinger, plunks Marks's glass.

"Oh? And, what are these?" Jerry asks picking up a plate with potato skins.

"My fee," Mark says smiling and taking one off the plate, biting into it. "And, my dinner," he adds after chewing briefly.

"Doc's getting smart," Jerry says putting down the plate.

"Yeah, smart-alec," Jeff says shaking his head.

"So, what did my you think of my performance, doc?" Frank asks nudging Mark slightly.

"Well," Mark says taking another bite of his supper, chewing, pausing, and swallowing, "you were good."

"That's it?" Frank says sarcastically. "All those years of school and the only thing you can come up with is, 'you were good'?"

"Would you like me to critique you on a personal or a technical level then?" Mark asks, smiling and taking a drink of his water.

"Technical for two hundred, please," Joe says.

"Well," Mark begins and rambles off many musical phrases and terms.

I look at Melody. She is smiling. She looks at me. This time, I reach out and caress her hand. I grasp it momentarily. She squeezes my fingers between hers.

"Look at the time," Mark says as he finishes his requested musical lecture.

My head snaps to him and my hand moves quickly from Melody's.

"You're going already?" Frank says. "We only did the one set. Next time, I'll settle for 'you were good.'"

"You can't go," Joe says, "we haven't saluted yet." He takes a gulp of an imaginary beer.

"I have rounds tonight," Mark says standing and putting on his coat. "Besides, I only have water, remember." He picks up his glass and swallows the last few drops.

"See you next week," Mark finishes. "It was nice meeting you." Mark waves to Melody as he turns to leave. With his short, quick steps, he makes his way toward the door.

"I'd better get going too," Steve says as he rises and puts on his coat.

"And, where are you going?" Joe asks.

"I have a date," Steve says downing his second shot.

"Anyone we know," Jeff asks sarcastically.

"Of coarse not," Jerry says.

"What do you mean by that?" Steve questions.

"Nothing," Jerry says laughing slightly.

"No, really," Steve says, "what do you mean?"

"You just have interesting taste in women and..." Jerry says and pauses.

"And, you never see any of them more than a few times," Joe adds.

"So?" Steve asks "I'm just playing the game." Steve takes a swing with an imaginary bat, winks in my direction, and turns to leave.

As all of us follow Steve to the door with our eyes, I see Jeff hold up one finger toward the bar.

Let's see...oh, yeah, rum and coke.

"Would anyone else, besides Jeff, like anything," Kirk says frowning at Jeff.

Frank and Joe ask for water. Cindy is still milking her first glass. I just nod to Kirk hoping he understands that I'll take my usual.

153

Chapter 8

"I'll just bring you what Bill's having," Kirk says winking at Melody. He then turns and heads toward the bar.

Melody's eyes widen as she looks at me. She still has not said a word.

"Was I that bad?" Frank says directing his statement to the entire table as he pulls out a chair next to Cindy and sits down.

"I thought you were all very good," says a sultry voice behind us.

We all seem to turn at the same moment. A tall blonde wearing a very short red skirt has her hand on Joe's shoulder.

She slips Joe a piece of paper and wiggles her way to a table toward the rear of the bar where she is accompanied by two other physically appealing women. They all wave to us.

I can only assume that everyone caught the entire act. Then again, it's not just us "guys" as usual.

"Way to go swiftis," my inner voice says. "You have a beautiful girl right next to you, and you let your eyes pop out of your head at the first temptation."

I turn around and catch Melody staring down at the table, biting her lower lip.

"Great! She thinks you're just another guy," my inner voice shouts. "Your poems seem so trivial now, don't they?"

I want to say, "you are much more beautiful," or "they can't compare with someone like you." Fortunately, I fight the urge. It would just sound too phony.

Instead, I turn to Frank and stare at him with those "help me" eyes.

It seems that Cindy and Jeff see my expression as well. All of them clear their throats as if about to say something.

154

Alone With Someone

Melody picks up her head and looks around the table.

"You know," Jeff says taking a deep breath, "this trip was a slight bit more bumpy than the last.

"Oh yeah," Joe says unfolding the small piece of paper he was just given. "Did you run into some of that bad weather? Or were you having too much fun with the stewardesses?" Smiling, Joe reaches across the table and shows the paper to Jerry who develops a very large grin.

"Well, a little bit of both," Jeff says grinning.

Melody still has not said a word.

I frown at Jeff as my eyebrows move upward, giving me that "what-next" look.

We are silent for a few seconds.

Kirk arrives with the drinks, and we all breathe a sigh of relief for some reason or another.

"Here we go," Kirk says as he places Jeff's drink in front of him. "So, what did I miss?"

No one says a word, but Jerry's head moves upward and toward the table in the back.

I do not follow his or Kirk's eyes. Instead, I keep my eyes on Melody, whose head is slanted downward and a frown rests upon her face. I place a hand on top of hers and wait.

She picks up her head. I just smile and shrug my shoulders slightly. Slowly, a smile begins to form on her face. Kirk places a mug, with the froth still settling, in front of each of us. Melody's smile becomes wider.

Joe clears his throat. I shift my gaze from Melody's sweet, innocent face to the center of the table where everyone has their glasses.

Chapter 8

With my left hand, I grab my mug and raise it. I motion for Melody to do the same. She follows quickly and we both move our drinks to the center of the table.

We sit motionless. Then, we click our glasses together and say "Salute," simultaneously.

I even see Melody mouth the word shortly after everyone else. I smile and move my glass toward my lips and pause before I take a sip.

Melody brings the mug up to her lips as well. Those full, red, enticing...

I close my eyes and take a drink, imagining those luscious lips touching mine; her soft delicate hand...in...my own.

I swallow and open my eyes slowly.

"I love root beer," Melody says rather loudly.

My eyes open the rest of the way very quickly, and my hand, which has remained on hers, moves involuntarily toward me.

I stare at her, my eyes widening and wondering. I swallow the beverage that remains in my mouth and start giggling. Melody does the same and takes another sip.

I look around the table, and before my eyes can reach everyone, my ears pick up their laughter.

"She speaks," Joe says and looks at Kirk.

"And...and...she loves," Kirk says nodding to Jerry.

"Rootbeer!" Jerry exclaims finishing the thought.

We all laugh.

Melody blushes slightly, but continues to laugh.

"Be careful," Jeff says just as Melody is about to take another sip. "If you laugh too hard, it might come out your nose."

Melody pauses and laughs slightly louder as a picture of such probably crosses her mind.

"Billie here says you play pretty well," Joe says continuing to make Melody part of the conversation, part of the group.

"Well, um, he..." Melody pauses still calming down from her fit of laughter.

"Bill is very sweet, but..." She pauses again.

"But, she's really not better than I am," Frank says, tooting on his mouth piece.

"Maybe you can sit in sometime too," Jerry offers smiling.

"Jerr," I say, my eyes widening.

Jerry just shrugs his shoulders.

"I could never play on a small stage like that," Melody says softly.

"Hey Kirk, can we get a bigger stage in here?" Jerry asks sarcastically.

"Sure, just give me a few weeks," Kirk responds, nodding his head as a phony grin forms on his face.

"I didn't mean it that way," Melody says blushing again and angling her head downward.

"We understand," Joe says pretending to slap Jerry in the air. "Hey, it's time for another set. Let's get going." Joe raps his sticks on the table.

I mouth the words, "Thank you," to Joe as he rises from his seat. He just smiles and heads toward the stage.

Chapter 8

"We pick on everyone," Jeff says. "It's just our way of saying 'welcome.'"

Melody picks up her head and looks at me. I smile at her, hoping she'll brighten up the room with her beautifully glistening smile.

"Thanks," she says to Jeff, though still looking at me. The corners of her mouth begin to move upward again.

"Sorry about the delay," Jerry says from the stage. "It's time for some requests. This one is for the lovely young ladies in the back. We can't exactly play what you asked for..."

"At least not on stage," Joe says in a comedic tone, as he winks toward the back of the room, and plays a "ba-dump-bump" on his snare.

The audience groans.

So, we can't all be comedians.

I no longer feel as if in a movie, rather in a dream, as I continue to stare into Melody's eyes.

What's racing around in her mind?

"So, have you figured out why she kissed you yet?" my inner voice interrupts.

My eyebrows scrunch in and downward as an inquisitive look forms on my face.

A slow, sensuous song escapes from Frank's and Jerry's horns, accentuated by the lower tones of Kirk's bass. Frank's higher pitched alto seems to ring through slightly more at first.

I feel a very warm tingling sensation on my right hand as a smile returns to my face. I look down and see Melody's hand on top of mine. My head moves slowly upward, toward her face. She has a rather sheepish grin on her face.

"Now, why..." my little voice starts, but I don't let it finish.

We have to get out of here.

"But, your friends are here," my inner voice says. "And, one of them is performing on this stage for the first time!"

The rhythm seems to pick up slightly, taking my heartbeat with it. I turn toward Melody and motion toward the door.

"Would you like to get some fresh air?" I say trying to pierce through the sounds of the music, though trying to stay rather quiet.

Melody just nods her head and reaches for her coat. Slowly, her hand moves from mine.

I rise, pick up my coat, and put my arms into both sleeves, but do not zip it.

I extend my hand, palm up, toward the door. I hope for Melody to move in that direction. She accepts my gesture, taking my hand in hers, and begins to walk toward the door.

As we walk past Cindy, I hear Melody say, "Thanks again. Tell Frank that he sounded great."

I just say, "I'll be right back."

Cindy smiles as if to say, "sure, whatever," and returns her stare toward the stage.

Melody and I finally reach the doors. I open one of them and wait until she walks through. Her hand slips from mine as she passes through the opening.

Chapter 8

We say nothing as we take a few steps outside. The wind has died down and a soothing scent seems to be riding the night breeze.

"You know, in a movie, it would start snowing," my little voice says sarcastically.

I look up and extend my right arm, opening my hand. I expect to feel the cool dampness of white fluffy flakes. Instead, I feel the cool smoothness of...of...

I look at my palm and see Melody's hand resting in mine once again. I close my fingers over hers and caress its softness. I turn my head and look at her innocent face. She blinks as I lower our hands and smile.

"I..." we both say at the same time, then pause.

"You first," Melody says.

I would rather you go first, but...

"I'm sorry if you felt uncomfortable in there," I say waiting for her to respond and address her issue.

"Address her issue?" my inner voice asks. "Are we in a seminar here?"

"Actually, I was more comfortable than I thought I would be," Melody says looking around.

"I'm glad. They're all great and..." I say and pause.

"And, very diverse," Melody says, continuing my thought.

"Yes, very much so," I say wondering what else there is to say. "There's a police officer..."

"Jerry," Melody says smiling.

"A pilot," I pause and look at Melody inquisitively.

"Jeff," she adds.

"A doctor..."

"Mark," Melody says moving closer.

"A barkeep and a..."

"Morning DJ," Melody whispers.

I blink my eyes very quickly. "How did you know that?" I ask.

"I wasn't exactly sure," Melody says, "but the way he said that last line, then hit the drums, I knew it was him. I started listening to his station a few months ago. He really wakes you up." Her eyes widen as does her smile.

"Most of the time he's trying to wake himself up as well. You have a good ear," I say. The urge to find a brick wall crosses my mind as it did in a similar circumstance. Of coarse she has a good ear, she's a musician.

"Thank you..." I say trying to come up with something else to say.

"Thank you," Melody says looking directly at me.

"So, do you think..." I begin a thought and stare up at the starry sky.

"Yes?" Melody says softly.

She said "yes!" She said "yes!" She said, yes?

"It was a question," my inner voice points out.

"Do you think it's going to snow?" I say still looking at the sky.

"Here we go again," the voice says somewhat disgusted.

Chapter 8

Even though I don't look at her directly, I can sense that a disappointed look has formed on Melody's sweet face.

"I mean, do you think it will snow next Friday? I was hoping we could...you're probably busy."

"I'd love to, but," Melody says hesitating somewhat. "But, we're doing a charity performance that night."

"I understand," I whisper sounding very disappointed myself.

"But, the Friday after that," Melody says as she moves even closer and takes my other hand in hers.

I look directly into her sparkling eyes as she continues, "I'm free then," she says smiling.

Just as the stars somehow mesmerized me a few moments ago, her eyes seem to be just as captivating, just as bright, just as welcoming.

"Do you think it will snow then?" I ask pausing a few seconds. "I was hoping to do some sledding." I smile and laugh.

Melody giggles briefly and says, "That sounds exciting."

"Actually," I say, "what do you think about horses?"

"I think they're rather large animals," Melody says maintaining the jocular mood and continuing to laugh.

I chuckle and shake my head. That's a line I probably would have used. It's just corny enough.

"We'll talk about it," she finally adds. "You do have my phone number, right?"

"Um, yes, I do," I say somewhat surprised by her comment.

Alone With Someone

Our right hands slip from each other, while our left ones remain clasped. We begin walking.

After only a few feet and a few moments of silence, we stop.

Melody turns toward me again. "Thanks again," she says. "I should go home and practice myself. They really sounded great in there."

"I'm really glad you were here," I say looking everywhere on her face, except in her eyes.

I begin to lean inward, stop, and say, "Do you really listen to Joe in the morning?"

Surprised somewhat and giggling, Melody says, "Yes, he's pretty funny at times."

"Oh," I say looking around and beginning to lean in again.

I stop myself and say, "Did you know someone else writes some of his lines?"

"No, I didn't know that," opening her half closed eyes.

Her eyes were closed? Why?

Once again, I lean toward her. Slowly, my eyes begin to close.

"Before you go," I say swaying backward and quickly opening my eyes, "I have another poem for you."

As she opens her eyes this time, a look of unsettled discontent forms on her face.

I remove an envelope from my inside coat pocket and hand it to her. She accepts it and begins to open it.

Chapter 8

"Actually, I would rather you read it later," I say sheepishly. "We could talk about it when I call you."

"Oh, OK," Melody says seemingly understanding my request.

I quickly grasp her free hand and kiss it lightly.

"Thanks again," I say, hoping this will suffice both of us.

Melody smiles, but a different gleam shines in her eyes. She folds the envelope in half and places it in her pocket. Melody grabs the handle of the car door and pulls it open.

I watch her slip in. I don't say anything. I can't say anything.

I want to ask her to stay. I want to ask if I can go home with her and listen; listen to her sweet music; listen to her soft voice.

Her car starts and the roar of the engine wakes me somewhat. I look around, still no snow. I move my hands together just below Melody's window and whisper, "cut."

My focus returns to Melody. Her window is now open.

"Did you say something?" she asks.

"What? No, no," I say swallowing hard. "Just out of curiosity... have you even thought your life was like a movie?"

Melody smiles and says, "I guess, at times." She pauses. "Um, would you like me to stay a while longer? I could practice later."

Yeah! Please stay!

"No, that's OK. You should practice..." I pause, then add, "Not that you need to practice...I mean..."

What am I doing?

Melody giggles. "Are you still going to call me?" she asks innocently and now somewhat concerned.

"I'll call in the next couple of days," I say hoping to reassure her of my sanity.

Where's that brick wall?

Breaking the silence, Melody says, "Bill, I really enjoyed tonight. Your friends are very nice. It's been a while since I was out on a..."

"Don't say it," I interrupt. "I mean, it's been a while for myself as well, but..."

Melody smiles and says, "Yes,"

We just stare at each other, and somehow, some way, we're still communicating.

"I..." we say at the same time again.

"I had better get going then," Melody says.

I take one step backward and wave to her as she rolls up her window and slowly drives across the parking lot, onto the street, and out of sight...again.

The thought of going back inside crosses my mind, but I delay making that decision as I attempt to remember the poem I had just given her:

Soothing Smile

Darkness is no more;
Ice dissipates into mist;
Walls of stone crumble;
The tallest buildings topple;
And, I literally melt
From the inside out.

Chapter 8

My head is sent
Spinning, spinning, spinning,
From just one,
Small,
Simple,
Sultry,
Comforting,
Glimpse of your
Soothing smile.

I sigh as I remember the actual inspiration, the sight, the feel, the emotional onslaught...

Sometime during the wondering in my mind, my body seems to have decided to return to my friends, because I am standing next to those familiar and welcoming doors of Kirk's. I shake my head, open a door, and walk inside. I wait for the door to close completely before moving again. As it hits my back, I turn around and look out the small panes of frosted glass. Light, white puffs fall from the night sky.

"Now! Now it snows!" my inner voice shouts.

I laugh inwardly and smile. Someone really has a sense of humor. I shake my head again and walk toward the table.

"So, when did you say you were going to call her?" my inner voice asks.

What time is it now?

Chapter 9

OK, OK. I'm standing by a stable, brushing a horse, it's somewhat chilly...and, I'm doing this why?

"If you can't figure this one out, we're both crazy!" my inner voice says sarcastically.

Great! Just great! Not only do I hear voices, but I'm also developing multiple personalities.

I look at the horse and expect to see its lips moving. Instead, the simple, yet proud creature simply stands there, periodically blinking.

Its eyes are large and seem to catch the sun's rays just right, causing them to twinkle almost rhythmically.

Melody's eyes seemed to sparkle even without the sunlight; those intensely illuminating mirrors radiating, engulfing me entirely. A small amount of content falls over me as I sigh and close my own eyes.

"Now you're comparing a beautiful young lady to a horse?"

Wonderful! It's bad enough having a little voice, but a sarcastic one...that's even worse!

"I'm sorry I'm so late," a soft voice says.

My eyes flip open, and I turn my head to face the refreshingly familiar voice.

Melody smiles and says nothing else.

The silence seems awkward, yet I continue to brush my horse.

"Are those the horses?" Melody asks, breaking the quietude.

"Um, yes," I manage to mumble. "Did you find the place OK?"

167

Chapter 9

"Yes. Yes, I did. The directions you've given me over the past week were great!" A smirk forms on Melody's face.

We've talked on the phone every evening since Frank's performance at Kirk's. It gave me something to look forward to, something to hope for. Melody called me a couple of times. For the most part, however, I called her, partly just to hear that soothing voice.

"And the lady at the little house sent me directly to you. She seemed to have a very large grin on her face. Does she know you?" Melody looks at me as if I had forgotten to tell her something.

"What? Oh, that was Linda," I say and pause.

Melody's eyes widen, her smile narrows, and I can almost hear her swallowing.

"Her son, Brian, is in one of my English classes," I say quickly, hoping that any thoughts she might be having have changed. "You know Brian. He was in the class Frank and you observed."

Melody's smile returns full force, and the twinkle, that sparkle, which I have been without, has returned to her large eyes.

"Do you do this often?" Melody asks as she moves closer and begins to caress the soft fur of the horse next to mine.

"Ride horses?" I say.

"No, making a fool out of yourself. You do that often, yes," my inner voice responds.

"Actually," I say shaking my head, hoping to shed the extra thoughts, "I usually come out here to think. It's so peaceful." I consider taking hold Melody's hand, but do not.

"It's rather quiet out here and very beautiful," Melody says looking around, still smiling.

Alone With Someone

Not as beautiful as you.

I surely hope I did not say that out loud.

Melody's face turns bright red as she begins testing the security of the saddle on the other horse.

"It looks as if you have done this before," I say hoping to break the slowness of our conversation. We talked and talked on the phone, but in person, where we can see and almost feel each other's emotions, we are held somewhat in check. Why?

"I rode a few times when I was younger," Melody responds.

"Oh yes, you did mention your camping experiences," I say remembering bits of our conversations. Funny, we really didn't talk about horseback riding that much...except for the directions on how to get here.

"We never got to ride at our own pace," Melody says. "We always had to stay in a straight line and keep to a path." Melody pauses for a few seconds, then as her eyes widen, adds, "we were never able to ride."

I stare at her momentarily and smile. "Well, today, today, you shall ride!" My eyes become large. This time, I do grasp her hands.

I run my thumbs over the back of her hands and say, "May I help you up?"

Melody clears her throat momentarily. She does not say a word, but nods, yes.

I too am surprised somewhat by my abruptness.

I help Melody climb onto her dark colored mare, then back away slightly, taking in the sight. Two magnificent creatures, one more alluring than the other.

Chapter 9

"There you go again, comparing her to a horse," my little voice says, interrupting my thoughts.

I smile at Melody and attempt to mount my own horse, which I have named Sugarfoot. I know the name sounds silly, but when I was younger, I had a Shetland pony with the same name. When this horse was born, I was asked to name it. Without hesitating, I said, "Sugarfoot." Of course Linda and her family laughed slightly, but accepted it nonetheless. Every few days I stop by to feed and groom him. Linda's other son, Matt, whom I taught two years ago, does a very good job with all the horses, but I feel somewhat responsible for Sugarfoot.

I shake my head and pat Sugarfoot on the side. He picks up his head, and we move toward Melody, who is sitting still as her horse nibbles on some hay.

"Sometimes hunger gets the best of them," I say moving closer.

"I understand that," Melody says, one hand on the reigns, the other brushing stagnant hairs from her face.

"You need to show her who's boss, without actually telling her," I say reaching out toward the other horse. I begin stroking its mane. "Come on Angel, you've had enough." I pat the creature a couple of times, and her head picks up.

"Is that her name?" Melody asks.

"What? Oh yeah, Angel," I say realizing how silly I must look talking to a horse.

"It's better than talking to yourself," my annoying little voice says mockingly.

"That's fitting. She is a pretty horse," Melody says, running her fingers through Angel's mane. "And, what's your horse's name?"

I blush at the thought of telling her. I try to think of something majestic like King, or Ali, or Rex...Rex? But just as I am about to say something false, Sugarfoot lifts his head and looks at me with one eye as if to say, "well?"

"His name...his name is Sugarfoot," I say smiling and alternating shades of red. Sugarfoot whinnies and bobs his head up and down after hearing his name.

"That's original," Melody says smiling. "He looks very playful."

"Oh, he can be," I say, patting his muscular neck. I clear my throat and add, "Are you ready to go?"

"Sure. Aren't we supposed to have a guide?" Melody asks, smiling.

"Nah. Linda has trusted me with her sons' education, so trusting me with her horses, well let's just say both can be rather delicate."

Melody does not say anything else. Instead, her eyes blink and sparkle as the rays from the second brightest star in our solar system reflect off them perfectly.

Sugarfoot moves his head toward me and proceeds forward a few steps as if to say, "let's go."

As we clear the stable area, I wave to the, um, how did Melody put it, oh yeah, "little house."

Melody and Angel are beside us as we reach the large gate. I look around for any other horses, position myself so that I can release the latch and open the wooden structure. I signal for Melody to pass and follow directly behind, closing the gate as quickly as I can.

I smile at Melody and say, "Shall we start out slow, so you can get used to the saddle?"

"Um, sure," she says biting her lower lip.

Chapter 9

I make a clicking sound and both horses move forward into the woodland area.

Clip, clop, clip, clop, crunch. One of the horses steps on a twig. It is just enough, however, to make me turn my head toward Melody, who has turned to look at me as well. A smile graces her face. We both shrug our shoulders.

"How about a trot?" I say hoping to speed this up slightly.

"OK," Melody says still staring at me.

"Just hold onto your saddle and reigns," I say reassuringly. "She'll do exactly what you ask her to do."

A look of content forms on Melody's face as she nods her head.

Again, I make a clicking sound and tap Sugarfoot. I loosely hold his reigns upward and signal for Melody to do the same. Sugarfoot begins to trot and Angel follows.

We are side by side. I turn my head toward Melody then look straight ahead.

"You know, if this were a movie..." my little voice says.

But, it's not.

"If it were though, the end credits would be rolling right about now."

The what?

"You know, the end credits."

Thank goodness it's not a movie. This isn't over yet. In fact, we've gotten to know so much about each other. Actually, now that I think of it, I know quite a bit about her, even though she just seems to add to what I start saying. I have talked only about my students and my classes.

Alone With Someone

"She has lived an interesting life though," my inner voice interrupts.

I steal a glance at Melody again. She shifts readily in the saddle and, a blank expression rests on her face as she seems to be taking in everything around her.

Beautiful...

Her gaze connects with mine. I jerk on the reigns momentarily, but it is just enough to slow down the horses.

I shrug my shoulders and attempt to look innocent.

Melody shakes her head. The look on her face seems to say she's not convinced.

I angle Sugarfoot toward her and Angel and say, "I figured we would slow down for a while. I was feeling like a yo-yo with a very short string."

Melody's smile widens as she nods in agreement.

We proceed along the banks of a slowly flowing and undoubtedly cold stream.

My thoughts drift back to bits of our phone conversations.

She loves animals, especially cats...

"You hate...rather, dislike cats."

She dreams of playing in a very large, well-known orchestra...

She started playing the clarinet in fourth grade...took up the alto sax, sophomore year in high school...was asked to play the bari sax in jazz band her senior year...oh yes, and she started playing the oboe...

"That sound was beautiful."

Chapter 9

Yes, it was.

She took the challenge of the oboe her freshman year in high school...too many clarinet players.

She was able to audition at numerous universities and was offered academic as well as musical scholarships. She has led a busy life.

"She's almost as busy as you are."

She did point that out during one of our conversations. Let's see, she mentioned her volunteer work at the animal shelter, and I brought up our writing workshops held at the school on Wednesday nights. They start halfway through band rehearsals, so I can help Frank, keep myself involved, and provide opportunities for other writers to share their work.

I look over at Melody. Her gaze is already focused in my direction. I smile at her. Her head seems to move back and forth as if shaking off a daze of her own.

Melody clears her throat and nods.

I pull gently on my reigns, and Sugarfoot stops. Angel notices this and stops as well. Just as I descend, I see Angel's head turn toward Melody, probably expecting her to do the same. I position myself next to both of them, so that I may help Melody down.

My timing is slightly off, however. As I reach out my hand, the only part not off the horse yet are her arms. I place one hand on her elbow and continue with my gesture anyway.

"Thank you," Melody says as my hand slides from her elbow to her soft, delicate hand. On first contact, there is coldness. As our touch lingers, however, warmth rushes quickly between us.

I lean toward her.

"Kiss her this time!" my inner voice shouts.

Alone With Someone

"So," Melody says raising her voice slightly and pulling back somewhat. "This is so beautiful. Do many people come out here?"

"Not during this time of year," I reply, somewhat perplexed. "It's still a bit chilly for the average horse rider around here." I chuckle at the thought of the type of people who ride horses around here, most of them are tourists. This is one of the few areas not amassed by plain, lifeless concrete or metal. Not too many people get out this way, let alone at this time...in a few weeks, sure, but now... Of course that's probably why I like it out here.

A grin fills my entire face as I say, "In fact, when I come out here, I don't even bring a book to keep me company."

A look of content emerges on Melody's face. She looks around at the trees, the grass, the horses. Sugarfoot and Angel have moved closer and are nudging each other with their noses. Since Melody and I are in between them, we are being pushed closer and closer together.

"Now, that's enough you two," I say to the horses as if they were children. "If you can't behave, we'll turn right around and go home."

I turn toward Melody, shrug my shoulders, and add, "They don't really get out that much either."

"I know the feeling," Melody says softly and giggling.

We stare at each other. We are both still smiling, but the looks seem blank and rather empty. My heart, however, is full of hopes, full of desires. We lean inward as if being pulled toward our individual centers of gravity.

I feel a small nudge in my back, but ignore it and continue to focus on my most recent delight.

My eyes are closed about halfway, when I am literally shoved toward Melody, who accelerates toward me as well. I manage to grasp both of her hands, diverting some of the force.

Chapter 9

It is too late though as we both fall to the damp ground. I tumble beside her, letting go of one of her hands.

"You didn't have to jump at her," my little voice says sarcastically.

Momentarily shocked, I look directly at Melody again. Her eyes are wide with surprise and her grip remains tight.

Then...laughter, uncontrollable laughter.

We are nudged together again, though not as forceful as before.

Propping myself up, I say, "I'm sorry," as I continue chuckling and blushing simultaneously.

"It's...it's OK," Melody says regaining some composure as she uses her free hand to support her head as I have. She looks at the horses and smiles.

The horses have moved away slightly and seem to be looking at us. Sugarfoot whinnies and stamps a front hoof. Angel does the same.

"Actually," I say still watching the horses, "I think they're laughing at us."

I turn my head toward Melody, whom I expect to be at least an arm's length away, instead her face is right next to my own. I look at our joined hands, which rest at her side.

I take a deep breath, inhaling her sweet scent, then collapse on the ground, causing our hands to separate.

I lie on my back and stare straight up at the "white fluffy pillows of the brilliant blue expanse." The music rushes back to me as do the many vivid images. I can not speak and do not even contemplate the task.

Alone With Someone

Again, I take a deep breath and become engulfed within the placidity. I feel the light, delicate touch of the clouds on my left hand and sense the presence of a true angel on my shoulder.

Her silky hair brushes my cheek as a cool breeze refreshes us. We do not dare speak one word, yet communicate, continuing to caress each other's hand and allowing the silence to translate.

"Do you..." we both say at the same time, disturbing much more than the quietude.

"You first this time," Melody whispers.

"Do you ever watch the movement of the clouds, then..."

"Then close your eyes and hear the music?" Melody finishes my thought.

"Yes," I reply as if she were asking the question.

"Incredible, isn't it?" Melody says moving her head slightly, though remaining on my shoulder. "How something so simple..."

"Something so pure, can bring so much peace of mind?" I add.

"Yes," Melody responds.

"Do you ever wonder what the music looks like," I say, finishing my own thought.

"All the time," Melody replies. "I usually try to identify it with something or someone I know."

Her grip tightens, then loosens.

"I do that with poetry as well," I say. "The more brutal the storm, the more bright the sun, or beautiful the person, the more intense the piece."

"Tell her she's beautiful," my inner voice coaches.

Chapter 9

"Do you..." I start, then hesitate as I angle my head toward hers.

"Yes," Melody says, responding rather than asking.

My gaze returns to the sky, and we lie here, absorbing the images...absorbing the togetherness...

"Absorbing the wetness of the cold ground," my little voice says, snapping me out of my daze.

"We should be getting back," I suggest as I begin pushing myself upward.

I pause and look deeper at Melody. Before she can move, I kiss her lightly on her forehead.

Melody's eyes close briefly. A few seconds pass, and she sighs softly.

"Do you know how beautiful she looks?" my inner voice asks. "Why would someone so beautiful, someone so special...why would she...?"

Melody removes her head from my shoulder and starts to stand. I push my self upward and literally spring to my feet, directly behind and very close to her.

Melody shivers and turns to face me. "Thank you," she whispers. Her eyes move quickly between the horses and myself.

Three high-pitched notes, one higher than the next, escape from my lips. Both horses pick up their heads and look at us. I clap my hands quickly three times, and they both trot to us.

Melody looks at me as if I just spoke to them in their native tongue.

I shrug my shoulders and say, "Actually, none of us get out very much."

She smiles and shakes her head.

Alone With Someone

The horses reach us, and I move to help Melody back into her saddle.

"Um, I know it's getting dark, but I was hoping that we could walk back...at least part of the way," Melody says then bites her lower lip.

"Sure," I say as hundreds of questions rush to the forefront of my mind.

We begin walking, reigns in one hand, happiness in the other.

"Just don't say anything," my little voice comments.

"Melody, can I ask you a question?"

"What? I'm sorry, what did you say?"

"Don't repeat yourself," my irritant exclaims.

"May I ask you a question?"

"Sure, what is it?"

"Um, well...I really don't know how to phrase it.."

We are quiet yet continue to walk.

"I think you told me on the phone," Melody says breaking the silence, "see the words before you use them."

"You remember that? I didn't think..."

"You didn't think what? You didn't think I was paying attention?"

"Well, actually, you didn't really initiate much."

"I didn't have to. You seemed to say so much..."

"I'm sorry. I ramble at times."

Chapter 9

Melody turns her head toward me. "No, no. So much of what you said, I was thinking. It was...amazing."

"Sometimes, I do ramble. I ramble when..."

"When you get nervous."

"Um, yes. I did notice though, how you...you..."

"Finished your sentences?"

I smile and say, "Yes, my sentences. How do you...I mean... when..."

"When even that little voice in your head doesn't know what to say next?"

She knows about my little voice? I don't think I mentioned that.

I stop walking and just stare at Melody. Since our hands are still together, she stops too, as do our horses. A look of concern forms on my face.

"What?" Melody asks. "We all have that voice. Sometimes, it's even louder than our normal voices," Melody finishes and clears her throat.

"I know what you mean," I say, tapping myself on the head.

"And, what exactly are you insinuating," my little voice interrupts.

Our eyes meet, and we begin to laugh. I tap my head a couple more times, while Melody nods hers.

Finally, I shake off the silliness and begin walking again. Melody and our companions move with me.

"What were you going to ask me?" Melody says looking straight ahead, away from me.

"Um, ask you?" I say trying to remember and forget at the same time. "I think we should ride the rest of the way. We're still rather far, and...and..." I look up at the dark purple sky, still illuminated by the last rays of sunlight. "And, it's getting darker out here."

"First, you're afraid to kiss the girl, and now...now, you're afraid of the dark!" my little voice shouts.

"That's fine," Melody says acceptingly, though the look on her face contradicts the statement.

I help her into her saddle again, and climb into my own. We are both quiet.

We look at each other briefly as we sit perched upon our still creatures. A smile forms on Melody's face. Then, she imitates the clicking sound I had made earlier and lightly taps Angel. I am jerked forward as we bolt off toward the stables.

I have managed to keep my balance and bend over slightly as I pat Sugarfoot on the side of his head. He seems to understand and we catch up to our counterparts. I straighten up and smile at Melody as we move ahead of them.

A few moments pass and we exchange the lead numerous times. I look ahead and realize that we are nearing the gate. I tug gently on the reigns and we slow down. Melody passes us again, but imitates my actions shortly thereafter.

We trot to the large wooden barrier, stopping briefly as I unlatch it. Melody goes through first and I follow, closing the structure and re-locking it. When I turn around, I see that Melody has not moved more than ten feet from me. There she sits smiling.

If I were any other person...any other person...

"You'd what?" my inner voice interrupts.

Chapter 9

I'd be able to talk to her...I'd be able to ask her...ask her...

"Ask her what?" the voice asks. "Don't tell me you're going to ask her..."

We reach the stables, and the horses stop. When I take a look around, all eyes are on me, Angel's, Sugarfoot's, and Melody's.

Quickly, I dismount and move to assist Melody. She has not moved and seems slightly preoccupied. She begins to descend slowly.

"Bill," Melody says, her voice arousing more than just my auditory senses...the horses ears pick up as well. "Bill, I was wondering..."

"Great! Just great!" my little voice exclaims. "She was probably wondering why someone like you would ask her out, especially because you have not a prayer for anything other than this single sympathy date."

"I was wondering why I can tell you so much about myself and complete many thoughts on the phone, but when we're together, I can't..."

"Can't seem to spit the words out as well?" I say completing her thought as well as my own.

Melody nods her head in agreement.

The silence feels comforting, yet unsettling.

I wish to tell her, explain to her why, but I can't explain it to myself, let alone someone else.

"Maybe," I say hoping to come up with an answer. "Maybe, we said so much on the phone..."

"There is not much else to add?" Melody responds.

We look at each other and end up shaking our heads in disagreement preserving the sacredness of the silent responses.

"So, how about the school's concert next month?" Melody says, her smile broadening as she stares at me.

Relieved, I say, "The band has improved greatly since your first visit. It should be a very good concert."

"Frank has done a great job," Melody says altering the subject slightly.

I smile, nod my head, and say, "See, we do have something to talk about."

Laughter, refreshing laughter, escapes from both our lips.

I grasp Sugarfoot's reigns and wait for Melody to do the same with Angel's. I take one step hesitantly and watch Melody as she does the same. Knowing that she is ready, I begin walking toward the horses' pens.

We stop just short of Angel's area, and I look at Melody.

"You are probably going to say 'no,'" I begin, "and you probably don't know what you're doing then, but I was wondering...well...I was wondering if you would accompany me to...I mean if you be a chaperone with me at the school's senior prom?"

There, I said it. I asked her. Now, she can say, "no," and I can go home, never worrying about talking to her concerning this again.

"I'd...I'd love to," Melody responds.

"I don't think she said no," my inner voice says seeming rather distant as my thoughts and excuses engulf it.

"I'm sorry...what did you say?"

"Yes," Melody reiterates. "In fact, I never quite made it to mine. I wondered what I really missed. I heard stories, believe me I heard stories, but never experienced it. When is it?"

"I didn't quite make it to mine either, but that's a very long story," I say smiling and shaking my head from side to side.

She said, "yes." I feel like one of my students must after his or her first date...

"Did you say 'date?'" my inner voice questions.

Well, I...

"So, when is it?" Melody asks again.

"May," I say smiling widely.

As I look at Melody longer, I notice her delighted expression has changed to one of concern.

"When in May?" she asks.

I tell her the exact date, feeling my own happiness slip away.

"I'm sorry," Melody says, turning away slowly. "That's...that's the week we perform down state. That's why our monthly concert is the following week...I thought..."

"That's right," I say hiding some of my disappointment and attempting to sound as if I actually remember those dates. "There will be another one next year." I can manage only a half smile.

"I told you not to ask her," my little voice taunts me. "You were fine until..."

We are pushed together from behind again. I grab Melody's smooth hands and stare into her soothing eyes.

Fits of silence engulf us.

"I should be getting home," Melody whispers as her face nears my own.

Alone With Someone

"Midnight must be hungry," I say and kiss her gently on her downward slanting forehead.

Melody lifts her eyes upward and blinks at me.

Slowly, she backs up, eventually letting go of my cold hands and aching heart.

"Wait," I say realizing she's leaving...again.

Melody stops, but is still to far away for me to feel her warmth.

"I almost forgot," I say, inserting my hand into my pocket and pulling out an envelope.

"Thank you," Melody says accepting the light blue object. "I'll read it when I get home." She smiles.

"You're welcome," I say still trying to hide my discomfort. "We'll see you at school."

I watch her walk backwards slowly. Then, when she is clear of the horse pens, she turns around and walks toward her car.

I think about leaving the horses and following her. I just close my eyes, however, and see her in my mind. I see her nearing her car and stopping. Instead of opening the car door. She stops and opens the envelope, unfolds the paper within and reads:

Chapter 9

Your Eyes
The intensity,
The radiance,
The beauty,
Within your eyes
Is amazing,
Simply amazing.
Full of dreams,
Full of desires,
Full of life.
They glisten
With an incomparable brilliance
And a youthful exuberance.
Soothing,
Comforting,
Calling.
A sole sparkle
Found within
Sheds light upon
My inner most self,
Brushing away the tarnish,
Tearing away the pain,
Allowing then to reflect.
Amazing,
Simply amazing.

I sigh and slowly open my eyes. I feel a nudge in my back and lurch forward, this time Melody is not there to hold onto.

My eyelids open the remainder of the way, and I stumble forward. I manage to spin around and see Sugarfoot's head bobbing up and down as if laughing at me.

"Even a horse laughs at you," my little voice says sarcastically.

Part of me wants to feel sorry for myself, yet I can't seem to refrain from letting out a burst of laughter. I lurch forward, attempting to grab

Sugarfoot's reigns. He backs up and bounces his head up and down again.

"Now, do you remember why you never went to your senior prom?" my inner voice asks. "You felt bad enough when you were turned down, at the last minute I might add, for your junior prom. Remember the pain, the sadness, the loneliness. Remember?"

Of course I remember. Of course I can still recall staying at home when all my friends, Joe, Jeff, Kirk, Mark, all went and enjoyed themselves. I never bothered to ask anyone to go.

I open a gate and watch the horses enter the area. I close the gate and move toward the parking area from which Melody's car should have disappeared from a while ago. I pick up my head and blink repeatedly as I watch her car pull away at this moment.

I smile and forget about the pain. I smile and remember how different I feel. I smile and remember how much more there is to do.

My inner voice tries to revert my thoughts again, "But, it's the prom. It's..."

It's only one day. Besides, the beats are just beginning.

Chapter 10

I can't believe I am still thinking about this. I told the students I was not going.

"You can go by yourself you know," my little voice suggests.

Yes, I know...but...

"But what?"

But, I would feel funny.

"You're supposed to be chaperoning the prom, not necessarily enjoying it."

What does that mean? I never...

"Yeah, yeah, you never went to yours. Get over it! The students think very highly of you and have asked you personally to be there."

I would really like to go, but...but I think I should bring someone. I think they are expecting it.

"Take one of your sisters then! Just go!"

Funny. Besides, they're both probably busy.

A wide smile forms on my thought enriched face, and I shuffle my feet as I look around the classroom. There is a small stack of papers on the right side of my desk, books to the left, and handwritten notes directly in front of me. I am sitting alone considering both the invitation I was offered today, by the students as well as the one I extended to Melody a week and a half ago.

"She said no," my obnoxious inner voice says. "Just move on. Besides, you still don't know why she kissed you. Or, why she went out with you."

Should it matter? I was happy. I wrote. I don't need to know why.

"So, you want to get hurt again?"
No. I just don't think this is the same situation as the ones before. This seems diff...special.

I smile again and shake my head, trying to stifle the little voice before it can get off another discouraging comment, and another brick is added to my walls of despair.

"Are you napping?" a slightly accented voice asks.

"What?" I say, turning my head.

Yvette, one of our Spanish teachers, is standing next to my desk, staring at me with her dark, enthusiastic eyes. She stands only about 5'3", but as her tanned skin and reddish-brown hair suggests, she is a very adamant individual.

"Did I wake you?" Yvette asks again, rephrasing her earlier question and trying to keep from laughing.

"No, no. I was just, um...thinking," I say trying to remember what I had forgotten to do after the last staff meeting. Yvette is also the head of our Communications Department and constantly pursues the answer to any question that was brought up during our meetings. I don't remember volunteering for anything last time we met.

"I just happen to overhear the seniors talking about their prom. Your name came up a few times," Yvette says and stares at me as if expecting to hear something from someone else in the room.

I am just smiling and nodding, not quite sure of where she is going with this and wishing to change the subject somehow.

"You are going, correct?" Yvette says nodding her head.

"Actually, no," I say, hoping the conversation will end here, but know I am not that fortunate.

"Bill, the students can request certain chaperones to head their prom. I've heard that they have asked you. Why don't you want to go?"

"I'm honored, really," I say trying to come up with a better excuse than I gave the students. "I just think they would be better with another teacher. I don't mind preparing and organizing, but someone else should be in charge at the prom itself."

"Well, that's better than what you told the students," Yvette says with a smirk on her face. "Now really, why don't you want to go? Why don't you ask the new band tutor? Frank says you two have been talking to each other for quite a while now."

"Well, I, um," I mumble as my face turns red. How many people has Frank told this to? Does the entire faculty know? No wonder they've been looking at me strangely lately."

"They've looked at you strange for quite sometime. You're just noticing it now?!?" my little voice interrupts.

"I believe she has plans for that day," I manage to eek out. "Besides, I think I'm a little too old to be asking someone to a prom."

"Have you asked her yet?" Yvette questions somewhat forcefully. "How do you know this if you haven't asked her?"

"Last I checked, she had a performance that night," I say reiterating the reason I was given. A small amount of sadness hits me, and I sign softly.

"So, you have asked her?" Yvette inquires, smirking again.

"Well..."

"Well, what?" Yvette says not waiting for me to continue. "Either you have or you haven't. I'll even ask her for you."

Chapter 10

The impact of her words hit me hard.

"No, no," I say abruptly. "You don't have to ask her. I know she has a performance, besides you don't even know what she looks like."

"You don't have to bring anyone then, just show up and enjoy yourself," Yvette says still pushing the issue.

"It just wouldn't feel right," I say frowning and looking away slightly.

"You know, you're worse than the students at times," Yvette says, slightly perturbed. "Do me a favor and just think about it some more. Or, at least come up with a better excuse for the students."

"I said I would help with everything," I say slowly rising from my chair. "OK, I'll at least consider the idea further, but..."

"Good, that's all I wanted to hear," Yvette says moving toward the door.

"But, I..."

"Oh yeah, she's about this tall, has dark hair, and large hazel eyes," Yvette says, smiles, and walks into the hall way.

I stand somewhat perplexed, then begin to laugh. I shake my head and move around my desk straightening the papers and books.

"Maybe, it would be a good thing for Yvette to ask her," my inner voice comments. "You may even find out why she..."

I begin to hum in the hopes of disturbing my renegade thoughts. Moving toward my chair again, I reach down and lift my brief case onto my desk. I pop the latches on both sides, continuing to hum louder.

As I put the small stack of papers and notes inside my leather traveling companion, I hear a soft sound behind me as if someone was clearing his or her throat.

Alone With Someone

"I need more than a few seconds to come up with a better excuse," I say smiling and turning around.

My eyes widen and my smile diminishes as I see not Yvette standing in the doorway, but Melody. I am very still.

"What type of excuse did you use before?" Melody asks, grinning.

"Um, I, hi," I say dropping half of the papers I was trying to pack.

"Hello," Melody says giggling and watching my clumsy act. "Are you trying to skip out on someone?" She points at the papers on the floor.

"Um, yes," I say, bending down to pick up some of the scattered papers, "my students. They were even more inquisitive than usual."

"Funny, the teacher I just passed in the hall on the way here said something similar," Melody says bending down to help me retrieve the remaining papers.

"I think her name was Yvette," Melody adds lifting her head.

Concerned, I stop and stare at her. I swallow hard and ask, "What else did she say?"

"Nothing, she just said hello and made a side comment about..." Melody says then pauses. "Are you OK? You look a little pale."

"I'm fine," I say and reach out to take the leaflettes Melody is holding in my direction.

We rise simultaneously. I put the papers in my briefcase and stare at her...at her "large hazel eyes." I can feel small beads of sweat running down my forehead.

"I think you should sit down," Melody says taking my hand and leading me a few steps to the chair.

Chapter 10

That familiar chill makes its way from my hand to my head. So many thoughts, so many ideas swirl around my mind. Desirous actions change places, each claiming to be more effective than the next.

My head moves slowly and my eyes focus on...on the clock directly behind Melody.

"Incredible!" my little voice exclaims. "The object of your obsession for the past couple of months has come here, stands in front of you, and you choose to look at...the clock! Incredible!"

Shaking off the extra voices, I let the only externally audible one escape, "You're here rather early, aren't you?" I smile, frown, and smile again. "Practice doesn't start for a couple of hours yet."

"I know, I just thought..." Melody says beginning to look around as well. "Are you sure you're OK?" She adds, her gaze focusing on me again.

I swallow and lick my lips, hoping to acquire some kind of additional moisture and wisdom. "I'm OK, really, just slightly tired...I guess."

The last time Melody was in this room, I had a plan...I was in control...at least somewhat...I literally had a script.

"You've talked to her how many times over the phone?" my little voice points out.

"I just thought..." Melody begins again. "I just thought we could talk?"

"You've 'talked' on the phone almost every day since you met!" my little voice interjects loudly.

"I mean...I just thought we could actually see each other again."

I want to tell her that I can see her every time I hear her sweet voice. I want to
explain to her how incredible she makes me feel without actually touching me. I want to show her how wonderful it is to see her.

Instead, I simply smile and shake my head,

"Actually, something you said during one of our conversations has stayed with me. Every time we talk, I find it more and more true," Melody completes this thought and looks at me as if I should remember what I had said.

I search my memory, but can't seem to recall anything pertinent.

"You mentioned how our 'telepathy' doesn't always translate very well over the phone." Melody says biting her lower lip, probably wondering whether to proceed with this line of thought. "You said you search for a clue, a sign of what to say next, during our comfortable moments of silence. Have you ever noticed how we seem to break those moments together?"

I hesitate before responding, trying to recall those instances. Images flash through my mind and my eyes widen, "I guess you're right, but..."

"Well, ever since you mentioned that, I've been thinking. I've been thinking about what you're doing and what expressions rest on your face."

"I do the same thing," I say amazed. "There are times when I've actually written down how you may look during one of our more 'involved' discussions."

Melody blushes and begins another thought, "You also mentioned that you 'need' to see your inspirations. Otherwise, they will eventually fade and you'll be left writing needless drivel."

"Wow, you pay better attention than my students."

We both smile.

After I've gotten off the phone with you, I take out an instrument and play. I don't play any familiar melodies; I just play, using our conversation as the base."

Chapter 10

"I think I understand," I comment, my eyes now focusing more on Melody than the clock. "I do the same thing with the words I write while we're talking. I'll then compose a poem or another short piece. While I'm writing, now don't laugh, I hear music in the background. It seems to keep the mood and the poetry fresh. Sounds silly doesn't it."

"Most of the time it's just the radio," my little voice comments.

I ignore it and continue, "My inspirations are few and far in between, so I take what I am given, even if it is the soft sweet sounds of a beautiful young lady." I grasp Melody's hand gently and smile.

"I, um," Melody mumbles.

"I know this may sound somewhat hokey, but even if we never speak again, your music and the friendship which we share will always inspire me." I sigh and pause. Somewhere in my body, despair adds another brick to its walls.

"Thank you," Melody says. "You know I've never felt so close to someone before. I've never felt so similar to anyone else, and to be honest with you..."

"It scares you," I add.

"A little," Melody says as she shuffles her feet. "There are so many things I want to do, so many things I want to see. Being with you reminds me of why I went into music, to enjoy and experience life."

I truly do not know how to reply. Is this a good-bye-thanks-for-everything speech? Or, one of those mushy things I've managed to stay way from?

"Maybe that's your problem!" my little voice remarks.

I look at Melody. Her eyes have re-focused on me.

"I am not sure," Melody says.

Alone With Someone

For the first time since we met, I do not believe I understand her, and it worries me.

"I'm not sure of what to do," Melody continues to hesitate. "I mean, you asked me to the prom, and..."

"It's OK," I say. "You have a performance that day. You shouldn't miss it. Besides, my students volunteered me to work on the theme and I don't think it'll be that great any way." I smile and hope Melody will do the same.

She returns my gesture and says, "It's not...oh never mind. Maybe, I'm just making assumptions I shouldn't."

"Hey," I say lifting her hand up and kissing it gently, "I will be here for you. You are...you are my best friend and I owe you greatly for the inspiration and my current level of sanity. However long you need to figure out what mysteries you are to fulfill, I will wait for you."

"Thank you," Melody says, sniffling back a tear. "I don't know if I'll ever..."

"Don't worry about what anyone else wants or needs, except you."

"Did you just say that?" my little voice comments. "I can't believe..."

"Friendships last a long time. Look at everyone at Kirk's. We've been together since high school and never worry about living up to someone else's expectations. That's why we're all still friends. We do what makes us as individuals happy." I pause and consider embracing Melody. Instead, I move slightly to my left, open my top desk drawer, and pull out an envelope. I hand it to Melody and say, "I didn't think I was going to see you tonight. We have a late tutoring session. Anywho, I wrote this for you and was going to give it to Frank, but since you're here..."

Melody accepts the envelope and looks at it briefly then looks at me. She opens it carefully and her gaze wonders back to me before actually taking out the paper inside.

Just as she pulls out the contents, a voice from the doorway startles us, "Hey, what are you two doing there?"

My head jerks toward the door and any contact I had with Melody is now severed. Frank enters the room and walks toward us.

"So?" Frank says, expecting some sort of reply.

My eyes focus on him now as a rather disgruntled look forms on my face. "So? Sew buttons on your underwear," I say, hoping Frank will get the hint and come back later.

Of course, he is inquisitive and stays, probing into the mood even more. "Funny, very funny. So, were you going anywhere? Or, were you going to order in?" Frank has that smirk again. You know that smirk that once said, 'I think I know something and will not come right out and say it.' Though in reality, he is most likely incorrect in his initial assumption.

Before responding to Frank, I look at Melody who had managed to remain focused on the piece from the envelope. She is still reading. Her expressions change constantly; eyebrows moving up and down; lips frowning, straightening, and smiling; eyes sparkling, glistening, radiating.

Out of the corner of my eyes, I can see Frank's mouth moving, but hear nothing except what Melody's voice would sound like if she were reading the piece aloud.

True Friendship

Acquaintances may come and go,
This all seem to know.
Friends stay together through thick and thin,
For it is the game of life they wish to win.
Many say friend to you they are,
But their loyalty and trust are well under par.
We all need someone to call our own,
But without friends,

Alone With Someone

We shall forever be alone.
Just as life's mysteries take time to be realized,
Our relationship may never be finalized.
And, those we care about,
Will always touch our lives.
Never alone are we,
As we try to answer life's plea,
To be forever happy and eternally free.

I sigh as I think of how relevant to our conversation moments ago, yet I wrote it days ago.

I look at Melody. She is smiling at me, and saying nothing.

I turn my head toward Frank, who is just finishing a thought of his own, "...so what do you think?"

My gaze wonders from Melody to Frank and back to Melody. "Actually," I say smiling at her.

"We were going to..." Melody says, returning my smile then pauses.

My eye widen as I continue "...get a bite to eat. Would you like us to bring you something back?" My eyebrows rise as if to say, 'don't even think about saying yes.'

Frank seems somewhat surprised at our actions as he stumbles with his response, "Um, a, I could...nah, go ahead. I'll see you when you get back."

"Shall we go?" I say, stressing the last word, bowing slightly and motioning toward the door.

Melody smiles at me, looks back at the poem, folds it, and responds, "We shall my friend. See you soon Frank."

I straighten up, turn toward Frank and say, "The first answer is no, the second is no, and the third is ask me later."

Chapter 10

Frank chuckles softly as Melody and I walk out the doorway.

Once in the hallway, I take Melody's hand and intertwine our arms. She leans against me, sighs, and says, "What are you doing after practice?"

"Calling a friend," I say, pulling her toward me and grasping her hand slightly tighter.

"I don't remember you touching your other friends' lives like this," my little voice says sarcastically. "And, what about the prom?"

"So, do you have a chaperone for the Spring concert yet?" I ask.

"Is this an invitation to something I'll be at anyway?" Melody questions smiling.

"Funny, I have to be there as well," I respond. "Maybe we should both have a chaperone."

"Maybe," Melody replies, "maybe."
We both laugh. A feeling of happiness and freedom falls over me. The construction on my inner walls have halted. In fact, the builders are nowhere in sight. We stop laughing, but a grin remains on my face as I cross the threshold with my "best" friend.

Chapter 11

A few last flustering notes flutter throughout the acoustically challenged gymnasium. An echoing eruption of applause follows shortly thereafter. My half-closed eyes open and the focus of my attention is quickly gained by a familiar voice.

"Thank you, thank you," Frank says bowing. He stands in front of the band at the south end of the auditorium.

As the applause dies down, Frank adds, "All the students have put much effort into this performance. From the freshmen, who first broke wind a few months ago..." Frank smiles as the audience groans. "...to the seniors who will improvise their own little tune in a couple of weeks when they arrive home late from prom."

Frank pauses and smirks, "Speaking of which, any additional donations or volunteers for the prom should be directed to one of our own English teachers, published poet, and all around nice guy..."

I tune out his words as I feel the many eyes focusing on me. Frank gestures toward the back of the gym, where I am standing. I am just about to raise my hand and wave as if to say, "Thank you, I am right here," when I realize that I am bound to another.

Before my head is able to turn and see who is standing next to me, Frank comments, "We would also like to thank one who has tutored and somehow tolerated many of our woodwind players. She has truly made a difference..."

As my gaze reaches the object of Frank's praise and that which my hand holds, my body temperature increases. From head to toe, I boil then shiver as the gentleness within my reach slips from my grasp.

Melody is beside me, blushing as she does when attention is brought to her, especially as much attention as fills this convert concert hall.

Chapter 11

My vision blurs as the warmth returns, shocking my system. My eyes gloss-over and are wiped clean almost instantaneously. I notice that the families of the performers and a few students are heading toward the stairs, which lead to the outside exits and away from their most recent confinement. The only part of my body capable movement is my head.

"Did anyone see you holding her hand?" my inner voice questions. "The students have left you alone for awhile now. They seem to have accepted the fact that you are just planning the prom and will not be attending."

"Hey, how was the concert?" A voice asks as a hand thumps once on my shoulder.

I turn my head and look at the foreign appendage, and trace it back to one of the band members, Dave. He plays the baritone and was in one of my English classes last year.

"Um, it was pretty good," I say, trying to find further justification.

"Just OK?!? It was probably the best we've played all year!" Dave exclaims, making a point and rustling my thoughts even more.

"You're right Dave," I say and smile. "It sounded great. You guys put much time into practicing those pieces."

"Yeah, and Miss M. helped us quite a bit. She helped Mr. A point out some of the smaller things that we were missing. She even played with us a few times."

"Yes, Dave. I remember. I was at some of those practices."

"Melody!" my little voice shouts.

I turn my head toward my original fixation. I do this more to reassure myself of her presence than anything else.

Alone With Someone

Sure enough, she is standing at my side, even closer than before. She smiles and listens to our words. She has that gleam in her eyes, as if she is thinking of something else.

"Speaking of being there," Dave comments, "since you're planning the thing, you are going, right?"

I am able to partially turn my body toward the smirking student. The most effective words race rampantly around my mind before I can reply, "Actually, no Dave. I am just organizing it. Did I not clarify that at the first three planning meetings?"

"Yeah, um, yes you did," Dave spurts out and continues. "We just figured you hadn't asked anyone yet." His smile widens as his eyes move from me to Melody, who is still standing along side of me.

I frown slightly and comment quickly, "Dave it has nothing to do with me asking." I pause for a moment and grasp Melody's hand. I look at her and add, "It has much to do with the fact that the only one I would even consider going with is busy that night." I smile at Melody, and she returns my gesture, squeezing my hand as well.

Before Dave can say anything else, I face him again and add, "And, you know how picky I am about my free time. When will I have time to write?" I smile contently as if to say 'that's enough, now go tell whomever sent you, no.'

Dave says, "Oh, well, um, a, we'll see you Monday then..." He turns to leave looking somewhat disappointed and confused.

"You all played very well tonight," Melody comments, probably hoping to change the subject and brighten up Dave at the same time.

Dave continues to move toward the band room, a little lighter in his steps.

I take a deep breath before looking at Melody.

"You know," she says, "he hasn't been the only one asking about the prom. Two other students, one whom I didn't even know, stopped me on the way in here and mentioned it."

"I'm sorry," I say, trying to understand why. "I didn't really want to go. I just thought..."

My hesitation betrays me.

"I just thought it would be nice...though not necessary."

"Bill, you know I would love to go..." Melody says as we both turn and begin to walk toward the band room ourselves. "What exactly have you told the students? You are planning the entire event and are not going to be there. This is not like you. You like to see, how did you put it, the fruits of your efforts."

"She knows you so well already," my inner voice comments.

We reach the doors to the band room and I stop. Melody does the same. We stare at each other.

"Well, you know our theme has to do with poetry," I say smiling as Melody nods her head. "I just told them that if I couldn't be accompanied by the angel who inspires me, I didn't want to go. I would be contradicting the theme."

Melody swallows hard and says, "So who is this angel you're talking about? I thought we were friends. You never mentioned anything about seeing angels." Melody smiles, and we both laugh.

I shake my head as we move into the band room. "You know," I say, "if I wasn't so sure, I would have to say it was actually a little sprite playing tricks on me. But, I'll give you, I mean her, the benefit of the doubt."

"So, did you enjoy the concert?" Frank asks from across the room.

"They sounded very good. There's still some rough spots, like the coda in the second piece, but overall they played well."

Frank and Melody stare at me inquisitively as if to say, "did you just say that?"

I shrug my shoulders and add, "What? You asked."

"I think he's been hanging around Mark too long," Frank responds looking at Melody.

"Either that or it's those figments of his imagination feeding him lines," Melody adds, staring at me.

I just shake my head and chuckle.

"Frank!" Cindy calls from behind us. "You're at it again aren't you?"

"What? Me? No," Frank replies laughing somewhat.

"How's everything, Bill?" Cindy asks as she moves closer.

"Just fine," I say and turn to make a face at Frank. As I turn back toward Cindy, I add, "How are the kids?"

"The same, there are none, unless you count the big one over there," she says pointing to Frank, who is returning my facial gesture. "How have you been Melody? We haven't seen either of you in a while. Have any jello lately?"

"Well, actually..." Melody responds and smiles at me.

We are all silent. I look at all of their faces, then say, "What?!? We were at a restaurant the other day and had jello for desert."

"Sure," Frank says sarcastically and winks.

Melody giggles and her eyes widen as she stares directly at me. "No really, that's what happened, but," she pauses. "After the jello came, we stared at it for a few seconds, and the waitress returned, shaking a can of whipped cream. Before she could even ask, we both shouted, 'No!' We covered our dishes and broke out in laughter."

"After the waitress left," I add, "we looked down and noticed the jello was cut into those little cubes. We looked at each other, then at the jello, and at each other again. I moved a napkin between the two bowls. Melody picked up a cube and placed it on the napkin. After a few moments..."

"We had a little pyramid of red jello," Melody finishes my thought, "and nothing in our bowls."

Melody and I look at each other, large grin form on our faces. Then we turn toward Frank and Cindy.

"I guess you had to be there," I say, holding back my laughter and temporarily tightening my grasp on Melody's hand which has not broken contact with mine since the attention was drawn to us in the gym.

"Sure, whatever," Frank comments.

"So," Cindy says, rolling her eyes slightly, as she moves closer to Frank, "how's the prom coming along?" A smirk forms on both of their faces simultaneously.

"Fine, thank you," I respond, the humor gone from my voice. "We still have a few things to finalize, but overall, just fine."

"Frank mentioned something about a poetry theme and a small dedication booklet," Cindy adds, hoping to obtain more information rather than news.

"Well," I say, attempting to keep my patience and not embarrass myself. "Well, the theme is Poetry in Motion as Frank has probably told you, and we will be putting together a small book with favorite poems of the students mixed with pieces by the students. That's about it."

"Frank also said that Robin, the senior class art teacher, is designing the cover, you're editing it, Frank's taking it to the printer and picking it up, and what else...let's see I'm forgetting something."

"Yeah, I think she forgot the why the tides are effected by the moon," my inner voice comments.

"Oh, yeah," Cindy adds, "something about you still not being sure if you are going to include a piece of your own, or even write the introduction."

Melody's hand finally slips from mine and she says, "You never mentioned the booklet, or you being asked to write something for it." She looks concerned and somewhat hurt.

"I, um," I begin and attempt to regain my composure. "Actually, I felt that this was a student thing, and I didn't want to deter from that."

"They asked you to write an introduction," Frank comments as if it is no big deal.

"And, and," I say moving my arm up and down, motioning toward Frank as if making a point. "And, I said I would, but would prefer one of them do it, especially since I wouldn't be there to read it as we discussed."

"That's right," Cindy says smirking. "Frank did mention the students wanted to kick off the prom with an introduction and periodically have other students read their own works."

I mumble hoping no one hears me.

"What was that, Bill?" Frank asks.

"Nothing, nothing," I reply.

Chapter 11

"We should probably get going," I say to Melody, who doesn't seem to know quite what to think. We have grown so close in so short of time, and every time she hears something about me or about something I may have done, a tiny piece of our togetherness, that special sparkle, fades. It takes so long for it to build-up again. It is never truly full force again.

"OK," Melody comments softly. "Thank you for the concert."

"Yeah, thanks again," I say to Frank and Cindy, who just shrug their shoulders as Melody and I exit.

We pass through the doors and I cradle her soft hand in mine. Melody stops and just stares at me.

"What?" I ask, though I already know the answer.

"Why didn't you tell me it meant that much to you?" Melody inquires, breaking our bond.

"It, um, doesn't really," I answer, trying to make all my words sound legitimate. "Part of my job is to have the students accomplish things on their own, and they are doing a great job with this prom."

Melody is silent then adds, "Who thought of the theme, originally?"

"Um, I did, but the students agreed with it," I say and take a deep breath.

"And, the booklet?"

I can do nothing else except smile and say, "Well..."

"OK, I'll be honest with you, I tried to design a prom I found ideal, one that I would enjoy attending."

We begin walking again.

"But, you're not?" Melody asks.

"Right," I reply.

"And, you really don't want to?"

"Well..."

We stop walking again.

"No, no, I'm just kidding. I didn't want it to be just another boring school dance. For the rest of their lives, these students are going to need to be involved and make the most of every opportunity. I just wanted to provide them with some of those opportunities."

Melody looks as if she is going to ask another question. She raises her hand, and one finger points outward. She refrains, however, and begins moving again.

We take a few steps and before she is able to clear her throat, I say, "Yes, I'm sure. Besides who would go with me? I have trouble getting a chaperone for concerts."

My eyes angle upward, and I move them from side to side. Melody takes my hand again and nudges me with her shoulder.

We reach the concession stand, which overlooks the gymnasium, and we stop. I should see how things are going with the clean-up.

I notice a student about Melody's height cleaning the counter. She has light brown hair, a few scattered freckles, and a small light-hearted smile.

"Hi, Cathy," I say.

"Oh, hi," Cathy responds as she makes eye contact with me. Her gaze shifts to Melody and her smile widens. "Hi," she says again.

"How's the clean-up going? It wasn't too busy, huh?" I ask.

"Actually, we did pretty well," Cathy replies. "I'm just finishing here.
Rob and Pat are counting the money..." She roles her eyes, "as usual, and
Laura, I'm not too sure where she is."

"Well, it sounds like you have everything under control here. See you
Monday," I say and prepare to leave.

Melody clears her throat and lightly tugs on my hand.

I look at her then back toward Cathy.

"She probably would like to be introduced," my little voice suggests.

"So, is this Miss M.?" Cathy asks before I can get out the words.

"Yes," Melody says as she breaks loose from my grasp yet again. She
extends her hand toward Cathy. "You are Cathy, correct?"

"I'm sorry," I say. "I wasn't thinking as usual. Cathy is the special events
manager for our student service organization, for which I believe I am
still the faculty moderator."

Cathy nods her head and continues to smile.

"Yes, and by the way, when's our next meeting?" Cathy asks. "We
haven't had one in quite some time."

"Well, um," I say trying to remember when the last meeting actually was
as well as select a good day within the next week or so. "I'm not too
sure, maybe after we finalize everything for your prom. If I am not
mistaken, you and a few other officers dragged me into that." A smirk
forms on my face, as if to say, 'so there.'

"Did you say prom?" my inner voice asks. "You better not have said..."

"Oh yeah," Cathy responds, as the smirk jumps from my face to hers.

"Here we go again," I mumble as I turn my head toward Melody.

"So, will you be going? Or do we need to tie you up and drag you there?" Cathy asks.

"You guys might enjoy that too much," I respond smiling. "Actually, I'm washing my hair that day, so..." I flip through the many strands on the side of my head.

"Funny," Cathy comments. "It's just a couple of weeks away. Besides, who will read the piece you're supposed to put in our dedication booklet?"

"I don't believe we decided on anything yet," I say, somewhat concerned. "I don't remember saying I would write something."

"What about that one poem?" Cathy questions.

"Which one?" I comment, playing along.

"Wait a minute, I think I have a copy of it somewhere," she responds, bending down and removing a small white piece of paper from underneath the counter.

She unfolds the writing, my heart races, and my blood pressure skyrockets.

"What poem is she talking about?" My inner voice questions, very concerned.

"Here it is," Cathy says and hands it to Melody.

I glance at the paper, picking up a few words.

"Where did she get that?" my protective conscious asks. "You must have left it in the submission folder after you wrote it the other day."

My mind creates an image of the piece and follows along with Melody as she reads.

Chapter 11

Glimpse of Eden

Beauty so serene
Can not be sculpted;
Innocence so sanctified
Can not be sustained;
Intensity so sharp
Can not be surmounted,
Except by
The vision,
The purity,
The light,
Who somehow engulfs
My entire realm of sight.
I am without
And she is within.
For now, however,
I sit satiated,
Hoping,
Praying,
Pleading,
For just one more
Glimpse of Eden.

Possible reactions enter my thoughts as Melody moves the paper slightly away from herself and says, "I can see why you may want this in your booklet." Her gaze shifts to me as her eyes enlarge and a pouting look forms on her lips as if to say, 'I never received this one.'

"Actually," I say taking the paper from Melody and folding it up, "it's not finished yet. I, um, must have put it with the other papers by mistake."

Before I can put it in my pocket, Melody takes it back and puts it in her little black purse, which hangs over her left shoulder.

Cathy mumbles something about a copy, then says, "You will at least think about it, right?"

Alone With Someone

"We'll think about it," I say shaking my head and taking Melody's hand. "See you later. Don't forget, your rough draft is due Monday."

I begin walking away immediately. Melody is close by my side. I hear more mumbling coming from the concession stand as we walk through the double doors just a few feet away.

Once outside, I say, "You know, you could have said something."

"You handled it very well," Melody responds and giggles.

"You think this is funny," I say and stop moving. "You're laughing, you're laughing." I start to chuckle myself.

Melody grins and says, "What? You mean, you don't have the feeling."

"We're being set-up," I complete the thought. "If you were any of the girls I dated in high school, I would be facing far less ridicule. You met my friends. They would have had a field day back then. You know they were well, less...well, younger and, and well, actually they were the same as they are today."

"Next time you angels decide to fall to earth, please consider somewhere else besides my head," I say shaking a fist toward the clouds, then tapping my head with it.

"I think it's cute," Melody says, taking both of my hands in hers and lowering them down to her side. "Your friends and students really care about you. That's a gift very few people possess."

"I know, I know," I say bowing my head and moving even more toward her. "I just wish they would care a little less at times. It leaves big bruises...see." I lift up my sleeve and point to a few faded sun freckles on my tricep.

I look at Melody and add, "Well, OK, maybe they're not that huge."

Chapter 11

I lean toward her, hoping she does not move or sneeze for that matter. My eyes are open only half way, and our lips touch. That instant surge of life resonates within me. I move backward a step and smile, content.

Melody brushes her tongue over her luscious red lips and says, "I'll be right back."

She breaks our connection and heads back toward the doors.

"Where? What?"

"I'll be right back, just wait here."

"Sure, that's what they all say," my inner voice comments.

Great! She's probably going to talk to someone else while she's in there, and decide to call a cab just to avoid me.

"If you're so concerned," my inner voice says, "then go in there and find her."

I'm not that concerned.

"Uh, huh," the obnoxious pang responds.

"Hey, Bill," a soft, hoarse voice says.

I turn around and see a short blond woman walking toward me. She smiles and her eyes squint. She bends her arm and moves it from right to left once.

"It's Robin and she's waving to you," my inner voice says, throwing me back into reality.

"Oh, hi," I say sounding somewhat disappointed and disturbed.

"Glad to see you too," Robin comments and looks around. "Where's your chaperone?"

"I, um, sorry. I'm just, um, she went back inside for some reason."

I try to remember when I told Robin about the chaperone idea. Oh yeah, I was helping her clean up the art room a few days ago. She asked about the prom, and I figuratively bit her head off. It had been a while since any one mentioned me not going. She just wanted to know if she could be of any help, and I jumped on her. After a few moments of silence, I explained everything to her.

"We've gotten a great response on the booklets," Robin says.

"Jerk!" my little voice shouts.

"What?" I say aloud.

"You mean you didn't know?" Robin asks smiling.

What did she just call me? No, no, wait a minute, she said something about the booklets. Oh yeah...where is Melody?

"Yes, we have," I say looking toward the doors again.

"I'm sure she'll be back," Robin says. "Besides, I believe they locked all the other exits."

"I'm sorry. I'm doing it again," I respond smiling. "You are designing the cover, correct?"

"Yep, almost finished," Robin replies. "Though I would like to see the introduction piece before I finish."

"Well, we're still debating that," I say, "I think it should be a senior who writes it, and they think I should."

"The poem!" my inner self shouts.

"Are you sure the other doors are locked?" I add, serious at first, then a wide smile forms on my lips.

Chapter 11

"It's been a while, huh?" Robin asks.

I just grin and nod once.

"Here she comes," Robin says, motioning toward one of the glass doors.

Melody is in rather lively spirits as she bounds toward us.

"Is she skipping?" my little voice questions sarcastically. "Yes, she's skipping! And, look, your dignity is in her hand."

What? Oh, the poem. Sure enough, there it is.

Melody finally reaches us. An ice-breaking, earth-shattering, worry-freeing, simply, comforting glimpse of Eden emanates from her full-faced smile.

She's done something.

"Great! What did she do now?" My little voice interrupts.

"Hi," Melody says extending a hand to Robin.

Robin returns the gesture, looks at me and says, "Hi, I'm one of the art instructors here..."

"You're Robin," Melody replies before Robin finishes.

"I see you have Bill's sentence completion down," Robin says smiling.

"Oh, I'm sorry," Melody responds. "We were just talking about you, I mean your name came up, I mean..."

"You babble also," Robin says giggling this time. "You two must be great at parties. Speaking of parties, what's this you can't go to the prom?"

"Well, so much for small talk," my inner voice says sarcastically.

"Robin!" I say projecting my voice though keeping the tone low.

"What?" Robin replies. "I just want to hear it from Melody. He did ask you, didn't he?"

"Yes," Melody replies. "We are going."

"I agree," I say. "I think we've had enough of this interrogation."

What did she say?

"I think she said..." my inner voice comments.

I turn my head quickly toward Melody who is still smiling widely.

"What?" I say delighted, yet confused. I want so much to run around yelling and screaming, but I need to hear the entire story.

"I believe she said you're going," Robin replies, continuing to grin.

"Well," Melody begins, "everyone here thinks we would be missing quite a bit..."

"Don't worry about them," I say stopping her short.

"Let her finish," Robin chides.

"Thank you," Melody says to Robin. "Anywho, after hearing everything today, and knowing how much effort you've put into the planning, I figured there would be other concerts. Besides, I'm allowed some personal time. So, I called Mr. Kay, and he asked if it was for, um, how did he put it, oh yes, that English teacher who smiles too much. I said 'yes.' He replied, 'well, have fun, but tell him to have you home before two.' And, here we are." The sparkle glistens brighter.

"Wow!" I say, stumbling for more words. "Wow! I, um, wow!"

"Kiss her, hug her, do something," my inner voice coerces.

217

Chapter 11

I hesitate for another moment, then break through my self applied restraints. I close my eyes, wrap my arms around Melody, and squeeze. I do not wish to loosen my grip, or open my eyes, or let her go, for fear of losing this small, significant part of reality.

An invisible force allows me somehow to open my eyes slightly, move my hands down to her waist, and lift her up. After a few seconds. I lower her down and our lips meet again.

Adrenaline rushes through my body. The walls of hope have solidified, breaking down almost all other barriers.

Robin clears her throat and says, "Well, now that we have that solved, I'll see you Monday, Bill. It's good to finally have met you, Melody."

"What? Oh, sorry," I say. "I'm just, a, um..."

Robin just nods her head and begins to walk away.

"Thanks," Melody calls to Robin.

Robin turns around, smiles, and says, "You may want to drive." We watch her disappear into the school.

As soon as the door closes completely, I turn to Melody and say, "Thank you. You know you don't have to..."

"Bill, I did say I would love to go with you."

"But, you may feel uncomfortable, not knowing anyone."

"I know Frank and Cindy, and after today, I don't think I'll have a problem with getting to know the other teachers and students."

Melody smiles.

"Besides," she adds, "I'm going with you, my teacher, my poet, my best friend."

Alone With Someone

"So much to do, so little time," my inner voice comments. "So where does that put you now? Are you really dating? Are you still just friends? You shouldn't feel happy; she just complicated your life! You didn't have this before!"

You're right, I didn't.

A very large grin forms as our arms intertwine and we walk. Melody rests her head on my shoulder. Her eyelashes flutter as the mirrors of our souls not only reflect the intense light, but become a part of it.

Chapter 12

The last few weeks have been...well they've been amazing, simply amazing. The perpetual motion and continuous action...making sure the students have everything...making sure I have everything. Would you believe that I ran around trying to match my cummerbund and tie to the color of Melody's dress. I spent a week trying to find something midnight-blue or close to it. The only problem was, I wasn't sure what midnight-blue looked like...exactly.

When Melody called me during a free period on Thursday, I admitted that I really wasn't sure how dark or how light the color actually was. She questioned if I had asked anyone at the rental places. I told her, "Of course, I talked to at least one person."

"And, what did he or she say?" Melody continued to inquire.

"It was a he. I mean, he was a he," I responded.

"Who, what was?"

"The person I asked was a he."

"So, what did he say?"

"Um," I hesitated as I recalled the encounter and debated whether or not to tell her that he said, "I don't work here."

Melody laughed as the truth made its way across the telephone lines. When we finally hung up, I still did not have a clue about midnight-blue.

When I went to collect my mail at the end of the school day, there was an envelope with a small rounded lump inside. I opened it and found a crayon. On its wrapper were the words, "Midnight-Blue."

Clapping and increased volume in music end my flashback, thrusting me into the excitement which surrounds me...I am here, I am at the prom.

Chapter 12

I turn and see a fairly tall, slim, dark-haired student with waving arms bound into the ballroom.

Many other students have moved toward the door and are chanting, "Ray! Ray! Ray!"

Ray was in my junior speech class last year and is an outstanding student. He is a natural people person. In fact, he seems to feed off the energy of others. The energy level here is very high.

Ray continues toward the stage where he will kick off the festivities. As he ascends the stairs, Jerry meets him and hands him a mike. Ray makes a couple whimsical comments and receives a few rim shots from Joe.

A feathery touch settles upon my still hand. A tighter grip takes hold of my heart as I turn and see Melody settling down in the chair next to me. In the far distance, I can hear Ray begin to read the opening poem, my poem.

I turn toward the stage as to not look directly at Melody. The words resonate in my mind and images of the angel by my side fade in and out. As the last few words reach us, I can stand my apparitions no longer, and I turn back toward Melody, gripping her hand slightly tighter. Our eyes meet and her smile widens, calming my thunderously thumping and ever-hopeful heart.

Ray finally finishes, looks in my direction, and bows slightly. Ray pauses briefly and says, "Tonight, tonight is our night!" Another burst of applause and shouting erupts. Ray waits and adds, "Tonight, there will be eating, dancing, and maybe even a few surprises, but, hey, this is our prom!"

Yes it is.

On his last words, more shouting ensues, and the band explodes.

Alone With Someone

I can feel the rush of enthusiasm engulf the room. I can feel the young hearts pound with excitement. I can feel...Melody leaning on my arm, emanating a soothing, comforting, warmth.

Before I can utter one word, Melody says, "Thank you," her eyes glistening in the dim lighting.

I smile, lift her hand upward, and gently touch my lips against her smooth skin.

"Are you paying attention to the students?" my inner voice questions. "Or, did you forget why you are here?"

Maintaining my composure, I slowly lower Melody's hand and say, "Let's take a walk around...have to make sure they're not having too good of a time." I need to elevate my voice somewhat because of the music, but know Melody hears me as we rise together.

Our table is in the back right corner, so we walk left toward the four sets of double doors where some students are still meandering in.

As we move around the room, eyes seem to follow us, but I am not all too sure whose eyes they are. Some students are dancing in the center of the hall, directly in front of the stage; some are sitting at their tables; others are just wandering around.

We near the doors and pause momentarily, taking in the entire room. I look at Melody, then back at the busy room before us. Part of me wants to just keep walking right out the doors, just to be alone with her, but...

"This is the prom!" my inner voice shouts. "You've been planning this event for years in your cluttered mind, and now that you are here, you want to leave?!?"

I know it's silly, but I realize that the only reason I ever wanted to go to the prom was to have a night to remember. Since I met Melody, I have had many memorable nights and days.

Chapter 12

I look up and see the oversized copies of poems written by the Romantic poets...Shelly, Byron, Keats. My eyes wander back to Melody, whose eyes are mimicking mine of just a few seconds ago. We stare at each other and a little smirk forms on each of our faces.

I am the one who says, "Thank you."

We begin moving again, this time toward the dance floor. As we near the stage, Ray bounds past us and the music begins to die down.

Ray takes the microphone says, "Food!" and points toward the rear by the kitchen doors, where servers are exiting with full trays.

I slightly squeeze Melody's hand and say, "Let's wait for them," motioning toward the stage and our tablemates. As Joe, Jerry, Kirk, and Frank set down and arrange their instruments safely until after dinner. I nod to the student standing behind a small stereo system on the other side of the stage. Chris nods back and presses a button in front of him. The theme of an old TV show escapes from the large speakers next to him. He nods again and gives me a thumbs up. Moans come from the quickly settling, yet still captive audience.

Chris was given this DJ opportunity because he was cheap, free in fact, but he is also a junior, who may not live to see his own senior prom if he keeps playing these songs.

The guys make their way to the stairs where Melody and I are standing. We are joined by Cindy, Nicole, and Crystol. As each friend descends, he kisses his counterpart on the cheek. Joe is the last one to step down and there is no one to meet him. He shrugs and opens his arms toward Melody. Before he can embrace her, I tap him on the shoulder and jokingly clear my throat. He shrugs his shoulders again and moves toward me with open arms. Melody smiles and taps Joe on the other shoulder, shaking her head. Joe frowns and drops his arms down to his side.

Jerry looks at the group and says, "Let's, eat!" With Nicole's arm wrapped around his, Jerry heads toward the table. He doesn't walk around the sides as Melody and I just did, instead, he walks right across the floor. Kirk, Crystol, and Joe follow. Melody and I hesitate. There is no one else out there!

Frank and Cindy motion for us to move, Melody looks at me, and we head toward the doors. We are, however, coerced to take the shorter, more open, route by hands pushing our shoulders from behind.

We take a few steps and hear a few crackles from the speakers as the TV tune ends and a slower, yet modern, one begins. Chris says, "Let's hear it for the band!" He pauses, looks at me, and continues, "and the teachers."

I shake my head and look upward. Melody tightens her grip on our still clasped hands. I want to lower my head, but for some reason, I can not.

We move through the tables of students who do not even seem to be interested in us. They are waiting for or are currently being served their soups and salads. I hear some positive comments about the quality of the meal so far, and hunger begins to push away some of those butterflies in my stomach.

We reach the table and reclaim our seats. As Melody and I sit, our hands separate. Our eyes move to meet each other. Melody smiles and for that moment I am held breathless. Smiles like this happen all too far apart. She smiles so frequently when we are together, but smiles like this one, smiles that for a split second make you forget who you are pretending to be, what you look like, and where you are; smiles that make the time apart, the time on the phone, all worth wild. It's a smile that just makes you happy.

We look at the table in front of us and notice bowls of soup already waiting.

"The soup is not very hot," I overhear Cindy say to Frank.

I pick up my spoon, dip it into the bowl, and lift out a small portion to taste. I bring the spoon closer to my mouth, blow on its contents, then surround it with my mouth. Hmm, creamy, rice, chicken, cold.

225

Chapter 12

I feel my bowl, lukewarm. As I reach for another mouthful, I look at Melody. An empty spoon is in her right hand and her left rests on the table; her eyes are wide and she is looking around at the group as if thinking about something.

I lower my own metal utensil back into the bowl, reach to hold her hand and say, "Definitely not café soup."

A small, yet somewhat loud burst escapes from her mouth. Everyone at the table stops eating and stares at us. I shrug my shoulders and simultaneously, though nonchalantly, caress Melody's hand.

She looks at her bowl then at me, seemingly waiting for approval for something. Before I can make any kind of response, the soup is taken from one side and replaced by a plate of salad from the other.

"I'm glad I was done," Joe says, his voice slightly elevated as the servers move from our table to the next.

I look down at my salad and frown. I really hope it is just the light making it look so dark. When I look toward Melody's plate, I think about how much dimmer the lights should be right about now. Melody is sorting through the leaves with a fork, finally sparing one. I look around the table, everyone else seems to be enjoying the salad. In fact, a carousal of different dressings has made its way around the table to me.

"I don't think anything is going to help this stuff," my little voice comments sarcastically.

I sigh and offer the containers to Melody, who frowns and shakes her head no. I place them in front of us and push my plate to the side.

Melody does the same and says, "I am not too big on salads anyway."

"So, Billie," Joe says, sipping from his water glass, "are we going to cooperate tonight?"

"Huh? What?" I ask.

"You know," Joe replies, puffing his cheeks, raising one hand toward his lips, and moving his fingers up and down.

"What?" I ask again, looking around the table, my eyebrows crunched together. There is no response from anyone. I reach for my water glass. Just as I take a sip, it hits me. "You don't...you wouldn't...I don't think so!" I say, almost spitting out the barely cool liquid.

"Even the water is not very good," my inner voice comments.

"You were supposed to wait," Jerry says, reaching behind Nicole to swing at Joe.

"You'll be fine," Kirk says.

"What are they talking about?" Melody asks smiling.

"Yes Frank, what are they talking about?" Cindy reiterates poking Frank.

"I don't know," Frank responds. Cindy pokes him again. "Really, I don't know."

"Nothing," I say as my wide eyes and flustered face move around the table.

"Don't worry about it Billie, we'll be nice," Joe comments, smirking.

"You're right, I won't worry about it," I respond, "because it is not going to happen!"

"Let's just drop it," Jerry says, leans back, and whispers something to Joe.

I glare at then until a comforting warmth settles against my already hot cheek.

"What is it?" Melody asks, sounding concerned.

Chapter 12

I smile and say, "Nothing really. I'll tell you later."

The main course arrives. Melody and I look at the foods on the plates...carrots, twice baked potato, and... I think that's chicken, at least that's what the menu said when the committee ordered it.

Conversation is kept to a minimum as we continue to learn what we are eating. Melody and I seem to take turns testing each item.

This wasn't exactly the way I envisioned my prom.

"It just started," my little voice chimes in.

The food is not the greatest.

"Everyone else seems to be enjoying it, look at Jerry," the voice rebuttals.

Jerry eats almost anything.

"At least he's eating, you're not even eating."

And can you believe them, trying to get me to...

"They were just playing with you," my inner voice responds.

I can't believe they would...

My thoughts continue to wander throughout the meal. I finally make an effort to shake off my continual cluttering figments and notice someone is taking away our half-empty plates.

Wow, I ate that much!

I turn toward Melody, smile, and say, "I think you start with dessert."

Melody giggles and responds, "Thanks!"

Alone With Someone

The table really is quiet, almost too quiet. Everyone seems to be engaging in small talk with those closest to them, but no large discussions. This is so unlike them.

"What do you expect, after you almost started throwing things at them for mentioning..." my inner voice comments, being cut short by a loud, echoing voice.

"OK, we'll play two more songs here, before the band takes over again. Enjoy your desserts," Chris says and turns to press a button.

"We haven't gotten dessert yet," Kirk says, pouting.

"Here it comes," Crystol responds. "You'll just have to eat fast."

"I don't think that's a problem for Kirk," Jerry adds.

"And, you're one to talk, Baby Huey," Kirk retaliates.

Big bowls are placed in front of us as Jerry says, "Just hurry up, some of you need the tune up time."

"What are you saying?" Kirk mumbles, shoveling a spoonful into his mouth.

Joe and Frank shake their heads.

I look down at the dessert, hoping for at least something edible. A light brown apple crisp type thing lies in the bottom of the bowl and soft melting vanilla ice cream is sliding slowly off the top. I look over at Melody who already has a spoonful up to her mouth. Her full red lips surround the metal object and a smile takes shape as the spoon is removed.

"That looks delicious," my little voice comments.

Huh?

Chapter 12

"The dessert!"

Oh sure.

Before my thoughts can slip further into the gutter, I feel a tap on my shoulder and turn to see Donnie, our Mechanical Drawing and Shop teacher, standing next to me.

"It's our turn," he says in a rather low, we-had-might-as-well-get-this-over-with tone.
My stare travels from him to Melody and then to my dessert. Without responding, I take a few quick bites of the edible sweet in front of me, rise, and say, "OK."

Donnie clears his throat and motions toward Melody. Without waiting for me, he extends his hand and introduces himself.

My face turns red and once again I whisper, "I'm sorry," to Melody. Before moving further, I hesitate, looking for something to add.

"We'll make sure she stays out of trouble while you're gone," Nicole says moving her chair closer.

The guys have already headed for the stage, leaving only Nicole, Cindy, and Crystol at the table with Melody.

"I'll be back in a while," I say to Melody as I take her hand and caress it. Her smile is soft and soothing...I don't want to go anywhere.

Donnie grabs my arm and mumbles something. I let Melody's hand slide from mine and walk away from the table with Donnie, not bothering to ask about his grumbling.

We are close to the double doors when I think about turning back. Before I can react, Donnie says, "They really did a good job with the decorations."

"Um, yeah," I respond, now just thinking about looking back.

Alone With Someone

"Bill," Donnie says as we head through the doors and down the hallway, "are you OK? You seem focused on other things. You seem like you don't want to be here, and from what I've been hearing..."

"And, what have you been hearing?" I ask, stopping short of the large external doors.

"Nothing, just that you seem to be more passionate than usual, which is hard to believe considering that you get more involved in the things you do more than anyone I know, and..." Donnie says, pushes open the doors, and motions for me to go through.

Once outside, he lights up a cigarette, and we begin our walk around the building, looking for students doing exactly what Donnie just did...irony.

We make our way around half of the building in silence, then Donnie says, "She's a very nice young lady."

"What?" I say, knowing exactly what or rather who is talking about.

"Melody, she seems very nice. She's a looker too."

I want to say, "Yes, she is. And, her smile, have you seen it? Isn't it intoxicating...and those eyes..."

Instead, I say, "Yep," and sigh.

"So, what's going on between you two?"

I stop moving again and look at Donnie, hoping for an answer from someone other than myself. I take a deep breath and say, "She's become my best friend, Donnie, and I can't explain exactly when or even why. Before you and Karen met, did you ever feel that you wanted to be alone with someone, and when you met that person, did you, do you, ever feel alone?"

Chapter 12

"Well, I'm not quite sure what you mean. I was married once before I met Karen. There were many times I felt alone with my first wife. Now, I like to spend time together with my wife."

"Exactly," I add and begin to move again.

"Well, buddy," Donnie replies, putting his hand on my shoulder and flipping away his extinguished ember, "that's how it is sometimes."

We reach the front doors and are greeted by Jeff. "Did you find anyone out there?" Jeff asks.

"No," Donnie responds.

"I caught a couple of students earlier and I don't think smoking was the only thing on their mind," Jeff says, smirking. "Such a great age, isn't it."

"Let's go back in," Donnie says, pulling a door open.

"You just missed the garters being removed," Jeff adds, following us inside. "Some of them really got into it."

"Do you think Melody had on a garter?" my little voice questions.

"How's the band doing?" I ask. "Are the students dancing?"

"They're doing well. In fact," Jeff adds, "they're very close to a break."

We walk back into the large, loud room. Many students have crowded onto the dance floor; some are still at their seats; and a few are standing around the perimeter talking. The band is playing a jazzy little tune.

I take a quick look at my watch...twenty minutes? It can't be. We were out there for twenty minutes? Melody was alone for twenty minutes! How could I...

I look toward our table, looking for my vision. I can feel the corners of my mouth angle upwards as my eyes meet with hers. Those large luminous mirrors shine through the crowd, through the dim lights, through time spent apart. I wave and move toward my beacon.

"Hey, where are you going?" Jeff asks. "You still have ten minutes."

"Oh yeah," I respond. Looking back at Melody, I hold up one finger and make small circles in the air as if to say, "one more time around."

Melody nods as Nicole taps her on the shoulder, drawing her attention.

"She was looking for you," my inner voice comments.

Before I am able to reply or dwell further, Jeff and Donnie say, "Let's go this way."

We begin a loop around the hall, heading toward the dance floor and stage.

I search for a thought, something to contain my wondering mind, something on which to focus. Nothing really. Unbelievable, so short an interruption and now nothing. I know my head is moving from side to side, but the details around me seem to be missing. I can see bodies and shapes, but can't quite make out faces.

We stop and before I am able to determine where we are, I hear the music stop, and a word appears in my thoughts, "hope."

For what? "Hope" for what?

"And now," Ray's voice crackles over the speaker system, "we have a special addition to the band for this next piece..."

The word fades, and I realize we are standing on the side of the stage. I react to Ray's words by turning my head and looking around. Who did they...

Jeff taps me on the shoulder and motions to the top of the stage stairs, where Ray now stands with a golden trumpet in his hand.

Chapter 12

I shake my head, "no."

Joe plays a marching cadence on his drums, a cadence similar to one we played in high school.

I can't believe they are doing this. I haven't played since...

"Last week," my inner voice completes my thought. "You played last week with that new CD you bought."

I haven't played in front of people since high school.

"That's longer than you've been on a real date," the annoying echo comments.

"I think he needs a little coaxing," Ray says, stepping down on a stair and extending the horn even more.

There is clapping all around us as Jeff grabs the instrument and hands it to me.
I want to push it away, but notice something very familiar about it...it's my trumpet! How did they...

As I take the shiny piece from Jeff, I look up on the stage and see Joe waving a key chain in the air and smiling. He's had those keys since my parents moved. I can't believe...

Reluctantly, I ascend the few steps to the top of the stage. The clapping and chanting die down as I reach the microphone. I look at the students and shake my head.
Joe gives a few clicks on his sticks, just as he would at the beginning of a song. I shrug my shoulders and blow into the horn, making a noise like a sick cow. I shake my head again and look at the trumpet.

"Actually," Jerry says into his microphone, "it would probably be nice to know what song we are playing, unless we want to play half and half, hoping it will balance out eventually. It's not like we've ever done that."

Alone With Someone

Jerry looks at Kirk as he makes his last comment and Joe provides a rim shot.

"We wanted to play something from when we were in high school, but figured it might scare you to know that we had music similar to yours," Jerry says, continuing to ham it up. "So, we thought we would play something all of us recently worked on."

What have we all worked on? Maybe, he means something Joe and he put together.

"You see, our guest here has written a few things that have inspired some of our songs. A couple of months ago, he brought in a little piece to one of our jam sessions. We read it and well..."

"What Jerry is trying to say," Joe interrupts, "is here it is..."

"Wait a minute," I rebuke, "I never really played this, I just..."

Before I can get out another word, Joe clicks his sticks, setting the tempo, and begins to lightly brush his symbols; Smooth sounds cascade from Jerry's and Frank's saxophones.
"You might as well try," my inner voice suggests.

I move my fingers over the valves on my horn, lift it to my mouth, blow some warm air through it, and lower it again. I look out onto the dance floor and see the students swaying to the music and faculty members standing around waiting for the show to start. My gaze wanders to the back where we were sitting.

"Where is she?" my conscious asks, concerned.

My eyes dart quickly to the front of the stage and just before they bulge back out. I see her. Melody has moved to a front table with the others, just as if we were at Kirk's. She is smiling.

235

Chapter 12

Somehow, I am able to hear the notes, the notes of the stanza right before
I need to play. I bring up my trumpet to my lips, take a deep breath,
count silently...2, 3, 4...3, 4...and play.

As the first note exits, I forget about the technical music aspects like the
beat and where the notes fall on the staff, which is my usual focus, and I
allow my feelings to take control. The words of my poem flash through
my mind as I continue to add to the initial imagery.

Alone with someone,
Is where I long to be;
Alone with you
Truly sets me free.
How much do we question;
How much do we debate;
How long do we wait,
Before our hearts
Stop making memories
Of our true soulmate.
My prayers have still been answered
Even if heaven didn't send you.
But, how can
Eyes sparkle so brightly
Without the stars above;
A voice sing so sweetly
Without nature's melodies;
And, how can
A heart beat so softly
Without the breath of an angel.
Alone with someone
Is where I long to be.
Alone with you
Truly sets me free.
How much do we question;
How much do we debate;
How long do we wait,
Before our hearts

Alone With Someone

Stop making memories
Of our true soulmate.

I stop playing, but the tune continues, now slowly fading. When I look toward Melody, however, the music in my mind increases in volume.

Somehow, I know other things are happening around me. This was definitely something I never thought I would or could do, and now here I am expressing much more than...

"All that English stuff, and he can blow a horn too," Ray shouts. "How about another one?"

I smile, shake my head, and bow to the guys as I walk toward the stairs, my trumpet cradled in my arms. The smooth sounds of Jerry's and Frank's own horns and the deep reverberations of Kirk's bass starting a new song, brings a small sigh from my focused mind.

How often does one actually get to do what he wants to do?

"For you," my inner voice says, "it seems to be very often. In fact, things seem to balance out for you quite a bit...are you sure the end credits shouldn't be rolling?"
Since this is my life, I am the writer, producer, and performer. The credits only roll when everything is the way they are meant to be, and besides, I still haven't danced with my inspiration.

Somehow, I have made it to the table where the ladies are. I stand still with my arm extended toward Melody.

She accepts my gesture and rises. We take a few steps in order to move to the corner of the dance floor. I take her left hand in my right, holding our arms slightly away from our bodies and place my left hand on the small of her back. She rests her other hand on my adjacent shoulder.

The music has become softer and we move. You hear about moving to the beat of each other's hearts, well if Melody's heart is beating as quickly as mine, we're not even close. My eyes wander and I see people smiling and enjoying the time together. The looks do not seem to be intended for us, rather the ones they are with.

My eyes rest on Melody's face. The brightness of her angelic aura has diminished somewhat and she seems more human. For some reason, I feel more comfortable now than I ever have before.

Melody notices the grin on my face and asks, "What? What were you doing?"

"Nothing, nothing," I mumble.

The song comes to an end. Melody and I move toward the table. I squeeze her hand, turn my head, and whisper, "Thank you."

A larger smile forms on Melody's blushing face.

I pull out a chair and offer it to her. "I need to take care of some odds and ends for the students, could you, are you..." I fumble with my words, trying to justify leaving again.

"We'll listen to the music," Nicole says, moving closer to Melody and pointing to the stage.

"Thanks," I say. I look at Melody and add, "after this is over..."

"I'll be here," Melody responds.

I turn and walk toward the doors, this time looking back and smiling. Now would be an OK time for those credits.

"But, you still have after the prom," my inner voice comments.

She'll be there, too.

Chapter 13

"But soft, what light through yonder window breaks," I whisper, moving toward a single still figure in the middle of the dance floor. I reach out to touch her shoulder.

"Does it scare you when someone knows you have entered or left the room without looking directly at you?" Melody questions before my outstretched hand can reach its destination.

I freeze and wonder if she really knows I am there or if she is just talking to herself.

"I, um, how did you know, I," I stutter.

"Your shadow," Melody says. "Besides, I think everyone else has left."

"I am so sorry," I respond. "I just needed to make sure everyone was…"

"OK," Melody says. "It's OK. Cindy and Frank just left. Besides, the quiet was nice."

"I am sorry for leaving you for so long," I add. "Things just got busy and, I, a, well…"

"It was OK. In fact, I thought I would feel very uncomfortable since I knew very few students and even fewer of the faculty, but with Cindy, Nicole, and Crystol here, I felt incredibly comfortable."

"But, I left you alone," I interject.

"It was like you were right over my shoulder the entire time," Melody says reaching up and back toward me.

I take her hand and add, "I'm still going to be sorry. Besides, after sitting through my wonderful musical blunder, I owe you quite a few apologies."

Chapter 13

"OK, I'll agree with you there," Melody comments.

"Stop, just stop," I say sarcastically, moving to the side of her chair and tugging slightly upward on her hand as if to say, 'please stand.' My heart beats faster, clouded and varied thoughts run through my mind as she slowly rises.

"Your chariot awaits," echoes a familiar voice behind me.

Melody stands completely. We both turn toward the doors. There, in a footman's costume is Michelle, a former student of mine. When she heard I was actually attending the prom this year, she insisted on providing the transportation herself. Her father owns a horse and buggy business, but she has been taking care of the business aspects of it since graduating high school two years ago. She is also attending a city college and working on a degree in Marketing and Communications, which she hopes will help her in opening a small publishing business of her own.

"So much for the quiet," I say and walk with Melody toward the door.

"She looks beautiful," my inner voice comments.

"Yes," I whisper.

"What?" Melody asks.

"Nothing," I respond softly.

"You do that too often," Melody adds. "What did you say?"

"Nothing really, I was just commenting on something that annoying voice said."

"What did it say?" She asks.

"Oh, look, we're here," I say hoping to change the subject. I extend my hand to Melody so as to help her into the red and white carriage.

Alone With Someone

Melody shakes her head as she ascends the small set of steps.

"She knows you are avoiding the question," my inner annoyance says.

I'm not avoiding anything.

I let go of her hand and dash to the opposite side and jump in. Melody
starts to laugh.
"What?" I say, a little out of breath, though not necessarily from the run,
rather from the jump. This thing is higher than I remember.

"You are too much," Michelle comments as she climbs into her seat,
which is slightly more elevated and further forward than our own. "If you
promise not to jump out, we will get going. The route is already set."

"I promise not to jump," I say. "But, if I'm pushed, the doctor bills should
be sent to the young lady to my right."

"Young lady, huh?" Melody says. "Don't you call your female students
that when you play that condescending father figure?"

"Well, um, I didn't mean…"

"OK, old man, you had better not have a heart attack from all that
running and jumping, because someone of my young age and experience
may not remember CPR too well," Melody says sarcastically.

"Well, OK," Michelle chimes in and swishes the reigns of the two horses
slightly. "If you two are going to fight, we'll turn this thing around and
go right home."

We pull away from the curb and I look at Melody. While my face is as
red as the cushion we are sitting on, a rather large grin rests on her face.

"I didn't mean…" I start to say.

"You know," Melody begins, "you may be getting old if you have to
even think about it." The grin remains and the whites of her eyes expand,

forming a soothing sea around those dark pupils and ever-sparkling irises.

"How could you get mad at someone with eyes like that?" the little voice returns. "Besides, you are older."

I sigh and say, "OK, OK, truce. You win. You're not young…I mean, um, you're a great age and definitely a lady."

"Then you," Melody says as she sits back and lightly leans against me, "you must be the tramp."

"When exactly did you become the comedian?" I ask laughing a little. "Besides, I'm not sure if my old bones can take your weight too long."

"Now you're saying I'm heavy," Melody huffs and moves in closer.

"Now, you need to stop," I respond giggling. I think about moving my arm and putting it around her, but I don't. Instead, I wiggle my hand to hers and add, "Let's just enjoy the ride. It's probably half over and I haven't seen anything yet."

"Do you need your glasses, grandpa?" Michelle joins in, her voice slightly elevated to compensate for the traffic around us. "We've just begun and the best part is coming up. Try not to fall asleep."

"Great, two of you," I comment and gently squeeze Melody's hand.

Melody doesn't add anything else except a sigh. I let myself relax and settle back into the comfortable seat cushion behind us. My eyes close about halfway.

"You know," my little voice says, "You have never really discussed the age difference."

What's there to discuss?

"Well, you are older."

Not by much.

"By at least three, if not four years…"

So.

"So when you're ready to retire…"

We'll be enjoying more vacations.

"But, she may still be working."

So.

"OK, let's think about it this way…when you were a senior in high school, she was in eighth grade! That's statutory…"

That is definitely enough.

"So," I say to Melody, breaking the argument within myself, "are you sure everything was OK tonight? I mean, sometimes I go a little too far with…"
"Everything went well," Melody interrupts. "I thought we were going to relax and enjoy the scenery."

"We are," I add. "Ah, don't all those bright lights look dazzling."

"Bill."

"Yes?"

"You're beginning to babble. Since you brought this evening up again…do you ever feel that someone you know, someone you know well, is right around the corner, but know that's impossible because they are halfway across the city in a meeting or something?"

"He or she is," I say.

"What?" Melody comments, moving off my shoulder and angling herself inward to stare at me.

"When you said, 'they are halfway across the city,' you should have said, 'he or she is halfway across the city,'" my voice hesitates and fades out on the last few words.

Silence.

"I'm sorry," I say, "bad habit. What were you saying?"

"Well," Melody continues and pauses, "that's how I felt tonight. Even though I knew you were running around for the students, every time someone stopped by to say hello, or when I heard a familiar song, you were there."

How can I follow that? I really want to tell her that I felt similar tonight. In fact, I have felt that way many times. As I drive home, as I walk to the grocery store, as I mail a letter, I swear I can smell her sweet scent in the cool breeze. There are times, when the feeling is so strong, I turn around expecting her to be there, but she's not…she couldn't be…she's at practice, at home, or tutoring. Just the thought, however, is enough for me to be engulfed by the energy and happiness she brings.

I want to tell her this, but would she, does she, really want to hear that? Would it frighten her as it does me sometimes? Would I babble so much that she wouldn't even be able to understand?

Instead, I just say, "Thank you."

"Here we go," Michelle's voice pierces the quietude. "This is the best part of your tour, I am told that a surprise and your car will be waiting for you."

"What?" I inquire. "Where will they be waiting?"

"Wait for it," Michelle responds.

Alone With Someone

"Yeah, wait for it," Melody echoes, smiling.

We round the corner. The steel and concrete veil of the city disappears behind us. The engine noises are replaced by the soft splashing of lakefront waves. And, a slightly cooler wind sends chills throughout my body.

"There should be a blanket and a few other things in a basket on the floor," Michelle remarks, her voice not as loud or strained as before. "Now, as long as I don't hear any screaming or crying, I'll be up here minding my own business and talking to the horses."

I slide forward and reach for the items Michelle had mentioned. I pull up the blanket first and hand it to Melody, who quickly covers herself. I shake my head and laugh as I reach for the basket.

I pull up the woven wooden container and slide back in the seat. I flip open one side of the lid and pull out a white cloth napkin. I look at Melody, then the blanket she has wrapped around her, and back to the napkin. I unfold the small cloth and place it on my chest and sit very still.

Melody looks at me, laughs, and asks, "What are you doing? What's in the basket?"

"Shh, I'm keeping warm," I respond. "I don't know what's in the basket, I wanted to make sure I at least got this," I say pulling the napkin off and waving it between us.

"Give me that and look in the basket," Melody says taking my only covering.

"Great!" I comment. "Now, I'm going to freeze out here. Well, let's see what's in here then." I bring the basket closer to me and pull out a bottle of non-alcoholic grape wine, a thermos with a label that reads, "hot chocolate," and a little card. I open the card and read it, "One to keep you warm and one to warm you up…your students." I smile and hand the note to Melody.

Chapter 13

She reads it and giggles. "Which one are you going to start with?"

"Well, since you warm me up just by being here, I was thinking about the hot chocolate, unless of course, you're actually going to share that blanket which is three times bigger than you."

"You're too much," Melody says, lifting up one end of the blanket.

I put the items back in the basket and slide closer to my beautiful friend. The distance isn't that far physically, but with every fraction of an inch I move, the warmer I feel. We've hugged, we've even kissed on occasion, but we haven't really been this closer for a long period, we haven't cuddled.

Melody lets the end of the blanket fall over me. I move the basket so that it sits on my lap above the covering. I have both hands on the handle, close my eyes about halfway, and inhale through my nose.

I know that I must look silly just sitting here, but I want to capture this moment. If I lost my sense of smell, I would miss her sweet scent; if I lost my sense of touch, I would miss the smoothness of her skin and the silkiness of her hair; if I lost my sense of sight, I would certainly miss her ever sparkling eyes. I would, however, still know that she is there.

"Are you OK?" Melody asks. "Bill, are you OK?"

"Um, yes," I respond. "I'm sorry, I was just…"

"I understand," Melody says.

"What? I, um," I reply, not understanding.

"You were having one of those moments," Melody responds.

"Huh. How did you…?"

"It's that look."

Alone With Someone

"What look?"

"The look that says, I'm paying attention really, just not to everything. The look that says so much more than a sigh, a laugh, or even a sentence."

I am amazed, simply amazed.

"I'm sorry," I say. "I hear that in old age, the mind starts to wonder."

"My mind wonders quite a bit these days," Melody comments.

"Well," I comment, "you must be older than I thought."

"Stop," Melody says and moves her hips quickly, bumping into me. "You know what I mean. In fact, when you were playing with the guys…"

"I've already apologized for that, please don't rub it in," I interject.

"It was nice," Melody continues. "I had one of those moments right after I read the lyrics Nicole gave me. Did you write them?"

"You read the lyrics?" I ask somewhat disturbed.

"Yes, Nicole had a copy and we followed along with the first part," Melody says.

"Did she say where she had gotten the words?" I ask.

"From Jerry, I guess," Melody responds. "I thought it was beautiful, but…"

Great. Wonderful. There's a 'but.'

"But, I was wondering why you didn't show it to me yourself." Melody says inquisitively.

Chapter 13

"Well, I," I fumble for words, more out of frustration rather than not knowing the answer. "It really wasn't finished. In fact, it still needs quite a bit of work as a song and a poem. I can't believe we played it."

"Bill," Melody says softly as her left hand wraps itself around my right even though I am still grasping the basket handle, tighter now than before. "I have always been flattered by your writing. I have never had anyone write me letters on a continuous basis, let alone poems. I don't always understand what you're saying or how far I should read into things, but I am always excited that you would share them with me."

I move the basket left and onto the seat, take Melody's hand in both of mine and say, "I made a promise to myself when I first started writing that when someone inspires me, I share the results of that inspiration with them. You have inspired me so extensively in such a short time; I would have trouble sharing everything with you, let alone thank you appropriately for each inspiration. I have written so much over these last few months and within each of those ramblings there are not only words, but little pieces of you." I bring her hand to my lips and gently kiss her knuckles.

"So, when you see a piece that is not necessarily complete, I worry that it may be missing the most important part, the connection here…" I move her hand again, this time to the left side of my chest.

I swallow hard, hoping I didn't "share" too much.

The silence entwines us as Melody bites her lower lip and attempts to say something a couple of times. Nothing audible seems to escape from her lips.

I lower her hand and release it. "I was going to save this for another time, but now might be a good time to share it with you…unless you've had enough of my babbling." I reach underneath the blanket and into my coat pocket, pulling out a folded piece of paper.

"Please," Melody says softly.

Alone With Someone

I unfold the paper and begin reading, the cool breeze subsiding, the waves barely audible, my heart thumping thunderously.

Most Recent Delight

Spring's gentle breeze
Sends sensations of youth
Throughout my entire being
As I attempt
To fully comprehend
The beauty I am seeing.
A lone bird begins to chirp,
Then many join in the song.
The notes seem to blend and flow,
Some short and others long.
Apart from this simplicity,
A true manifestation can be seen,
Smiling, Laughing, Being,
Life,
My life.
All I ever was,
All I am aspiring to be
Is there to behold
In this
My most recent delight,
Whose loveliness engulfs
My entire realm of sight.

I feel the urge to tell her more, to tell her what goes through my mind, but something is stopping me. Something always stops me.

I do, however, manager to refold the paper and offer it to her. A small smile graces her face. I wonder if she is having one of those moments, or is that a look of concern.

"Thank you," Melody says as she leans over to take the paper and hug me.

Chapter 13

We've hugged before, but this one seems different. She seems closer, yet somewhat distant. Her smooth cheek brushes against mine. I want to whisper something in her ear, but I don't. I can't. Our embrace lingers as the wind whistles by carrying its own message.

Did she just say…? I must be hearing things.

Melody pulls away slowly. The look on her face is similar to my own, happy, but wondering.

"Did you…" We say simultaneously.

"Never mind," I respond.

"Never mind," she replies.

We sit still, not necessarily knowing what is next. I turn my head and notice we are on the beach itself. Our pace has slowed as we get closer to a dimly lit patch of sand.

"Are you two still alive back there?" Michelle asks. "We have arrived. I was told to let you out here."

"Where's here?" I question. "And, who told you to let us out here?"

We have come to a complete stop and Michelle is climbing down from her seat. "Well," she says, "here is by that bright spot over there with candles, a radio, and a basket. Who would be your friends."

"Whose friends?" I ask. "My friends wouldn't do all of this, it would require work and thought on their part."

I smile and look at Melody. "It must be your friends," I say taking her hand again.

"Couldn't be my friends," Melody comments, "most of them are still in jail."

"I'm kidding," Melody says, noticing that my eyes have gotten wider and my smile has slowly faded.

"Well, I don't know," I say. "I really haven't met any of your friends. Besides, you only mention them when we are on the phone."

"Speaking of jail," Michelle joins in, "here comes a nice police officer now."

A man of about medium height and large build bounds toward us on a horse. "Good morning, we were expecting you a little earlier. Is everything OK?"

"Um, everything is going very well," I respond. "But, um, who were you expecting?"

"You are Jerry's friends?" the officer asks.

"Is Jerry one of your friends, right?" I ask Melody. "Because, after tonight, I'm not sure how much of my friend here is going to be."

"I'll take that as a yes. My name is David. I'll be patrolling the area. You should have this section pretty much to yourselves for at least a couple of hours, compliments of your friends and the CPD."

"Again with these friends," I say sarcastically. "Next time we go to the prom, Melody, could you provide the entertainment, please."

"Everyone out," Michelle shouts. "Free rides are only one way. Are you going to jump out or use the stairs?"

"I think we'll use the stairs," I respond. "Can we keep the blanket? I think the young lady here has grown rather attached to it."

"Sure, I don't think the horses will mind if you keep their blanket," Michelle responds giggling.

Chapter 13

"She was kidding," I say as Melody and I stand. I help her wrap the blanket around herself so as not to trip over it and point to the stairs.

We reach the ground and take a few steps away from our transportation. I turn to thank Michelle for the ride, giving her a little hug. Melody does the same.

"So, David," I say looking up at him, "are you going to be very close, or just around?

"I'll just be around," David responds. "In fact, I'll be patrolling the area, so I shouldn't disturb you at all. There is food and your favorite wine over there and a little radio turned to your favorite station. Your car is just around the corner. Enjoy and if you need anything, holler. After all, we are here to protect and serve."

"You know if you weren't supposed to say that, I would have to tip you," I say. "Thank you again."

I put my right hand around Melody and with my left, motion toward the dimly lit area. "Shall we?"

Melody nods and we walk through the fresh tracks left by the horses and carriage. As we get closer, we hear the music from the radio, see little snacks set out, and glasses already filled with a purple substance.

"This is so nice," Melody comments. "Did you know they were going to do this?"

"No," I say. "Sometimes, they surprise even me. Usually, it's painful, but you are right, this is very nice."

We reach the preset area and sit down on the blanket, which covers the sand.

"Well, I could feed you these grapes like the slaves did with Cleopatra…Or," I say, "we could each try to let the other take little sips from those wine glasses, or we could…"

Alone With Someone

"Let's just enjoy the moment," Melody whispers.

"Or, we could do that," I say moving closer to her.

"And now, here's a little dedication for Bill and Melody," a voice on the radio breaks in.

I hesitate briefly, but as the music begins, I move my arm around Melody's shoulder. She lies against me at almost the same time, and my arm slips to her waist.

"You know," I say, "since we just missed Friday at Kirk's they will expect us Saturday."

Melody doesn't say anything. The look on her face says she is enjoying the moment. She looks happy.

Things seem so quiet, so peaceful, so right. The only difference between this moment and just about every other is that my vision hasn't faded and we are here together. I feel happy.

Chapter 14

My mistress's eyes are nothing like the sun, tis true,
They are a far more brilliant hue.
Coral's redness may be debated only among sunken ships,
But they may never taste as sweet as my mistress' lips.
If snow be white, then true purity befriended the seven,
And her silken hair was certainly spun from the clouds of heaven.
Her sweet scent is synonymous with what a fresh breeze brings,
And her voice chimes in time with my delicate heartstrings.
If on Earth there a goddess be,
I am truly fortunate, for she is with me.
Alas, a poet's pact I break and abuse,
And, as my own words prove, I have fallen for my muse.
I offer no excuses for what my mind has endeavored to create,
But open my heart no matter how long the wait.

"I know," I say, "I always seem to give you these things either at the end of our time together or close to it. I just wanted you to know…well, I just, um…actually, it's a response to one of Shakespeare's sonnets, which…well, it wasn't very flattering…"

"Bill," Melody interrupts. "Stop, just stop, you're babbling."

"I know. I just can't seem to…never mind, let's get in there. Hopefully, they are in the middle of a set."

It's only been a couple of hours, I know. I still feel happy, but this seems different somehow. Maybe it's my lack of sleep. I spent some time on that poem even after I dropped off Melody and drove home myself.

I motion toward the entrance of Kirk's and wait for Melody to move first. I watch her face as she walks past me, hoping for a small glimpse of the sparkle in her eyes. Good, it's still there. My gaze travels quickly to her lips, hoping to see a full smile, a grin, or even a smirk, but I am met with a straight line.

I do not move as a cold breeze rumbles over the quiet parking lot. "Is," I hesitate briefly, "is everything OK? Did I…"

Chapter 14

"Everything is great," Melody says, her now fake smile widening. "Last night was wonderful. Tonight will be fine. Stop worrying."

"I just well…you seem…was the poem," I stumble over my words but start to walk toward the doors, hoping to change the mood. Did she just say, "stop worrying?" I usually tell her that. But, I really should stop worrying. After all, it's only Kirk's.

I take a deep breath, open the door, and say, "After you, my lady. Our audience awaits."

She curtsies and says, "Yes your grace."

We walk into the friendly confines. Music meets us. I grin and glance at Melody, who now has a similar expression.

We reach the table, and I pull out a chair next to Cindy, wait for Melody to sit down, and follow suit between her and Jeff.

"Out too late," Jeff leans toward me and whispers.

I shift my body toward him and reply, "With the paid chaperone and armed guards surrounding us, you should know more about what went on last night then we do." A smirk forms on my face as I move toward Melody.

"Let the games begin," I whisper to her, taking her hand which rests between our chairs. "You tell them about the passionate love we shared, and I'll just sit here and blush." Melody swings our hands toward me and hits my leg. I jump a little.

The music stops.

"You know I bruise easily," I comment as a mug of root beer is placed in front of each of us.

Both hands move toward our drinks. We lift them, click them together, and move them toward our lips, still watching each other's actions.

"What, we're not good enough to drink with any more?" Jerry's voice sounds in front of us.

Quickly, the mug moves away from my waiting mouth, and I look in the direction of the voice. Jerry, Joe, and Frank are pulling out chairs and sitting down.

"Well," I respond jokingly, "we didn't know how long you blow-hards were going to be up there."

"Has that ever mattered?" Joe comments, smiling and turning toward Melody. "You know, I don't think I like the influence you have on him, young lady. He seems to be forgetting about his friends and tradition!"

Melody smiles and says, "Well, I'm not sure if he is hanging around with the right crowd these days, with all this drinking and loud music…"

I am somewhat surprised at the quickness and sarcastic nature of Melody's comment, but interrupt saying, "All right you two, that's enough fighting. I'll turn this place around and we'll go right home."

"See," Joe interjects, "he's forgotten, we're already home." Joe's arms are raised and stretched wide.

"Well then," Jeff joins in, "I would like to negotiate an increase in my allowance."

"You all need to start forking over your allowances," Kirk chimes in as he sets down drinks in front of Joe, Jerry, and Frank, then sits down himself. "The landlord is threatening to turn off the heat."

"Speaking of heat," Jerry says looking toward Melody and I, "how was last night?"

"Speaking of last night," I say, hoping not to blush too much, "what kind of friends would throw me to the wolves then try to set up an evening, telling me to enjoy myself with more people watching our every move than the president has excuses."

Chapter 14

"What?!?" Joe comments. "Now, you're ungrateful. Can you believe this? We give him the evening he never had, an evening he's been waiting for, for years, and he questions our intentions!"

"Everything for him. Everything we've put up with," Jeff says, "Listening to him complain about never going to the prom, and not knowing what to do even if he did go. We gave him all the answers, and still he complains. I can't believe he's still complaining."

"Don't forget about the smiles and head bobbing," Frank pipes up.

"That's right," Jeff continues. "We put up with that for weeks. Besides, the helicopter got some good shots of you two on the beach. We'll have them tomorrow."

"OK, stop, just stop," I say giggling. "Thank you. Are you happy now? I said thank you. Can we drink now?"

I raise my mug, Melody follows, then Jeff, Joe, Jerry, Kirk, finally Frank and Cindy. "Salute," we say simultaneously, clicking all the glasses together.

This time, I manage to take a small sip of the dark liquid and look over the top of my mug before setting it down. As my eyes pass each person, I think of how fortunate I am to have such good friends. Completing the half circle of the table, my gaze settles on Melody, and I think of how good it feels to be so fortunate.

"By the way," Cindy says setting down her glass and looking at me. "I never told you how well you played yesterday."

"That's because he didn't," Kirk jabs.

"You're brutal," I say. "Thank you Cindy. It was my last public performance. I'm going to leave the performing to professionals." I take Melody's closest hand, smoothly caressing the top with my thumb, "And, I'm going to leave the public humiliation to my students. Some of them were a little more wild than I expected, especially toward the end."

"The students actually were not that bad this year," Jeff interrupts. "Do you remember last year? And, did you see that new math teacher? What's her name, Trixi or something?"

"See her," Joe adds, "she was hard to miss in that slinky red dress, and that red hair…wow! I bet she knows how to really party."

"Her name is Samantha," I say, quickly taking another sip of my root beer. "And, her dress wasn't that bad."

"Even Billie noticed her," Joe says. "So, is she single?"

"She is a very nice young lady and not your type," I comment.

"Oh?" Joe inquires. "And, how would you know?"

Melody's hand goes limp under mine. I wish the landlord would turn off that heat right about now.

"I, um," I stumble for some reason and look at everyone, ending on Melody. They seem interested in what I have to say, especially the angel next to me. "I work with her. Her classroom is down the hall from mine. And, she helped me with the prom setup…" my words trail off at the end. Both my hands move to encompass my drink as I stare at it. For some reason, I feel guilty and am not completely sure why.

"You've been holding out on us," Jerry says winking.

"Stop," I say, "you're killing me. We're colleagues. Besides, Frank works with her too." I look quickly at him and hope for some kind of support. As I wait for Frank to comment, other thoughts enter my mind, like: how beautiful Melody is; how incredible she makes me feel; and how no one else can or has supplied me with inspiration the way she does. I can't and don't verbalize any of them as we continue to wait for Frank to say something, anything.

Cindy nudges Frank and stares at him.

Chapter 14

"What?" Frank asks. "She teaches at the same school for god's sake. We see her everyday. What's there to say? Besides, the most beautiful woman is right here next to me." Frank takes Cindy's hand, brings it to his lips, and kisses it.

I want to do the same to Melody, but am not sure right now if she will be as distant as before or as cold as this frosty beverage in my hands now.

"Now you're killing me," Cindy says.

"Besides," Frank adds, "she's too young for me."

Cindy squeezes his hand and nearly knocks him off his chair as she shoves him. There is laughter around the table.

"So, how old is she?" Melody asks softly.

The laughter stops and everyone stares at me again. I want to look into Melody's eyes and let all my worries just disappear, but for some reason, the biggest worry remains, what if the radiating sparkle isn't there this time. I just don't want to take that chance.

"She is the same age as you are," I mumble, still looking at my mug, running my thumb along the top.

The usual warmth between us has slowly dissipated. I even have trouble smelling her perfume. I didn't do anything. I haven't even thought anything. Why is this like this? Who brought this up?

"Well," Joe says, "since you have already found your soulmate, you'll have to introduce me to Samantha one day…"

This time I manage to look at Melody. She has that fake smile on her face and she is staring blankly ahead.

"Not if I get to her first," Jeff comments. "I wonder if she goes for jocks."

"You play golf!" Kirk interjects.

"Golf is a sport," Jeff replies, "and a very complicated one at that."

Great! Small talk. I look around the table slowly.

"Hey," Jerry jumps in, "did I mention the audition I have in New York?"

"No, you haven't," Cindy responds, seemingly agreeing with the subject change. "Tell us about it."

When exactly did I lose control? When exactly did I become this stupid. I should just reach over...things went well last night, didn't they? Did I go too far? Did I not go far enough?

"It's next week," Jerry begins. "I met them a few days ago. This group was performing at the community college down the street from the station."

"What were you doing at the community college?" Kirk asks, implying other intentions than learning.

"My job," Jerry responds swinging at Kirk. "Anyway, I listened to them play a little and went back when they had finished. I talked with Paul, the lead vocalist, and he mentioned they were losing their tenor sax player, Mike, to some marketing firm in Albany or something. So, they were flying back to New York to audition people. I commented on how great they sounded and what a shame it would be to lose someone as talented as Mike. It would throw off the chemistry of the group. They would have to find someone who felt the music the same way each you them did..."

But I have. She is incredible. She's intelligent...she's beautiful...she's, she's inches away from me. Why can't I even move...OK, all I need to do is slide my hand off my mug, to the table, and over to hers. Where's that little voice when you need it? At least then I had an excuse, now I don't even have that.

Chapter 14

"So," Jerry's voice fades back in, "I'll be there next week. Maybe, Billie will sit in for me."

My left hand has slid off my glass, and I freeze. "What?" I ask. "Didn't I just say that one stint of public stardom is enough for one decade?" I grab the sides of the table and readjust myself in the chair. My hand is closer, but not close enough.

"Great! Thanks a lot pal," Joe comments. "When were you going to tell us? And speaking of breaking traditions, who have you been hanging around with lately?"

"This is a great opportunity, Joe," Jerry replies. "We've both talked about playing professionally and jamming for a bigger audience. This is a great group. They're doing well, really well."

"Yeah, we've talked about jamming all the time," Joe says, "but we were going to do it as a group. You, me, Kirk, and then add one or two more. What happened to that?"

I look down at the table and notice that my slightly trembling hand is up against Melody's. I lift it slightly…

"I have an audition in New York too," Melody blurts out.

My hand falls the short distance it has risen, my eyes widen, and a frown forms on my face. Joe and Jerry have stopped arguing and all eyes are on Melody.

"That's good," Cindy chimes in. "Who's it with?"

Silence.

I manage to move my head and look at Melody's face. She licks her lips and says, "I'll spare you all the details, but it's with one of the larger orchestras there. I had a call on my answering machine after we got in yesterday, I mean this morning."

"Wow, that's great," Frank comments. His eyes meet mine, and he adds, "Isn't it great, Bill?"

"Yes, it is," I say smiling and faking my sincerity. I move my chair back a little and my hands return to the mug. "That's so great. When is it?"

"Um, well," Melody says, "it is next week, too."

"Wow," I comment. "That is exciting. What are you going to play? Maybe, Frank can help you pick something. And, Jeff, he knows some people in New York. Do you need a hotel room?"

"I'll be fine," Melody replies. "I picked out the pieces this morning and called a couple of friends who live in New York. I will probably stay with one of them."

"Well, if you need anything, I'm sure we could arrange something," I say trying to add excitement to my voice.

"Yeah, if you need a room," Jeff jumps in, "I could probably get you an airline rate somewhere."

I can't believe I am trying to be excited about this. I can't believe I am trying to be excited about my inspiration leaving for any amount of time. What if she does well? Why wouldn't she do well? Why am I not thinking well here? This would be great for her. It is what she wants, isn't it?

"When are you going?" Jerry asks. "I'm heading out on Thursday."

"They want me to be there by Thursday night," Melody responds. "But, we were…"

"Nonsense," I say recalling we were going to go horseback riding on Thursday evening. "You can not let an opportunity like this pass or even wait."

Chapter 14

"Let me know what flight you'll be on," Jerry responds. "Nicole wouldn't mind if you joined us. She's going to drop me off about noon or so."

"That would be nice," Melody says. "I'll find out details over the next couple of days. Thank you."

"Maybe Bill wants to bring her," Joe comments.

"Well, actually," I say hesitating somewhat, "I have school and the students are brutal with substitutes."

"I could sit in on your afternoon classes if you really want to…" Frank begins a thought.

"That's nice of you to offer, but we're in the middle of my lesson plans, and I have papers to return and discuss. Besides, we'll spend time together Wednesday," I respond.

"Actually," Melody says, "with practice and reorganizing my schedule for the week after that…"

"So you'll be gone for a week?" I inquire, turning to face her completely.

"Nine days," Melody responds. "I think it's going to be nine days. That's if I make it all the way through."

"And, why wouldn't you," Cindy comments.

"Yeah, Bill has always told us how amazing you are," Kirk comments.

I look at Kirk and shake my head.

"What?!" Kirk exclaims. "You do. I have never seen you…" he pauses and looks around the table. "OK, then I'll just go get us another round."

"Well," Jerry pipes up, "we've rested long enough. Let's get back up there. Besides, we'll have to play a little longer to make up for the drinks this week."

264

Alone With Someone

Joe and Jerry rise and head toward the stage. Frank stands up and whispers in Cindy's ear before moving to the stage himself. Kirk puts down the tray he just picked up and joins the others.

I look at Melody and try to say something, anything before the music begins.

Silence again.

"We can go when I get back," Melody whispers, her face toward the stage, a soft smile on her face, and her hand next to mine on the table.

If I reach over, right now, will she let my hand stay? Will the warmth accompany the softness? If she doesn't, if it isn't, the walls that have deteriorated so slowly over these last few months, will surely grow so much quicker, so much stronger. That's something I'm not willing to risk at this point. I have been able to feel so much. I have been so inspired. If I tell her what I am thinking right now, not only may I lose the inspiration, I may also lose someone who has become one of, if not my best friend. I should just smile and stay as close as possible, but avoid prolonged contact. If I get too close now, she might be able to sense my hesitation, my fear.

Some of the warmth between us creeps back in, though it feels slightly different. How long can I go without that feeling?

The melodies emanating in front of us meld.

Chapter 15

So, here we…I mean, I, am again. Sitting here as we…I have done so many times before. You know, so many people wouldn't think twice about this. It would be just a normal part of their lives. For me, however, this is brutal. I have grown used to the routines in my life and when something or someone enhances that routine, I appreciate the entire event even more.

I look at the mug in front of me and watch as my fingers run across the top of it. Where is everyone? I pick up my head and look around. Many familiar faces surround me, but none of which have helped make this more than just a bar; none of which have made this a place where my closest friends gather regularly to relax and unwind; and none of these faces make me feel at home.

Jerry, of course, has flown to New York. Joe decided to finally ask out his producer and may show up later. Mark had some medical convention in Florida. Steve, well Steve thought it necessary to find his ancestral roots or something and took off for Europe, though I am not too sure where exactly. Even Frank, who usually walks here with me, even he made other plans…he and Cindy are going to see a movie, a movie for god's sake! And, Kirk, the owner of this clean-well lit place, is at his house, relaxing…relaxing!?! Who else? Who else has deserted me when my strongest inspiration is challenged, questioned, lessened.

I lift my mug, take a sip of the frothy substance, and sink down in my chair, resting the glass between my chest and stomach.

"Well, there's Jeff," a distance voice sounds.

Yeah, there's Jeff. He'll be here. He wouldn't let me sit here alone, listening to this lifeless music over these poor tinny speakers. Jeff will be here.

I pick up my head slightly and look toward the door.

"Nothing," the inner echo chimes.

Chapter 15

Great! Not only am I sitting here drinking alone, listening to bad music, missing her, but I'm hear voices again. I thought I only had these problems when I am immediately inspired. Where were you last week when I needed to express the rush of emotions, the fluster of my heart, the swirls in my mind after one of, if not the best night of my life? Where was my conscious when I needed it?

"I was here," the inner voice responds. "You chose to ignore me."

I frown and change positions in my chair. I move my beverage to the table again and hunch toward it, staring blankly ahead at the empty stage.

"You are inspired one way or another every day," my little voice continues. "Sometimes it's a happy and energetic inspiration like when you think about those big beautiful eyes…"

Ah, yes, the mirrors of my soul. The corners of my mouth move slightly upward at the mere thought of those glistening panes. A sense of warmth encompasses me and I sigh.

"Sometimes, however, it is depressing and discouraging, like right now. And, sometimes, you just choose to ignore everything in between because it is not as extreme as you would like it."

I sit up in my chair and take a drink. I'm not an extremist. I deal very well with regular, everyday things.

"Yes, you do," my inner self comments. "You actually like your routines. When was the last time you wrote something about your daily events? When was the last time you wrote something, anything about teaching?"

I need to think about this one. I must have written something. Oh, yeah, I wrote that one piece…what was it…'Stop Wasting Time, Teach."

"And, that was when?" I question myself.

When I was student-teaching. Yes, when I was student-teaching.

"And, you thought you could change the world then," my inner reasoning responds. "You were tired of all the things you were told you couldn't do when teaching and decided you would do it any way."

Yes I did. Many things didn't work exactly the way I thought, or rather hoped they would, but the students respected me for trying…I think.

"You were inspired then," the little voice points out.

But, I am very passionate about education and providing students with opportunities to learn. Why haven't I written anything major about this since my student-teaching?

"Just as external beauty is not the sole means of inspiration, passion is not the only source needed to maintain an inspiration. You need courage and a sense that any emotions you experience will be shared, otherwise it all fades."

But what about the depressing stuff I write? It's some of my better ramblings.

"While depression may be considered a lonely emotion, it actually feeds on what makes you most comfortable. Those daily routines become drudgeries. The friends you turn to in the hopes of snapping you out of that mood, actually add to it with condolences on your loss or by repeating old stories which have gone from fond memories to boring repetitions."

But, I want to maintain my inspiration. She is amazing. She makes me happy.

"That's the funny thing about inspirations," my inner voice responds. "You can control the passion and most of the time, the courage, but you can't control the emotions you receive. It's only when the other person feels as inspired by you as you are by her, can reality truly take root."

I nod my head and think about all of the socializing I have done since high school. All of the inspirations have stopped when either I lost contact with the person or when I got the speech…the speech that makes men shudder…the speech that says you are the kindest, gentlest, sweetest person…or translated, you are a nice guy and a good 'friend.' Ah, yes, the dreaded "f" word. That's it. That's when the inspiration either drops right off or begins to fade. The emotions are not shared, the passion can not compensate for it, and the courage simply dissipates.

"Has she returned your emotions?" my little voice asks.

Of course she has. We've done so much together. We've shared so much. She makes me happy.

"But has she really returned your emotions?" the inner being interjects.

Well…I guess so. I have shared, well I have been, um, well I have been happy.

"Happiness is more of a state of mind than an emotion. Either you are happy or you are not. Do you like her? Do you love her? What do you feel about her?"

She knows what I am thinking as I think it. She completes my sentences. She excites me, entices me, enthralls me. She makes me feel…well, she just makes me feel. I can not say exactly what I feel, but for the first time, I can truly say that I feel.

"Sometimes, however," my inner reflection comments, "sometimes, just feeling is not enough. Have you told her about anything you are feeling?"

She knows how I feel…doesn't she? Of course she does. She knows so much of what I think.

"That's just it. She may know what you think and even think the same way, but how can she know what you feel when you can't express it entirely yourself? Do you think she knew what you were feeling when the guys mentioned Samantha?"

Alone With Someone

What? What does Samantha have to do with how I feel about her. Besides, I didn't really feel anything, except maybe concerned about what she was thinking.
"Did she know that?" the little inquisitor questions. "She was going to New York right after you mentioned that. What do you feel about her." Well, um, well, we hug, we hold hands…she even kissed me.

"But, who did she kiss? The poet? The comedian? Or you? Which one is you?" I ask myself. "And, whom did you kiss? A gorgeous young lady? An inspiration? Or someone who's name you have not spoken or thought of this entire evening? Did you kiss Melody because she is Melody, or because of what she represents to you?"

Well I, I never really thought of whom I was kissing. In fact, I stopped wondering why she kissed me. I guess it didn't seem to matter after a while. We get along so well. We do so many things together.

"And, what do you feel?" my inner consultant reiterates. "Write it down right now. Take out a piece of paper and write down what you are feeling right now. Don't write that she has helped you feel, write about how you feel even without her here."

I take a sip of my root beer and hesitate at my own thoughts. There is noone here. I might as well write. I reach down and open my backpack, pulling out two blank pieces of paper. I put my hand into my pants pocket and pull out my pen. I twirl the writing utensil with my fingers and look at the white slates on the table.

Think…think…

"Feel," the little voice corrects.

Chapter 15

I can feel the warmth radiating through my being,
As I ask if I am only dreaming.
These sensations are found in one source,
Bringing about joy and never remorse.
When one has lived in sadness for so long,
Only joy can follow to make one strong.
Simple, yet corrupt, is everyday life
As we attempt to deal with even the smallest strife.
Eventually, the time may come
When we truly feel the beat of the same drum.
As I reflect, I can see
Just what my manifestation means to me.
I make no promises here, except those which lie above
My soft heart and dare I say it, love.

I pause and look back at the last word, thinking of scratching it out. However, a rush of acceptance hits me and it stays. I scribble "My Happiness" at the top of the paper and scan all the words. I smile and nod, not only in agreement to the message of the piece, but also in agreement to my inner self.

"You're at that again, huh?" a familiar voice behind me comments. "Isn't Melody in New York?"

"What? Huh?" I ask, turning my head from left to right, finally seeing Jeff as he sits down and holds up three fingers toward the bar.

"Is it just you?" Jeff asks. "What do you have there?"

I look down at the poem I just wrote, scan the words yet again, smile, then fold it in half. "Nothing, just some ramblings." I say moving it toward my backpack on the floor.

"When did I lose my reading privileges?" Jeff comments. "What are you writing about? You probably haven't seen her in days."

"It's just some feelings." I respond, my eyes widening. "Besides, I don't actually have to see her to be inspired."

"You know," Jeff says, taking a swig of the beer which has mysteriously appeared before him. "Sometimes, you worry me when you write. You become a different person."

"What do you mean, different?" I ask and polish off the remainder of my beverage.

"Well," Jeff starts, "for example, your jokes are different. They aren't really funny. No really, you are more agreeable. You don't seem to care much about anything else. And, and, this is the part that scares me, you become somewhat sensitive to everyone's feelings. I'm not just talking about you're friends' feelings. You defend everyone. Like when we mentioned what a babe that new math teacher is."

"Wow," I respond. "When did you notice this? Besides, I just thought you wanted to know Samantha's name."

"Yeah, sure, OK. But, you've done it in the past," Jeff replies. "It's just worse this time. You really like her, don't you? I mean you should. Melody seems very nice. You two complement each other well."

"Wow," I reiterate. "What brought this on? I mean, thank you. Aren't you the one who says something only if I am acting like a complete idiot, or I'm just not understanding something?

"Bill," Jeff says, "you seem so happy when you're with her, but you also hesitate when it comes to showing her how you feel."

"I've shown her how I feel," I respond, recalling the recent conversation with myself. "I've even broken my own rules and held her hand before she offered it to me. I've been very emotional…haven't I?"

"Bill, you hesitate way too much with Melody," Jeff comments. "Holding her hand? Holding her hand? Bill! Melody is incredibly beautiful, if you don't let those emotions out of your little world, she'll either give up or find someone else."

"See, he gets it," my inner voice says.

Chapter 15

"What are you saying?" I question somewhat confused by both Jeff and my own thoughts. "What brought this on. I mean, I've been sitting here, by myself, then you just come in here and tell me what a fool I am being."

"Stop," Jeff says sarcastically, trying to lighten the mood. "I just think you have something unique with Melody and I would hate to see you lose it. Relationships are so different today."

"Different from when?" I ask. "We're not that old."

"Well," Jeff begins, "romance may have been important in the beginning of relationships even up to when our parents were married. Now, however, if you don't make more of an impact initially, the romantic stuff may not mean very much."

"People are in such a hurry these days," my little voice agrees. "Very few people even know what romance is."

"Well, I, a," I stumble. "I hear what you are saying, but I think Melody and I are OK." I reach into my bag and pull out the poem I just wrote. "Here, read this. I'll give it to her when she gets back."

Jeff takes the folded paper and reads it as he sips his beer.

Is everything OK, really? What is he thinking? Which part is he reading right now? I do really care about her.

"She has a name," my inner voice points out again. "Remember, passion, courage, and sharing emotions."

I stare past Jeff and nod my head, not necessarily knowing the reason why.

"Well," Jeff says, putting the paper on the table, "it's pretty good."

"Pretty good?" I say. "I know it's just a first draft, but does it say anything?"

"I think it does," Jeff comments. "But…"

"You think it does? But what?"

"But, why don't you just tell her what you feel?" Jeff says.

"The poem does that," I respond.

"Why don't you just tell her?"

"What's wrong with the poem?" I ask somewhat concerned now.

"There is nothing wrong with the poem itself," Jeff replies. "But, if you care about her that much, tell her. She needs to hear that you care."

"Then I will read it to her," I say and giggle a little.

"Seriously," Jeff interjects. "Unless you tell her and show her, she may continue to wonder with whom she is spending her time. Is it this romantic poet who can only communicate in writing? And, if so, does he really believe what he is writing? Or is it an insecure wimp who doesn't know what he wants?"

"Are you calling me a wimp now?" I say sarcastically. "I know, I know. I had a similar conversation with myself before you got here about how to maintain the inspiration."

"She's a woman, Bill!" Jeff exclaims. "You are going to have to make up your mind. Either you tell her you care about her, or you try to maintain your precious inspiration. Each one come with a risk, but you are the one who must make the decision."

"Why can't I do both?" I question. "If she is the one, she will inspire me all the time."

"And, you can," Jeff responds, "but you may never know if she is the one if you don't get there. And, why do you need to know that now?"

Chapter 15

"I guess I don't," I say. "But, what if I lose my inspiration, what if she doesn't feel the same?"

"Then, you find out what you're missing and move on from there. You've seen the rest of us either push too hard with girls or not push at all."

"I know that's why I have hesitated so much with Melody. I've seen Jerry marry his high school sweetheart; Kirk click with Crystol after one date; Joe, Steve, and you come in with so many different girls; and I've seen Mark's career take precedence over dating. I envy all of you, but am still not sure how to express what I feel. And, how do I know when I'm actually feeling it?"

"What have you got to lose?" Jeff asks. "Hell, even Mark has gone out with a couple of female doctors and a few nurses recently."

"You're kidding, Mark?" I say smirking. "That little…why didn't he say anything?"

"Whoops, that's not important," Jeff says as if he wasn't supposed to tell me. "You know what I mean. I'm just tired of you not appreciating what you have. You know what you need to do. Just go ahead and do it. Don't be stupid!"

"How about I just," I begin.

"Just tell her," Jeff interrupts. "No gifts, no flowers, no poems, just tell her."

"When did you become so insightful?" I ask. "Thank you though. I just need to make sure. What if…what if…"

"Whatever," Jeff says chugging the remainder of his drink and waving one finger toward the bar.

I half smile, half frown. Jeff would never go there if he didn't really believe what he was saying. In fact, he's the one mainstay my confused and debateful conscious has relied on since high school.

Alone With Someone

"Hey there," another voice says in front of us.

I look up and see Joe standing next to a young woman with blonde hair.

"Hey, what are you two talking about? It seems too serious for this place," Joe says as he pulls out a chair for the young lady.

"Women," Jeff responds laughing and nodding at Joe's companion.

"Oh yeah, sorry. This is Tonya, my new producer," Joe comments and sits down himself. He motions for two drinks. "It looks pretty dead in here tonight. How long have you two been here?"

"Too long," I reply. "So, where did you go for dinner?"

"We sort of skipped dinner," Tonya responds grinning.

"You don't have to follow all of their examples," my little voice comments.

Jeff and I smile, shaking our heads. I guess she's not shy.

"How about that?" Jeff whispers to me.

"What?" Joe asks.

"Nothing," I say chuckling.

"So, when is Melody coming back?" Joe asks, changing the subject somewhat.

"Not soon enough," I comment, raise my freshly filled mug and wait.

Chapter 16

"So, tell me again why I have my eyes closed," a soft familiar voice pierces my dreaming happiness.

"She speaks," I exclaim. The laughter of small children surrounds us. "You've been rather quiet all the way here."

"We are supposed to be horseback riding. I've been looking forward to this since I had to cancel out original date."

"She said date," my little voice comments.

"Well," I respond, "since you changed our original date time, I decided to change our original date place."

"So where are we?" Melody asks.

"Yes, where are you two?" my inner voice questions something other than our location.

I notice her eyes start to flutter as if trying to open, but staying closed just enough not to really see anything other than flashes of light. A little girl races past us, and I see Melody smile.

"Hey now, no fair peeking. We're almost there."

"Where?"

"Watch out for that log...step up...OK, we're here. You can open your eyes now."

I want to see her face when she realizes how ridiculous this adventure is. I want to hear her comments as she connects what she has heard to what is bounding, bouncing, and beaming in front of her.

Nothing. Then a grin forms on her face and widens. With each burst of laughter, with each sway of the swings, with each slide on the metal chutes, Melody's smile becomes bigger. Her eyes expand and the ingrained sparkle twinkles brighter. A small giggle escapes from her supple lips. She squeezes my hand tighter and shakes her head.

"This is your inspiration," my inner voice comments. "Moments like these make those routines of yours all worth while."

"Yes," I say out loud.

"Yes, what?" Melody asks still shaking her head.

"Sorry, another conversation," I respond. "So, would you care for the slide or the swings first me lady."

"Bill, you are too much," Melody responds. "What happened to the horses? What happened to the river?"

"Well," I say, pointing around the playground, "the horses are right over there. See those metal things bobbing up and down. And, let's see…oh yes, the river is right there next to the sandbox. Or is that just a puddle from the rain yesterday? Oh well, it's water, right."

"You come here often, don't you?" Melody questions giggling.

"Well, if you must know," I comment and start to laugh myself.

We look around, but my true focus is on Melody. She is still smiling.

"Actually," I say breaking the moment of silence, "since you were gone last week and most of the guys were doing other things, I needed somewhere to spend my time. I didn't want to sit at home alone and be depressed. I wanted to find a place where everyone was happy. I ran across this park the weekend you left. I've played on the swings and even went down the slide a few times, but most of the time, I've just watched."

"You know," Melody begins, "people would worry about you, sitting out here by yourself watching children play."

Alone With Someone

"You just need to stop," I say whimsically and nudge her.

"What's gotten into you?" Melody says and stares at me as if I'm possessed. "I wasn't away for that long."

"Last week," I respond, "last week, I really had to find things that made me happy. Even when I did, it wasn't enough. It just didn't seem right. Being happy didn't mean I was feeling anything. In fact, the only feelings I had were because I was missing you." I pause and look at Melody.

"Um," I continue, "did I just…well, never mind. I am babbling again, don't mind me. Babbling, that's what I seem to do when I'm happy. Or at least when I want others to think I'm happy. And, right here, at this park, right now, with you, I am happy. So, your trip was good, huh?"

"You're scaring me now," Melody says laughing. "In fact, you're driving me crazy. How much caffeine did you have while I was away? Did you start eating chocolate again?"

"You really need to slow down," my little voice warns. "Or you're going to blow it."

"I'm sorry," I say, "I just well, I just feel that…How about going on the swings?" I motion forward.

"You feel what?" Melody questions.

"Nothing, sorry. How about them swings? Look there is no one over there."

"You're killing the mood," my conscious warns. "Slow down and tell her how you feel."

I think I'm showing her how I feel. Besides, I'm sure she can feel my heart racing through our hands. I am holding rather tightly.

"OK," Melody replies moving forward, "but you have to stop starting sentences and not finishing them. Otherwise, I won't let you come back here and play with the other children."

My smile widens temporarily, and we move toward the swings.

"Would you prefer this one or this one?" I ask bowing and gesturing to the two seats in front of us.

"I'll take this one," Melody responds and sits down.

"Excellent choice," I respond and place myself in the one right beside her.

"So, really," I say, "how was your trip? We haven't really talked about it since you came back. You've been much quieter than usual."

"You made me keep my eyes closed all the way from the house," Melody responds. "And, I'm afraid of the dark, remember."

"I'm the one who's afraid of the dark," I comment and sway toward her, bumping her slightly.

"Bill, I can't imagine you being afraid of anything," Melody says and begins to swing a little higher. "I haven't been on one of these in years."

"She's changing the subject," my little voice interjects. "Besides, if she knew you as well as you think she does, she would know that you are petrified right now. You always ramble when you're…"

"These are the things that make life more interesting," I say raising my voice slightly and trying to keep up with her. "You just need to let that child out sometimes and allow it to explore, or play on the swings. Most of my goals and dreams come from that little kid."

Melody slows down a little and says, "I thought your little voice helped you with that?"
"Why do you think it is called a 'little' voice?"

"Great, now you both are making fun of a non-existent being," the topic itself retorts.
I laugh and slow down even more.

"So, how do you know?" Melody inquires and just about stops her swing.

"What?" I ask not quite sure of the exact question let alone the answer.

"How do you know when to follow your inner child, little voice, whatever, and when your adult responsibilities need to take precedence?"

I stop my swing completely and stare at Melody who is biting her lower lip and staring blankly ahead. "What brought this on?" I ask.

"Nothing. I was just wondering," Melody replies and resumes her previous motions.

"Not only is she changing the subject," the inner voice comments, "but she is avoiding something."

"The child," I say catching up to her movements.

"What?" Melody questions looking toward me.

"The child," I reiterate. "Dreaming comes from that child. You should listen to what he, I mean she, has to say."

"But what about…" Melody starts.

"About money, making your parents happy, and responsibilities," I finish the thought and slow down my pace again. "If you are doing something you enjoy, the money will be a result of that. If your parents supported you through those wonderful high school years, no matter how good or bad you were, you will never be a disappoint to them. They've seen the wonders of growing pains and the ups and downs of hormones. For the most part, they've been there and have already made some of those same decisions themselves. If you are following a dream, the responsibility of fulfilling that dream will be with you until you actually do it."

Chapter 16

I pause and look at Melody. She is staring blankly forward again; her swing has just about stopped; and her feet shuffle in the gravel beneath us.

"That child has gotten us this far," I continue, "why can't we go a little further with it."

"But," Melody pipes up, "but, children are always moving, always growing, always looking for different things. They never seem to be content. My mother always talked about when I grew up…if I never grow up, when will I know I've made the right decisions? When will I be content with what I have and with what I've done?"

"I tell my students that when we stop learning, we stop growing," I say moving toward Melody's swing. "When you stop growing, you become complacent. I don't think you could ever be complacent."

"But why?" Melody responds. "I don't always take risks. In fact, I'm rather safe in my decisions. I gravitate toward things I do well. Even with my music, I know what instruments and songs I play well and stick with them."

"You went to New York, didn't you?" I say contemplating holding her hand. "You went to prom with me and ate that somewhat semblance of food. That was a risk right there. And, you do something I can only do in the classroom, perform before a large group of people."

"But, how do I know whether it was a good decision or not?" Melody asks, looking directly at me and waiting for a response.

A small amount of hesitation cascades over me as I peer into her inquisitive eyes.

"Well," I say clearing my throat and wondering myself. "I guess you can't answer that unless you make the decision. Since you would have decided on something, it has to be good, because you are amazing." I reach to hold her hand.

Alone With Someone

"Hi, Bill," a tiny voice interrupts my thoughts and movements.

I push the swing slightly away from Melody and see a little girl with light brown hair in pigtails standing before us.

"Oh hi there, Tiffany," I say, the pitch of my voice elevating slightly. "Would you like to go on the swings?"

"Yes, please," Tiffany responds and moves closer to me.

I rise from my seat and help Tiffany up into it. She scoots back a little, turns her head to the right, and tugs on my arm, which is resting on the chains. "Do you know that girl?" Tiffany asks and points toward Melody.

"I can't believe you," my inner voice comments. "You just told her she is amazing, then proceed to ignore her for a little girl."

I lean down and say, "Her name is Melody. She is my best friend…besides you of course."
Melody moves her swing over to Tiffany's and says, "Hi Tiffany. How old are you?"
"I'm four years old," Tiffany responds. "Are you Bill's girlfriend? My mommy was wondering if Bill had a girlfriend."

Melody's eyes widen and the look of surprise she had when Tiffany first approached us has turned into one of amazement. Melody laughs and looks at me, shaking her head. "Well, he is my best friend. Maybe you could be my new best friend, since Bill seems to prefer younger women."

"My mommy said he didn't have a girlfriend," Tiffany says. "My mommy is the same age as…"

"So where is your mommy, Tiff?" I inquire cutting off her last words. My face is extremely red and my embarrassment level is incredibly high. I can't look at either Melody or Tiffany. Instead, I gaze around the playground.

"She's not here," Tiffany responds.

Chapter 16

"Thank goodness," my little voice comments.

"She's picking me up later," Tiffany continues.

"How did you get here?" Melody questions, slightly concerned.

"Suzie's mom," Tiffany says and points to the monkey bars. "She says you don't have a girlfriend either."

"Great!" my little voice exclaims. "Everyone thinks you are a crazy single guy preying on the mothers of the children you play with at the park."

I wave toward the monkey bars in order to acknowledge Suzie and her mother. "Well," I say "how about if I push you and Melody for a little while?" I pull the chains of Tiffany's swing and let them go. "How's that?"

"Higher," Tiffany responds giggling and kicking her feet.

I give her a little push and then another. I look at Melody and smile. She has a look I've never seen on her before. If she were any other woman, I would say she looks jealous, but she isn't any other woman, she's Melody. And, what would she be jealous of, Tiffany?"

"Can I push her now?" I ask Tiffany, pointing toward Melody.

Tiffany shakes her head 'yes' as I give her one last push. I move behind Melody and place my hands on the middle of her back. Leaning toward her right ear, I whisper, "She's a cute kid, huh?"

Melody shakes her head and a single brief semblance of a laugh makes its way back toward me.

"That said, yeah, right," my little voice comments. "She's thinking about something."
"I thought you like kids," I respond giving her a small push.

"I do, and yes, she is very cute," Melody responds sitting rather still on her swing.

"Now me, now me," Tiffany beckons, kicking her feet aimlessly.

"Hold that thought," I say to Melody and move back to Tiffany.

"High! High!" Tiffany exclaims. "Push me high!"

I give her a small push and energetically say, "Do you want an underdog?"

"Yes! High!" Tiffany shouts.

"Ready, here we go," I say moving back and forth with the swing. I grab the chains where they meet the seat, and pull backwards. I rush forward veering to the right slightly, careful not to push her too high. I stumble forward intentionally and fall a few feet in front of Melody's swing, looking only at the ground.

I hear giggling and pick up my head. Melody is moving her head from side-to-side as if not sure what to think. She continues to move back and forth, maintaining her motion.
"Are you two laughing at me?" I say hopping to my feet. "You are laughing at me. I think you need a push too, my friend," I add pointing at Melody.

"You're killing me," Melody says watching me move behind her. "Bill, not too high. Bill!"

"How high should she go Tiffany?" I ask as I give her a few more pushes with my left hand.

"High! Very high!" Tiffany exclaims.

"Bill!" Melody shouts, still laughing. "You're having too much fun with this."

Chapter 16

"Hey," I comment, "this is the only way I will be able to push you around."

"You are definitely enjoying this too much," Melody says turning her head toward me.

"Ready, here we go," I say just before Melody's swing moves away from me. I rush forward, using just enough strength to get underneath. My surge carries me a little further this time, but I perform the same stumbling routine, plopping down on the cushioned grass, facing the swings again.

"Again, again," I hear Tiffany shout, but see and feel only Melody's happiness.
"Tell her," my inner voice whispers.

"Pushing young girls, Bill?" another female voice disrupts me from behind as I attempt to stand.

I turn away from the swings toward the voice. There in a white blouse, red skirt, and jacket to match, stands Kelly, Tiffany's mother. Her sky blue eyes are somewhat magnified by the thin glasses resting on her pert little nose.

"You really have a problem," my inner voice exclaims.

"Kelly, how are you?" I say bowing slightly. "Tiffany said she was here with Suzie and her mom."

"They brought her here," Kelly responds looking toward the swings. "I just came to pick her up."

"Melody!" my little voice screams.

"Oh yeah, sorry," I say trying to cover up my embarrassment and error, "this is Melody, one of the most amazing, talented, and beautiful young ladies I can honestly say I associate with."

"Well, it got Kelly thinking," my conscious responds, "but I'm not sure about Melody. You probably should have looked at her."

I turn quickly toward Melody and see her dragging her feet in the gravel in order to slow down her swing. She slowly comes to a stop and rises from the swing. We all move toward each other.

"Nice to meet you…Kelly was it," Melody says extending her hand.

"Yes, same here," Kelly responds accepting Melody's gesture.

"Mommy! Mommy!" Tiffany shouts excitedly. "Bill gave us puppies!"
"Um, underdogs," I mumble.

"Yes, I saw," Kelly replies smiling and shifting her gaze between Melody and me.

I am not sure why, but it has just gotten warmer out here. I am not sure of what to say.

"Tiffany," Kelly calls, "we should be going home for dinner now."

"But mom," Tiffany whines, "I want to play some more."

"You've been playing with Suzie all day," Kelly responds. "It's time to go home."

"How long have they been here?" my inner voice questions.

"It was good to see you again, Bill. Thanks for playing with Tiffany," Kelly says, lifting Tiffany from the swing. "It was nice meeting you too," she adds looking at Melody.

"Can Bill come home for dinner?" Tiffany asks innocently.

"Um, I, well," I stammer.

Chapter 16

"I think Bill is going to play some more with his other friend," Kelly responds.

"Thank you," I say and move toward Melody. "We're headed to the slide next."

"Oh, OK, bye," Tiffany says softly and turns to leave with her mother. She seems somewhat disappointed.

"Bye," I reply, waving a couple of times. I turn to Melody and say, "She is a..."
"Cute kid," Melody finishes.

"Yes, she is," I add and look at Melody's face.

"She has something to say," my inner voice says.

I am not sure how to ask, but blurt out, "What's wrong?"

"Nothing," she replies as we walk toward the slide.

"Melody, I know when you have something to say," I add. "What is it?"

"Nothing really. I'm just tired," she responds.

"Now, you know she is not tired," the little voice comments.

I do not want to push it. I need to say what I planned on saying.

"Are you too tired to take a few trips down the slide?" I ask.

"Well..." Melody responds.

"Good, let's go!" I exclaim, taking her hand and leading her up the steps. I follow immediately behind her.

She reaches the top and starts to sit down. "Wait!" I shout startling her a little. "Look around," I say.

"Why?" Melody asks, a small smile forming on her face.

"Just look, please," I say, my eyes widening.

Melody scans the land below and says, "Bill, I…"

"Didn't you ever do this when you were younger?" I ask cutting off her thought. "You felt so tall, so far away from everything, so excited, not only about where you were, but what you were going to do next."

"Bill, I…"

"OK, you can sit down now," I indicate.

Melody smiles, shakes her head, and lowers herself onto the metal chute. "Just don't push me," she says looking back at me.

"Oh, you're no fun," I comment and look away briefly.

Melody pushes herself from the top and slides down.

"She still seems distant," my inner voice says.

I follow the same ritual Melody had just moments ago. Stand up, look around, smile, sit, and slide. I hit the ground and bounce once on the balls of my feet.

"I'm sorry. I'm being so childish," I say looking at Melody and reaching out to take her hands. "I just need to share some things with you, and wanted to make sure we weren't interrupted too much, and we had some fun."

I look at her for a response, but see nothing significant. She is looking right at me and waiting.

"I know we've talked about inspiration before, but I just wanted to show you another element of it," I say and take a deep breath. "For the past six months, I have felt so alive, so young, so inspired, and I attribute it to

291

one source. I have never felt so much and yet not be able to truly explain what it is that I am feeling. At times, it has worried me, even frightened me, but I felt so comfortable with the source it didn't matter. Like the swings, I have gone back and forth with many of my feelings, and like the slide, there have been a few ups and downs, but we still manage to land on our feet. I've just been so happy since I met you. We have grown so much together. I, well, I, um…"

"Bill, I'm going to New York…"

"I love you," I finish my thoughts.

Silence.

"Did you just…" we say simultaneously.

"You have got to be kidding!" my inner voice exclaims, just now catching what Melody said.

I can't look at her, I can't say anything. I just can't…can't believe…

"Bill," her voice cuts through my disbelief. "I didn't think…"

"So, your audition went well then, huh," I say trying not to think about what she just said, what I just said.

"Bill, this, this is my dream," Melody comments. "Ever since I can remember, I wanted to do this."

"What?" I ask, still confused. "What have you wanted to do? I just, a, um, I'm not too sure."

"There are just so many opportunities," Melody responds. "My music has been everything for me. My music has been my lone solace, my one consistent happiness, my constant inspiration."

"Great! Now, she's got an inspiration. Where did this come from?" my little voice comments sarcastically.

Alone With Someone

"Melody, I..." I begin to say and pause.

"My music has always been there for me...that is until I met you," Melody continues. "We have done things I have never done with any of my friends let alone any of the boys I have dated. Just coming here today, helped me realize how special our relationship has become."

"And, she's going to New York!" my inner voice rips.

"Everything we've done, everything we've talked about, every poem you have given me," Melody says, her voice elevating slightly with each example. "Everything, Bill, has been amazing."

"But, you're going to New York," I say out loud this time and stare directly at her.

"There are times," Melody continues, "that I can't believe I have a friend like you. You always make me laugh; you talk to me when I need to hear someone else's voice; you listen when I need to vent or just babble; and you put me on a pedestal. I don't have to do anything extraordinary when I am with you. I can always be myself. You make me feel like a member of your family, especially around your buddies."

"Did she say friend?" my inner voice questions. "I'm pretty sure she said it. How many sleepless nights have you had for this? She's going to New York!"

"I thought about talking this through with you," Melody says, "but after today, after everything we did and talked about, the light went on, the little voice shouted out the decision. I thought you would understand."

"Why after today?" I ask. "I'm not sure what we talked about or could have done..."

"You said that if I made a decision, it had to be good, and I should listen to what the child in me has to say. Well, the child said it loved music. And, when I saw you with Tiffany, it just hit me."

Chapter 16

"I'm sorry," I say. "I'm still not sure what helped you decide."

"It was Kelly," my little voice says, mocking me. "Melody thinks you…"

"You were wonderful with her," Melody says. "It made me think about so many things, but most of all, it made me think about what has gotten me through life so far."

"And, that's your music," I say softly as if finally understanding something.

"Yes," Melody responds. "And, when Tiffany's mother came to pick her up…"

"See, it was Kelly," my inner voice pushes.

"…It made me think about responsibilities and how many I would be fulfilling in New York. It made me feel uncomfortable initially, but…"

"Good, there's a 'but.' Thank goodness for 'buts,'" my inner voice comments.

"So," I interrupt, "how long are you going to be gone? A few weeks, months, a season?"

"Well," Melody replies, "I would actually have a solid career there."

"Career?" I say. "That sounds like an adult response not a child response."

"Bill, I thought you would be happy for me," Melody replies.

Happy? The poem I wrote at Kirk's flashes through my mind, and I remember that I left it at her apartment yesterday. She must have read it by now.

"I am excited for you," I say, "but I can't say I'm all too happy right now."

"Bill, you've been my teacher, my confidant, and my best friend," Melody says, taking my hand. "I see you doing the things you love, teaching, writing, just being yourself, and I know I can do the things I love to do as well."

Didn't I say, I love you? Didn't I say I cared? I want to ask her these things, but can only say, "But…never mind."

"You're just going to let her leave?" my inner voice retorts.

What can I say? What can I do? She's made a decision. I can't change her mind for her. Besides, we already went to prom, what is there for her to stay around for, if she can be happy…

"You could ask her to m…"

"So," I say breaking up my own thoughts, "you'll be here for a while yet, right?"

"Actually," Melody replies, "the next season starts soon and I need to find an apartment, get settled, and just take care of many other odds and ends. I'll be helping Frank with the last school concert next week and probably leave after that. I should be at your school everyday until the performance, tutoring and stuff. We could have lunch together."

"She's going to torture you now," the inner voice says.

"Wow, I, a," I stutter, but nothing else comes out.

"Please, tell me it will be OK," Melody says. "If you say it, somehow I know I made a good decision."

"She didn't even think of your feelings when she made this decision," my inner voice says. "Did she care about your feelings?"

Then again, did I really know I had feelings until recently.

"Say something!" my inner voice echoes.

Chapter 16

"You'll be fine," I find myself saying as my head lowers, and I hear the internal walls being reassembled.

Melody gives me a hug and takes my hand as we begin walking toward the car, her eyes wide open, my eyes fighting back tiny tears. I look at her face briefly. A wide smile graces her lips and a newer sparkle glistens in her eyes. This time, however, it's not for me.

We step over the log boundary of the park and something I wrote years ago flashes into my mind:

Live once
Fool Self
For eternity

For now, the symphonies are suppressed.

Chapter 17

"She's been here almost everyday this week, and you've had lunch with her each of those days. Still, you do not know what happened in New York to make her…"

There are moments when I wish I could truly just shut off little voices. Sure, I can ignore them when I become overjoyed and over-confident, but if I could truly ignore them, I wouldn't have to deal with contradicting myself every time I turn around.

"You also wouldn't have the fore warning not to make mistakes over and over again," the rambler chimes back in. "You are losing possibly the strongest inspiration you ever had and you don't want to be bothered? What is the problem here?"

The problem is, I was happy and now, well now, I am not.

"Way to go Romeo."

What is that supposed to mean?

"Well, you are supposed to be the romantic poet, and all you can come up with here is, 'I was happy, and now I am not.' What is that all about?"

If I show that I'm depressed, then she'll know.

"You are getting old…and stupid."

I am not old!

"Well, then just stupid. You finally are ready to share your emotions with someone, and after one road block, you stop. That's stupid."

I don't see it as stupid. She evidently doesn't share the emotions. Otherwise, she would have responded differently when I said, "I love you."

Chapter 17

"I don't think she heard you. Besides, how should she have reacted?"

Hugged me, slugged me, something. Instead, I get nothing, except me reacting to her going to New York.

"Maybe she didn't hear you! Why didn't you say it again?"

One of the important aspects of an inspiration is for the sharing of emotions or whatever, right?

"Of course. We had this conversation at Kirk's when everyone was gone."

Exactly. When she didn't respond to what I said, the inspiration faded. The sparkle changed.

"So, you're not feeling anything for her right now?"

Well, not really for her, for the inspiration.

"Right now, what are you feeling?"

Right now?

"Yes! Write it down."

I look around my cluttered desk for a blank piece of paper and wonder why I am doing this, why I am here in my classroom, and not in the bandroom where I am usually after concerts.

"Just write!"

Alone With Someone

Are You There?

Are you there?
My ears are open,
Fill them.
Are you there?
My arms are wide,
Find them.
Are you there?
My hands are free,
Grasp them.
Are you there?
My heart aches,
Soothe it.
Are you there?
I am cold.
I am alone.

"See, you miss her already," my little voice chides.

"It's not about her!" I say out loud and toss my pen down onto the desk.
A lone tear streaks down my cheek.

"Not about whom?" a soft female voice inquires.

I turn and see Melody standing in the doorway. "Um, no one," I say
faking a smile. "Come in. I was just grabbing some things."

Melody moves toward me and says, "We were wondering where you
went after the concert was over. You usually stick around at least a little.
Or, at least until I pack up my things."

"Just had to grab a couple of things," I say holding up some pens and the
paper I just scribbled on.

"What do you have there?" Melody inquires. "Is that a poem? Can I read
it? You haven't given me many since prom."

Chapter 17

"It's nothing," I say, fold it, and put it in my pocket. "Besides, I really haven't been writing much."

"Oh," Melody responds and sits down in the chair next to my desk. "Why haven't you been writing?"

"Can you believe this!" my inner voice shouts.

"Well, I haven't really had the time, I guess," I say, knowing how large of a lie it really is.

"So, it doesn't have anything to do with me going to New York?" Melody asks, moving her chair closer to mine. "I mean, I've only seen one piece since I returned."

"Well, I, a," I stumble for any actual thought.

"Tell her what you've been thinking!" my inner voice demands. "Tell her about the inspiration, about how much you care, about how much you will miss her. Tell her!"

"I guess I am a little confused," I say trying to look behind her.

"Confused?!?" my inner voice yells.

"Confused?" Melody questions. "I'm not sure what you mean."

"After all this time," the little voice comments, "she's not sure what you mean? The woman who knew what you were going to say before you said it, the woman who completed your sentences, is not sure what you mean when you say you're confused."

"Well, yes," I say. "I am confused. I know how much you've wanted this opportunity, but, well, I was just wondering about…about…"

"Us," Melody says.

"Yes," I respond. "I mean, I know what you said about your music and your inspiration, but my inspiration has been so strong, yet so soft, it has touched my perpetually pounding and thunderously thumping heart so much, I've had trouble explaining it, let alone accepting it."

"Bill, you have told me how your inspirations fade after a while, and to be quite honest with you, this has worried me."

"But, I don't believe the inspiration fades. It may change, but it wouldn't completely fade."

"That's what worries me, Bill," Melody replies. "The time we spend together has been amazing. In the back of my mind has always been the question of how long the intensity could last and how much longer the inspiration would be there. My concern has always been how we would continue to connect after the initial specialness has faded."

"I never really thought of it fading," I respond.

"But, I have," Melody adds. "Instead of waiting for it, plus this incredible opportunity, I just thought…"

"You thought what?" I ask.

"I just thought, I would try to preserve the original inspiration," Melody says convincingly. "I didn't want the images we created to fade. Prom was so wonderful. I just thought if we captured those moments, the inspiration would stay true to the original intensity and not fade."

"Now she's lecturing you on inspiration and intensity," my inner voice comments.
I hesitate and try to recall all the conversations we've had, hoping to remember where I've heard this before. "Ah, yes," I say. "The original inspiration. We talked about that when you took my gloves."

"What?" Melody questions giggling.

301

Chapter 17

"Your February concert, Frank, Cindy, cold, restaurant, jello…remember?" I respond.

"Oh, yeah," Melody replies. "I gave those back, didn't I?"

"Yes, three weeks ago," I respond and smile.

"Sorry," Melody says still giggling.

"Anywho, I remember talking about capturing the inspiration from the music before anything changes it," I say.

"Yes," Melody replies seemingly recalling the same conversation. "You said after dessert and our conversation, you couldn't write about the music. The inspiration had changed."

"Those are temporary glimpses of Eden," I say partially citing a piece I know she has read. "I haven't seen the inspiration we've shared as fading."

"Bill," Melody says, "have you ever seen the end of any of your inspirations?"

"Well," I say and pause. "Usually, I just try to appreciate the fact that I am inspired. I try not to be concerned about when it is going to end. In fact, it's when the thought even crosses my mind, I seem to lose that inspiration. If it was particularly strong, however, the inspiration changes to the opposite of the original."

"See, and that's what has worried me," Melody says. "It's when it changes, what if…"

"Melody," I interrupt, "while the original inspiration is important, it has changed since I first heard your music and met you. It has grown. Every time we talk or do things together, a fresh, new wave of intensity hits me. I've written about everything I've seen and experienced. I've shared every complete and even some incomplete pieces with you. You've read much more than I originally intended."

"But, doesn't the change worry you?" Melody asks. "What about the original inspiration?"

"What worries me," I reply, "is not having you here."

"We will still talk," Melody comments.

"Yes, but the phone doesn't enhance the inspiration. Sometimes, it stifles it," I say trying not to sound too pathetic.

"I am so fortunate to have a friend like you, Bill," Melody says. "I don't think anyone will ever take what we shared away from us."

"No one, but what about something?" I question.

"What thing are you talking about?" Melody inquires.

"Well, the distance, the different environments, the time," I respond.

"We can talk on the phone," Melody begins. "Besides, I know I'll need you to help me adjust to my new environment. I appreciate your opinions. We are so alike. It's like hearing myself think at times."

"But what about the time," I ask.

"I'm not sure what you mean about time," Melody replies.
I want to tell her that the time apart is actually what alters my inspirations, not necessarily other people or events. The time which lies between me and the inspiration creates the distance, provides for additional conflicts, and simply disrupts the original pure thoughts. I want to tell her that the little thing we seem to kill at whim, that which we never seem to have enough of, is the biggest agent of change for my inspirations.

"There's a one hour time difference between New York and here," I say instead. "When I am just waking up, you'll probably be leaving for work. And, when I get home from Kirk's, you'll probably be going to bed…"

"Bill," Melody chides, "you are just too funny. We'll talk. Who knows, things may not work out as well as I'm hoping."

"You'll talk alright. When she finds some guy and starts dating," my little voice chimes in.

"I have trouble believing that things can't work out for you," I say. "Things always seem to work out for me. Since we are so similar, you should have no problem once you settle in."

"But it's that settling in period I worry about. What if I don't play well and…"

"Melody, please," I interrupt, "You are incredibly talented. I've seen you have a complete set read, interpreted, and tweaked within days of getting the music."

"This is different," Melody says, a slight sound of worry still in her voice.

"It's not different," I comment, "just new."

I look at her downward tilted head and smile.

"But…" she tries to say something as her head lifts up.

"But, it's just new," I say reassuringly. "Look at horseback riding."

"We didn't go last week," Melody says and smiles.

"Yes, but the first time we did, you were worried," I say. "You didn't really say anything, but when we started out, I could tell you were worried. Not because it was different, but because it was new. By the time we were by the river, you were hoping on and off Angel as if it didn't matter."
"But if more people sense I'm worried," Melody says biting her lower lip, "well, it's New York…"

"New York is not very different from Chicago," I say trying to sound even more convincing. "It's just…"

"New," Melody finishes.

"Exactly. It says it even in the name, New York," I respond. "Tall buildings, too much traffic, cold in the winter, many people. In many ways it is similar. It's the experience that is new."

"Are you making her feel good about going?" my little voice questions. "You are encouraging her. I can't believe this."
I shake my head, hoping to shed the errant thoughts. "You have a couple of friends there already right?"

"Um, yes, but they…"

"You are further ahead of how many other musicians who moved there and didn't know anyone," I add.

"They go out quite a bit after work and stuff, and I…" Melody says then fades out.

"Good," I say, "then you'll have something to keep your mind off worrying so much about so little."

"And, something to keep her mind off of you," my little voice jabs.

"I haven't gone to clubs in a couple of years," Melody comments. "What if, well, let's say they dance, and drink, and…"

"You are too funny," I say. "You're even worrying about things not associated with your music. Relax and enjoy yourself. You're way too young to be worrying so much."

"But this is a big change," Melody says still seemingly searching for more reassurance.

Chapter 17

"Here's the change thing again," my inner voice points out. "Do you think this is what she was talking about all along?"

"I think, you just need to do it and be happy with your decision," I say. "You should never look back with regret on any decision you make. It causes life to be a rather unbearable state rather than the mystery it truly is."

"Oh brother," my inner editorial board comments.

"Even now," Melody says, "you make me feel like I can do anything. How, why, do you do this?"

"What?" I say innocently, though she has already boosted my sliding ego.

"How do you stay so positive?" Melody inquires.

"I try to learn from my mistakes," I respond. "Besides, I am not always positive."

"There are times when you hesitate," Melody comments, "but you always look at the good things, the things that make you happy."

"Not always," I respond. "When I'm alone with my obnoxious little voice, I debate the silly things, worry about them for 30 seconds or so, then just start laughing. The most serious subjects make me want to laugh, and I can't explain why, other than it all seem easier to deal with."

"You know," Melody says, "some would say you are repressing your true feelings and should seek counseling."

"Who are these people?" I say sarcastically. "I'll take them on with one hand tied behind my back. Where are they?"

"See you're avoiding the issue," Melody says laughing.

Alone With Someone

"So, you're one of them," I say raising my hands to my face as if getting ready to spare. "Ok, put 'em up."

"Stop," Melody says giggling now and taking my half fists in her hands, lowering them. "So, what are we going to do on one of the last nights together?"

"Well, I'm pretty tired and have a headache. Did I mention that I need to wash my hair, take out the garbage, and argue with my little voice some more?" I say playing to the mood.

"Bill, really, what are we going to do?" Melody questions, squeezing my hands tighter and smiling.

I hear one of my knuckles crack and say, "You may need to take me to the emergency room if you keep squeezing my hands that hard."

"Bill!" Melody says raising her voice slightly and tightening her grip again.

"OK, OK, I give up," I say moving one hand out of her grasp and cradling one of hers.
"There's a new miniature golf place down the street. I think it's open until midnight. We could tease all the teenagers."

"First the park and now miniature golfing," Melody says. "What exactly happened while I was in New York? You seem to be digressing. What's going to happen when I'm there for months? Really, what would you like to do?"

"You know what," I say, "I'm not too sure, but I do need to grab some things out of the computer lab. Why don't you think about it while I go get them?"

"Alright, but you need to think of something too," Melody comments.

"I will. I will," I say rising from my chair, letting go of her hand, and taking my keys from the desk.

Chapter 17

"Yeah, right. You'll still be thinking of her," my inner voice comments.

"I'll be right back. Read a book or something," I say as I near the door.

I close my eyes about half way and try to hold onto the picture of her sitting in my dimly lit room. I need to capture these moments much better than I have been.

I reach the computer lab, move my keys to the door, open it, and enter. I take the disks off the corner of the first table and pause, remembering something else in the room with Melody.

"You left that out?" my inner voice questions harshly. "You did. It was folded, but it had her name on it."

The poem I wrote last week as a goodbye is sitting on my desk directly in front of her. I try to recall whether or not it was in an envelope or not.

"I'm pretty sure it wasn't," my little voice says sounding somewhat concerned.

I scan the scene again in my mind. It is out of the envelope. I try to remember what I actually wrote, hoping it won't spoil the positive mood swing I think we just had.

"It's fine," my inner voice says. "Besides, she won't open it."

But, what was in it?

"You've just made her feel better about moving, and now you're worrying about whether a poem you're going to give her anyway is going to change the mood. You really do need help."

I've made many mistakes in the few relationships I've had. One of the biggest has been my inability to remain objective after my inspiration changes greatly as it just did.

"Don't worry about it," my inner voice comments. "You have this last night with her. Capture what you can and accept the change. You really haven't been given a choice here."

Yeah, I guess. I will just relax and enjoy myself. I've done this before.

"Actually," my inner voice points out, "you really haven't been this close before. But, hey if you keep in touch, who knows."

Maybe, I could move to New York.

"She never suggested that, did she?"

Anywho, I should get back there. I toss one of the disks into the air, catch it, and walk out of the computer lab. I close the door, makes sure it is locked by pulling on the handle, and walk back to my room.

It sure is dark in here.

"That's because there are no lights except at the ends of the hallway," my inner voice comments sarcastically.

I reach my room and hop in, hoping to startle Melody. She is standing by my desk, swaying back and forth slightly.

"Hey there," Melody says calmly. "Are we all set?"

"Yep," I respond moving toward my chair. "Did you decide where we are going?"

"Actually," Melody replies, "I did. And, if you don't mind, I'll drive."

"Um, well, I'm not sure about actually getting into a car with you," I say and chuckle.

"I'm not that bad of a driver," Melody says and fakes a pout.

Chapter 17

"OK, whatever," I say and collect some of the things on my desk. I pause at the folded letter. It doesn't look disturbed. I put all of the other items in my backpack and zip up the bag itself.

I look back at the paper I avoided, and place it in the envelope that was underneath it. I lick the flap, close it, and extend it to Melody. "Here, this is for you. But, you can not open it until tomorrow."

"Why?" Melody asks taking the envelope and folding it once. She puts it in her purse and waits for a response.

"It's too dark in here to read anything," I reply. "Besides, it's just that lasagna recipe you've wanted."

"Stop. It is not," Melody says and moves toward me more.

"You're right," I say. "It's my will. I needed someone else to have a copy. Oh yeah, I left everything to my students."

"Bill," Melody says giving me a little push.

"OK, let's go," I say and reach for my backpack.

Melody takes my arm before it reaches its destination and hugs me.

"What is this for?" my little voice asks somewhat astonished.

"Thank you," Melody whispers in my ear as she slowly pulls away.

Small shivers shake my body, but they cease just as quickly as they began.

"Shall we go?" I ask, picking up my backpack this time, and extending my hand to Melody who just nods her head.

As we leave the room, I turn off the few lights that have remained on and the words of last week's poem return to the forefront of my mind...

Alone With Someone

Melody,
If you would be so kind to extend me a bit more time for this simple
expression and rhyme...

Experiencing living from the inside out
May leave one in constant doubt,
Of life and what it may bring.
But, if we continue to question
The gifts we are given,
We are left with nothing on which to cling.
We may never be alone together,
But, for now, alone maybe better,
For appreciating how amazing angels can truly be.
It is when we look into the eyes of such a cherub
That we may see a glimpse of heaven,
And, when we spend time with our best friend,
We may experience remnants of eternity.
Though I know,
I will be missing you while being without,
Your soul's shadow will remain within
And settle as a precious part
Of my ever-hopeful heart.

Chapter 18

"This is definitely not a movie," my inner companion says. "Because if it were, the end credits would have most certainly rolled by now."

I really need to stop worrying about endings. There are so many things I need to see, hear, experience, feel. Besides, endings allow for new beginnings.

"She's been away for about a month now."

I could give the exact amount of time.

"Why would it matter?"

Exactly. I have come to rely heavily on others for my inspirations, but over the last month or so, I have learned to appreciate what those people share with me, but realize that my happiness is found mostly in the illusions of my own mind.

"And yet, you still have an annoying little voice."

Of course, it helps maintain my sanity.

Bump-bump, bump-bump, baaaaaaaaa, bump-bump.

I pick up my head and look to the right. The sidewalks are filled with people, some old, many young, all gathered around watching. There are no deserters here. Red, white, and blue streamers are draped over the outstretched branches of the trees on both sides of the street. Coming toward us, though still a bit away, playing an energetic marching tune are trombones, trumpets, tubas, drums, flutes, clarinets, and saxophones.

The students parade by and the notes vibrate through much more than the space between us. I shiver slightly and close my eyes, trying to feel and relive parts of the past few months.

Chapter 18

Brief images of the things Melody and I did together flash through my spacious mind. I try to focus on her…her eyes, her lips, her hair, her voice…Nothing. My visions do not include her, why?

"No oboe," comments my inner self.

I open my eyes and shake my head, laughing.

"Well, at least your not nodding and smiling," a familiar voice says as a hand plops down on my shoulder.

I turn and see Frank standing next to me. He motions for me to walk with him and the band. I shake my head and say, "I'll meet you at the end."

"Come on," Frank insists. "I need someone to make sure they are in step as they play."

Frank moves past me as the clarinets pass. He signals me to follow again. I take a few, short, quick steps, then a couple of long strides in order to match his pace.

"They look pretty good," I say finally catching up to Frank.

"It's not how they look, but how they sound," Frank says signaling to the drum major to play their second song once this one is over.

"They sound very good. The tunes are pretty simple, but they sound good," I comment as another drum intro starts the next song.

"Now you're a critic," Frank responds giving a small down beat as the students blast the initial notes.

"It's the same set you played last year," I say justifying my earlier statement.

"So, are you going to Kirk's later?" Frank inquires, looking back at me, but still moving.

"Of course," I respond.

"Just making sure," Frank says. "We seem to be losing people everyday from our little group."

"Yeah," I reply as my mind wonders slightly to the first time Melody came to Kirk's. I still can not really see her.

"Yeah, Steve decided to stay in Europe for a while; Jerry and Nicole are moving in the next month; Mark got another grant…"

"And, you and Cindy are expecting a new member to your family," I add and pat Frank on the shoulder.

"I'll still be there for a while," Frank says as an incredibly wide grin forms on his face.

The song stops and the drum cadence takes over again.

"So, how are you holding up?" Frank questions.

"Fine," I say. "I've stopped most of my daydreaming and the nightmares have ended all together. OK, I'm kidding. I am fine. This too shall pass."

"Bill, it's not a cold," Frank says. "You spent so much time together, it's OK to feel s…"

"I am fine," I say cutting him off, my eyes widening and a frown forming on my face. "We've talked since she's left and she is doing well, incredibly well."

"Whatever, Bill," Frank says and signals for their last tune.

"Really," I say waving my hands in the air, "she is doing what she has always wanted to do. She is happy. Why would I be sad? I can say that I miss her and our closeness, but I truly do feel things happen for a reason. We will keep in touch and who knows. Sillier things have happened, especially in my life."

Chapter 18

"Well there's always young redheaded colleagues," Frank comments, winking at me and motioning to our left where one of our math teachers is standing. Frank waves to her and she returns the gesture.

"I don't think so," I say and wave myself. "She looks beautiful, but my inspirations and insanity are not always influenced by mere beauty."

"Now you're getting too deep," Frank says. "Just listen to the music. We're almost at the end of the parade route. Was this a quick performance or what."

"Inspirations," my inner reflection says, "true inspirations, are influenced by so much, but no matter what initiates them, you always experience the joys of life and intricacies of living even after they are altered."

The last song is a bit slower than the other two, but pure and simple nonetheless. The basic melody mediates through the summer breeze and scrolling lines of simplicity flash through my inner vision. These are the results of my inspiration, my own ramblings…

Let Me Not Begin Anew

Let me not begin anew.
Let me spend my days with you, or you, or you,
My friends, my companions, my creations.
Losing you would be a great devastation.
You are my entire being,
The results of my dreaming.
With every word I breathe,
You are able to achieve
New invigorating life
To help me deal with all the strife.
I need, I want, I feel,
Only what I believe real.
That being you
To whom I will always remain true.
So, go forth
And let your intensity be shown.
For with you,
I will never be alone.